FALLING IN LOVE WITH MY VAMPIRE CAT

~

☦ A SWEET, FANTASY ROM-COM ☦

CAMILLA EVERGREEN

☦

Copyright © 2023 by Camilla Evergreen
This book is licensed for your personal enjoyment only. This book is a work of fiction. No part of this publication may be reproduced, distributed, or transmitted in any form by any means, including photocopying, recording, or other electronic or mechanical methods, without the proper written permission of the publisher, except in the case of brief quotations embodied in critical reviews and certain other noncommercial uses permitted by copyright law.

If you are reading this book and did not purchase it from Amazon.com or receive a copy through Camilla Evergreen, Anne Stryker, or associates of Gossamer Wings & Ink Press, please report this to the author at authorcamillaevergreen@gmail.com.

Thank you for respecting the hard work that goes into publishing a book.

None of the characters in this book are actual people. Any resemblance to real individuals is coincidental. The mention of actual celebrities, songs, movies, or brands included in this book do not necessarily reflect the author's actual feelings or ideas about those individuals, creative works, or companies.

Edited by a Strange Little Squirrel
Cover Art by House of Orian Graphics

Reader Expectations

Heat Level: Fade-to-black, innuendos, no cursing, sensual description, mentions of sex

Notable Tropes: Forced proximity, enemies to lovers, only one bed, "damsel in distress" (I'm a damsel, I am in distress, I cannot handle it **sobbing**), not-so-secret pining, chosen one (as in, the cat chose her), soulmates, fish out of water

Triggers: Magic, vampires, blood, references to fantasy violence, loss of a loved one

Style: First person present, single POV

Stress Level: Low, apart from the fantasy violence in chapter 1

Ending: HEA

This book is if cottagecore and fantasycore had a tiny, silly baby.

Do not read this book if you are expecting angst, action, or sparkly skin.

Warning: Floppy kitties. No third-act breaks. First-, second-, and third-act breakdowns.

Hope you enjoy. <3

*This book is sponsored by Wendy, who gave me Taco Bell.
Wendy is the best person ever.
If everyone were like Wendy, there would be peace on Earth.
Thank you for being you.*

Prologue

This is the first and last time I *go outside*.

Books are better than people.
You might say, *Obviously, Willow. Have you ever met a person? They suck.*
And to that I would say, *Fair point, random voice in my head, who I have conversations with, because I like to, and not because I'm lonely* at all. *But you know what's* also *better than people?*
Roosters.
And now—if you have ever once had the unfortunate displeasure of meeting a rooster—you understand my sheer, utter resentment of humankind. The broad depth of my distaste. The unending pool of disgust every time I see a human. Or, OR—worse—every time I see a *child* because *a child* implies that the humans are *breeding*.
My lip curls as I cozy up in my window seat with my latest epic fantasy novel. Taking a deep breath and shudderingly turning to the final page in the epilogue, which has just waxed poetic concerning the main character being pregerrnanate with twins, I decide it was a mediocre read. Clichés by the boatload. Questionable world-building at best. Insufficient action in favor of making out in the closet *while the literal world burned.* Andddd language so simple my inner monologue hasn't slowed once since I opened the tome this lovely summer morning.
I flick the book closed, sigh deeply, and lift my elegant, gilded gold teacup. Dainty pink lilies adorn the glass bowl

filled with chocolate milk, and sunlight pours through the empty portion, scattering rainbows across the pearl white shag carpet of my living room. Beyond my window, chickens cluck in their penitentiary, which spares them from the foxes and coyotes in the woods surrounding my peaceful abode.

The creek burbles.

Birds trill.

I haven't had—or made—a phone call for half a dozen moons, minimum.

All is at peace, as it has been ever since I inherited this place from my grandmother, moved in, and started fixing it up to suit me. Rest in peace, Monica Harding. You will always be the only person I have ever liked.

Care to know the sad part?

My mediocre book was *still* better than people.

Dare to ponder the *sadder* part?

I slump into the window seat's plush pale pink and *sprawl*, dismal.

I, Willow Harding, must traverse through yonder wood, come upon ye olde town, and purchase sustenance, lest I survive off eggs and garden-fresh veggies for the rest of my days.

And I *could*.

I *could* survive off eggs and garden-fresh veggies for the rest of my days. Summer produce is plentiful. If I get to the eggs in time and make sure *not* to take them from my *brooding* hens—shudder, shudder, help, I will never recover from the mistakes I have made—I can survive happily for a *good long time* without *any* human interaction.

The PROBLEM?

I sniffle and sag a little deeper into the soft cushions.

No cow.

No butter.

No cheese.

It's a miracle I have not succumbed to depression or drowned myself in the creek that runs near my property. Mayhaps this eve I shall don my *I'm a ghost in a Victorian mansion* gown and lie in the chilled water, staring up through the canopy at the starry sky.

'Tis what nature intended, I'm sure.

Dragging myself from my seat in a spill of my lace nightgown, I trudge to my bedroom. Since it's summer, I veer toward the white half of my black-and-white closet, pluck an off-the-shoulder dress with a flowing skirt and sleeves off a hanger, and top it with a pearl white princess line corset. I cinch the laces before pulling on matching knee-high boots that add a gracious three inches to my petite five-foot-two frame. Glancing in the mirror, I make sure the two streaks of white hair that contrast my long dark locks and frame my face are on proper display. Once upon a time, kids made fun of me for my poliosis. Now, I don't have to buy bleach to match my summer wardrobe.

The moral of the story: sometimes curses become blessings in the end.

Twisting on my heel, I snatch my shopping basket and my purse and step out into the sun.

Immediate regrets.

They hit me with such force I barely make it down the cottage steps and to the large flat stones leading toward the narrow forest path. As soon as pine needles crunch beneath my boots and branches protect me from the evil, horrible, no good, really bad (but actually, ily, thank you for feeding my garden, babe) sun, I take a humid breath.

My lungs are not meant to be *damp*. Yet here we are.

"Summer," I mutter. It's the worst time of the year.

Hot.

Children are home from school.
Sweat.
Sweaty *children.*

A prickle of *nope* shoots down my spine, and I hope Martyn's Grocery Mart isn't cramped.

For a small town with nearly everything I need within walking distance, Mountain Vale, Virginia sure has a lot of children and people. And *cars*. Whenever I march my way through my forest path and wind up at the quaint downtown streets, every spot lining the two-way road is full.

I hate cars.

They robbed me of an era of horse-drawn carriages.

Sunlight returns in full, wicked force when I step from my forest path onto the concrete sidewalk and peer at what could moonlight as Small Town USA. Distress burdens my very soul as I squint into the bustle.

People.

Walking.

Chatting.

Laughing.

Going in and out of shops.

Toting crinkly plastic bags around.

While walking and chatting and laughing.

"What fresh sensory—"

A yowl cuts my revulsion short, and I scowl. The cause of disruption shall rue the day it interrupted my quippy one-liner.

Another yowl draws my march toward an alley between the only good place in this town—AKA the bookstore—and the obligatory nightclub. It's too early for drunken nonsense.

Irritating laughter hits my ears as I stomp into the shaded narrow strip. Red brick towers on either side of me, confining three children beside a mud-green dumpster.

"You think it's dying?" Too much mirth saturates the morbid words.

I freeze as the sight turns my stomach up in knots.

Beside stacks of week-old refuse, the children hover over a puddle of dark fur.

One boy lifts a nearby rock in both his grubby hands, a vicious smile curling his round face. "Maybe we should put it out of its misery?"

My stomach lurches, and I charge, wrap my hand around the child's arm, and bury my nails into his flesh as I yank him away. The stone tumbles harmlessly from his grasp. Wild panic flashes through his eyes as he looks up at me, then his ruddy face pales.

"What do you think you're doing?" I demand.

"It's the witch!" he yells.

Another of the boys jumps to his feet. "Run!"

"Ow!" I shriek when the last of the monsters kicks me, scuffing my boot. "Rude!"

"Let me go!" Sticky, gritty hands pry at my fingers, so I toss the brat away from the lump of fur.

"She came for her familiar! My mom told me black cats were evil. Come on! She'll curse us!"

They scramble while I contemplate cursing in a totally *non*-supernatural way. The only thing holding me back is a dull sense of *not my monkeys, not my circus*. You don't teach monkeys that aren't yours how to do a swore without parental permission. It's the law.

Gram used to tell me I should be considerate with children, gentle. They're *learning* how to people, and isn't peopling hard?

Yes, it is.

But, counterpoint, children aren't as stupid as we give them credit for. Some (read as: *most*) of them are fully aware they're monsters.

If I were a witch, I'd hex everyone under sixteen so they could never be anything other than polite. The speed with which I would banish children to training camps until they *both* came of age *and* completed a base-level common sense test is astounding.

It's also why the ones writing my plot did not put me in a position of power whereby my villain arc would lead to dictatorship.

Honestly, missed opportunities, guys.

Puffing a strand of white hair out of my eyes, I lower myself into a crouch by the cat and set my shopping basket down on the pavement beside us.

Otherworldly allure enraptures me as its silken fur shines even in the shadows. Blinking the sensation off, I reach slowly toward it. "Are you all right, little guy?"

Weakly, the creature opens its eyes. One blue as a clear sky. The other green as the lush earth.

My lips part. "Wow." My heart rate kicks up a notch. "You're beautiful." I graze my fingers through its soft fur. No collar. No visible blood. It seems all right, if lethargic. And on a day like today where the world is the equivalent of a goat's armpit, who can blame it? There's a reason I wear all white in summer, but this little guy can't exactly change its fur for the seasons.

"Are you all right?" I murmur.

Before I can pet its head, it swipes at me, slashing my wrist with its claw.

Heat blooms, and I wince, jerking my hand back. Red beads.

"Okay, wow. I'm rescuing you. You're almost as bad as the male lead in the book I just read."

Its dark head tilts.

"Yeah. You heard me. You're what we call an *alphahole*. All jerk and thinly-veiled narcissism. You can't go around hurting others because others have hurt you." I sigh. "Trust me. You get charged with less aggravated assault if you keep your violent actions as violent thoughts. Repeat after me: I'm too hot for prison. They'd devour me like a baked bean."

The cat mews.

I smile. "Very good."

Sniffing when I reach for it again, it lifts its head, finds my wrist, and licks the wound.

"I accept your apology. And I hope that you don't have any diseases. That does kind of hurt, though. You have a little sandpaper tongue, don't you?" Before I can pull my hand away, its precious little bean paws wrap around my wrist, claws pricking but not piercing.

It licks. It love bites. I develop an unnaturally close bond in the span of approximately two seconds.

My black heart swells.

It flops onto its back when it's finished sandpapering the wound it caused into an angry red. Boneless. Wiggly. Purring.

"Oh my. Are you trying to seduce me…mister?" I pet his lil belly and beam. "Scandalous. I'll have you know I'm already in an abusive relationship with an animal. His name is Clucking Disaster. He only ever attacks when my back is turned, and he insists on having a harem of side chicks." I lean in close, murmuring, "I'll let you know if I turn him into chicken nuggies. We can share."

With a sigh, I stand and brush off my skirts. "Well, I should probably…"

He climbs into my basket.

My heart hits my ribs.

He gets comfortable, closes his multicolored eyes, and lets his low purr rumble.

Drawing my fingertips together, I press them to my lips.

"I'm the chosen one." I swallow hard and shove down a sudden spike of feeling like a female lead. I can do this. I can breathe through this. He'll probably jump out when I lift the basket anyway, right? Right. Of course. We've not forged a lifelong attachment just now. That's some goofy book nonsens—

Physically defeating my squeal as he does not—in fact —jump out the moment I lift the basket, I turn carefully out of the alleyway.

I have a cat in my basket.

I have a *cat* in my *basket*.

Everything other than his eyes is a pitch black that calls to the depths of my soul. Even his wee toe beans are jet little pads. He needs a name.

Something dark and mysterious. Maybe from mythology. Hades? No. Too common. Maybe—

No. *No*. Bad Willow. Naming him implies *keeping* him. And have we even seen our house? Animals belong outside, not on the pink, blue, and white furniture. Causing mischief. Knocking over little glass teacups of chocolate milk.

He *could* be an outside cat. He could totally be an outside cat. Keep the chimkins in line. Put the appropriate level of fear into Clucking Disaster.

But it's *hot* outside, especially in summer, and look at his poor shiny coat. So dark it's swallowing 99.999% of all visible light. If he weren't in the shade earlier, he'd have been toastier than tarmac. A real burnt baked bean.

Who says he's even going to stay with me for very long?

Cats are angelic beings who abide by their own rules.

He's just taking a nap.

Yeah. He's just taking a nap in my basket. Afterward, he'll trot off, and I'll see him every now and again traversing in the corners of my vision. I'll upward nod his way. He'll ignore me. Because he's a cat.

When he slips out of my basket right before I enter Martyn's Grocery Mart, I assume that's the end.

Except it isn't.

Because he follows me in, trailing behind me as I peruse the aisles. When a little girl notices the *pretty black kitty* on my heels, his fur stands on end and he hisses until the cretin's mother tugs her away, muttering about how *pets shouldn't be allowed in stores*.

"Didn't stop you from bringing yours," I mumble as I place a bag of flour in my basket.

The cat eyes me.

I eye him. "What?"

He looks elsewhere.

"That's what I thought." He knows I'm right. He's a good boy.

Even though my wrist stings a little from his claw attack, he's still a good boy.

He's such a good boy that he follows me through checkout, back up the street, in and out of the bookstore, then down the forest path home. I stop at the front door to my cottage and stare at him when he sits on the porch, curling his tail around his paws.

His eyes look deep into my soul.

I chew my bottom lip.

What if a fox gets him?

What if I never see him again?

If he doesn't know that this is *home* yet—and how could he possibly?—then he'll disappear in the middle of the night.

The idea of never seeing a cat I've only just met ever again disrupts my internal organs more than I think it should.

Basically, whoever decided to give humans feelings is dead to me.

Sucking in a deep breath, I open my front door.

He doesn't move. His gaze flicks inside my pristine abode, then back up at me, as though he's waiting for a clearer invitation, some sort of verbal contract that claims *yes*, it's okay for you to come into my perfect little home and let your midnight zoomies destroy my carpet. I would love to clean shed fur off my white couch every day, never getting all of it, no matter how hard I try.

It's all I aspire to do for the rest of my life, really.

"Would you…" I begin, so foolishly. "…like to come in?"

A flicker of something dastardly sparks in those beautiful, mismatched eyes of his, then he stands, and he enters, and I don't know it yet, but my life changes.

Forever.

Chapter 1

The regrets I have are plentiful.

Five years later

A faintly-exhaled curse slips into my ear, whispered in the silkiest tones I've ever heard. The hypnotic quality sets my nerves on edge, making my heart hammer, thunder, stampede, then stutter.

I'm dreaming. This is a nightmare. Oh. Okay. That's cool then. Nightmares are interesting. Some of my best brain stories have started as nightmares. I just need to figure out how to win. I love the HD. Practically BluRay in here. My brain really got a great budget for the visuals on this one. In fact…it's not just the visuals. I can feel everything. Breath against my ear. The cold, hard forest floor against my back. It's…damp…cluttered with day-old snow.

And then there's the—

Pain.

"Stay with me, starlight." Lips graze my cheek before an icy touch slips over my waist, planting against my side. My nightgown…

It's soaked in something warm, cooling quickly.

Every slender finger of the large hand imprints into my skin, spanning nearly my entire burning stomach.

Am I shaking?

Am I breathing?

Am I really here at all?

This dream's budget must be running out, because the winter sky shining through the trees above me blurs.

The press of fingers deepens. "No." The word is eerily calm, seductively demanding.

My cells obey it, and my vision clears even as the pain heightens.

I whimper, like some kind of damsel in distress. Pathetic. I never greenlighted myself on that archetype. *Clearly* I'm the stoic, cynical one who hates everything—apart from a handful of things that allow me to be *hashtag relatable*. My lips part, gape, and I try to tell the nightmare figure that I'd like to wake up now, but I can't get any words out.

It hurts so *much*.

I don't think I'm breathing.

The man whispering in my ear lifts his head, and my struggling heart squeezes.

One right blue eye. One left green eye.

I'd know those eyes anywhere.

They're what I've woken up to for the past five years.

My kitty. Lord Keres, Master of Mischief and Darkness, Greek god of brutal death…just ask the local population of small creatures.

Oh wait.

You can't.

He's murdered them all.

Is that…is that what's happening right now? Am I being *murdered*?

A troubled smile curls his soft lips, and his cold knuckle skates up the slender column of my throat—wet. He utters another curse word as he tips my gaping mouth closed with a finger. "It's okay. Don't worry. It will be over soon." Looking a touch pained, he curses again and cups my cheek in his wet hand.

Is that... It can't be. Please tell me the wetness is not *blood*.

Slick, he slips his thumb across my cheekbone and swears. Breathless, he swears and swears, looking half drunk and half scared. "Relax, starlight."

Again, my cells obey him. My heart slows, and my mind panics where my body can't.

"That's my girl. Everything is okay." He taps my nose with a cold wet finger, and a droplet of *something* slides down the side to my cheek. "I'll take care of the—" He curses. "—who did this to you, and you'll never have to be in danger again. This is a *good thing*." His voice makes my body *want* to believe it, but logic demands I take note of the tension in his expression, the slightly forced quality of his smile. The *fear*.

He's lying. He must be lying. Lying through his... fangs.

He swears. "—you're so—" Swear. "—beautiful." His lungs fill, and the pain spreading in my limbs grows more taut. "The first moment I saw you I thought I was dead. You looked like an angel. You made me believe in soulmates the second you smiled at me. I would have hoped to make this sweeter for you. Less...forced." His eyes close, and something very near agony knits his brows. "Still, don't worry. I know you. Every inch of you." His lips meet mine, and air fills my chest—burning, hot and cold and sharp. "I'll take the best care of you, starlight." He kisses me again. "There. You can rest now. Just remember: everything is *fine*."

First of all, I don't believe him.

Second of all, cultic vibes much?

Third of all...I don't think I want to sleep anymore, but my body isn't agreeing with my brain. My eyelids grow heavy despite the fact I'm fighting them. A frail whimper escapes me as my eyes shut and sleep overwhelms.

The last thing I feel is an open kiss against my cheek. Then the cold, the hot, the night, the *man* are all...gone.

★

I gasp awake in my bedroom, staring at the ceiling. Everything is—normal. Creepy *normal*.

The sort of normal that lingers in the air during a funeral.

My chest clenches as I sit up and look at my nightgown.

I am dry, warm, in my cozy daybed canopied with lace, surrounded by soft pink walls. Sunlight pours through my window. Pillowy clouds traipse throughout the winter sky. My chickens brave the chilly morning beyond their roost in order to create their clucky ruckus. Clucking Disaster (the fourth) crows.

So...

The problem is...

This isn't the nightgown I put on when I went to bed last night. I have *never once in the past five years* woken without Lord Keres standing on my chest, staring deeply into my eyes. And...I smell food. Breakfast food.

Someone is cooking in my kitchen.

In books, there's a *moment*. Fancy people in college courses call it the *inciting incident*. I call it the instant *crap hits the fan*. The *moment* instigates the *clean up the crap storm*, which is otherwise known as the rest of the book or series.

With a blurry recollection of last night streaming behind my eyes, I think crap's hit the fan.

I do not want to clean it up.

My lifestyle has not prepared me for anything more traumatic than walking all the way to the grocery store only to discover my favorite reading snack is out of stock. I'm built like a damsel in distress with the disposition of a cactus. While I'm not adverse to physical activities, I draw a firm line at tending to my household.

Care for my chickens? Not an issue. Plant a garden? Good times. *Learn how to sword fight?* Nope. Nopity, nope, no.

What did I do to deserve the lead role in *anything*, much less the kind of *anything* that comes with vivid memories of bleeding out in my front yard? I'm against this.

Therefore, I must not encounter whoever is in my kitchen. I'll take an impromptu vacation, head to Florida. Wait for this to blow over. Yup.

I'm sorry, chickens.

However, if you didn't want to be abandoned, you should have thought twice before being two measly dollars a piece.

Grabbing my purse, I head for the window.

"Starlight?"

My heart lunges before I can fully prop my leg on the sill. Whipping my attention behind me, I find *him*.

Since it's broad daylight and I'm no longer *bleeding out in my yard*, I'm able to get a better look at his chiseled, otherworldly features. He's...he's...

Definitely my cat. But also definitely *not* my cat.

Jumbled curses dance around inside my skull, and I close my eyes for a moment to hold back tears. I was so ready to accept that my head was a twisted garbage can willing to anthropomorph my pet into a sexy man with no concept of personal space. I was prepared to find a therapist in Florida and be diagnosed with too much shifter romance. Prescription: stop hanging out in the trash section of the bookstore. Read a sweet and clean once in a while. Beg authors everywhere to stop putting smut in YA or start religiously and reliably calling it New Adult.

Sincere concern floods not my cat's mismatched eyes. "You should get dressed before you go out."

He's so attractive it's offensive. Long ink-black hair falls around his pale cheeks. Faintly pointed ears pierce the straight curtains. His physique is lean, toned, muscular, bearing hints of danger that confirm he's a predator at a single glance. He's tall. Even if I weren't on the smaller side, he's *tall*. And fit. No doubt a six-pack hides beneath the apron he's wearing. The *frilly white* apron he's wearing. *My* frilly white apron.

There's something far too intimate in the understanding he knew where to find my apron.

He continues, "You should also eat before you go anywhere. You're still recovering."

Recovering.

My heart beats feebly in response to the mention I have something to *recover* from.

I press myself back against the wall beside my window and scan him from head to toe.

He's tall. Beautiful. Pale. Lethal. Some sort of power tangles itself in his voice, reaching my ears like a wicked melody.

The memory of *fangs* slices into my brain, hitting me between the brows, and I know what he is.

I slap my hand to my mouth. No. *Nooo*.

Please, please no.

Slowly, I crumple against the carpet, dropping my purse and hugging my legs to my chest. My years of being a fantasy romance reader could never prepare me for this. "I've been good. I-I don't understand." Threading my fingers into my hair, I stare blankly at the floor and grip the roots. "I only *think* terrible things. I've never *actually* tried to hurt anyone." My eyes narrow. "Well. Except that one time. But that brat Christie was *asking* for it. And the scissors they give you in kindergarten aren't sharp anyway." My teacher made me sit alone after the attempted stabbing. My parents called it *The Incident* until I was in high school. I've *more* than done my time for that crime.

I do *not* deserve the punishment of encountering a *vampire* in my real life.

That's what some might consider cruel and unusual.

Nausea sweeps up the back of my throat, and I groan, sinking onto my side against the rug.

With inhuman speed, not my cat lifts me into his arms and carries me across the hall into my bathroom. His cool fingers sweep back my hair before I vomit uncontrollably in the sink.

When the water runs, I make the mistake of looking in the porcelain bowl.

My knees go weak.

"Shh," not my cat murmurs, much too close while my head's spinning. "It's all right."

"I don't believe you," I croak. I'm no doctor, but I think vomiting blood is *not* all right. "I *refuse* to ask what's going on. That's the next step in story progression. I won't do it. I'm going to go back to bed. Disengage. Then what will the story gods do, hm? Kill me off? Make it a tragedy? Nice try. There's no point to it if my death wouldn't incite some sort of emotion. Scr—" I vomit again. "*Screw this.*"

Not my cat supports one hundred percent of my weight as he strokes my back. It doesn't feel nice or comforting. Not even a little bit. And I'm not being sarcastic, for once.

In case you missed it, *there's a strange man with fangs in my house holding my hair back while I puke up blood.* Nothing about this is okay, all right, or *endearing*. At base-level, the power discrepancy between a mythical being and the human girl who gets roped into their charm makes *every one of these kinds of stories deeply concerning.*

Do I read this kind of plot by the thousands?

Scoff. Duh.

Would I ever in a million years want to *experience it*? Hard. Pass.

Weakly, I hit my fist against the counter. Give me back my quiet life in the woods where the most drama I have to deal with is whether or not my rooster is coming for my ankles.

I can barely handle a phone call with my parents once a quarter. I'm not built for forbidden romance.

Not my cat pins one white lock of my hair behind my ear. "I think you're a little delirious, starlight." His voice seeps into me, beckoning. It coos and coddles, encouraging me to believe him.

I throw off a shudder. "Lies." I stumble away from him. "Evil." I make a cross with my hands.

Not my cat glances at my hands, then rolls his lips into his mouth, biting back a smile. Probably literally. I hope his fangs are pricking his stupid pretty—

Before my thought finishes, he's leaning into my space, and my back hits the wall behind me. Cornering me, he tilts his head. Tenderness gleams in his mismatched eyes. His fingers snake up my forearms, break my cross, slip over my palms, and twine. He pins me to the wall, traces his thumbs up from my wrists to the tips of my thumbs, back down. "I'm not evil, actually. That's propaganda from the dark ages."

The dreamy glaze overcoming him sends my stumbling heart into outright panic.

I. Am. Freaking. Out.

Aren't I? Am I? No, I totally am. Right? *Freaking out* is an emotion, and I'm feeling it. Do not be misled by my façade of calm irritation. I can curse the people running my plot *and* freak out at the same time. I am obviously capable of more emotions than sarcasm.

It's called *multi-tasking*, which—for the record—I am *also* definitely capable of.

It does not overwhelm me to the point of tears at all.

Eyes burning, I gulp down a stinging sniffle.

How in the world are the female leads in my stories just chill with this? What do they put in main character water? Liquid stupid??

He is *so* tall. Threateningly tall.

I'm used to feeling small, confused, and generally uncomfortable whenever I leave my house, but *my house* is the place I crafted for *me*. Everything here is safe, designed, thought out. Every detail, every color, every decoration. It's all planned and coordinated. Familiar. It's all *mine*. I redid every inch when I inherited it after high school at eighteen, and the biggest change I dared make since I perfected everything at twenty-one was…

Adopting a cat.

I knew change was bad. I *knew* it. But I fell for toe beans.

Decidedly *evil* toe beans.

"I'm not evil," he reiterates.

The atoms making me up latch onto the words as they caress every exposed centimeter of my flesh. "Get out of my head," I hiss.

"Starlight—"

"No." I force down another thick swallow that tastes faintly of iron and strongly of acid. "I am not interested in anything your existence prompts. I want to read books, grow tomatoes, and yell at my rooster. I respectfully decline the plot, in any form it might take. Mine is a life of blissful rest. Nothing ever happens, and everything is good."

Faint lines at the corners of his eyes deepen as he looks at me. "Do you never get bored?"

"I *read*."

"You never want to…" He bonks his forehead gently against mine—something I thought I taught Lord Keres to do. "…experience what you read?"

I snap my teeth at him. "Back off with your frivolous displays of affection. They shan't fool me." I've just decided. YA vampire novels should be outlawed. Honestly. What kind of message do the authors think they're sending to impressionable teenagers? Boundaries are a *suggestion*? You can still fall for the guy who *wants to eat you*?

Story gods have mercy.

If this *thing* is my cat, he's been watching me sleep for five years. *We've* been sleeping *together* for five years. He's been to the *vet* with me, once a year, for *shots*.

I *knew* I should have neutered him.

Why didn't I neuter him?

Am I an irresponsible cat parent? Or did he use freaky vampire magic and keep the thought from ever crossing my mind?

His hold on my hands tightens, and his forehead hits my shoulder. His chest shakes, silent laughter overwhelming him. Releasing me once he's composed himself, he plunges his fingers into his hair, cuts the dark strands back, and peers down at me.

The freak looks like he's posing for a calendar when he says, "Everything is fine."

"Liar."

"Why don't you give me a chance?"

Oh ho. Yes. Of course. What a *fantastic* idea. Give the blood-sucking vampire *a chance*. That never ended poorly for anyone ever.

If there's one skill I've mastered in my twenty-six years

of life, it's *not* giving people a chance to hurt me anymore. That ship sailed a long, long time ago.

I cut a look toward my bathroom mirror and flinch at the sight of two people.

He angles himself to look in the mirror as well. Exhaling a laugh, he says, "Okay, first of all, that myth about vampires not having reflections relied on mirrors having a silver backing, which is outdated. Second of all, the idea was that foul beings couldn't interact with holy metal, and, once again, I'm not evil."

He can repeat whatever he wants to as many times as he likes. My stubborn skill set is maxed out. I poured every drop of experience into it, heedlessly ignoring other things.

Like charisma.

Which, arguably, does make ordering a pizza impossible (a big sad). But I've managed.

The point is: he's evil. And now I'm hungry.

Before I can fold my arms, he grabs my hand and totes me out of the bathroom, through the living room, to the kitchen. Sitting me in my spot at the cushioned window nook, he sets the table in front of me and puts a slice of bread in the toaster before cocking his hip against the robin egg blue counter. "Ask your questions," he says, conversationally.

I look out the window, at the sunlight, which is shining across not my cat's diamond-cut cheekbones. It does no burning. It doesn't even make his pale skin glitter. All the myths. Curses. Don't tell me the rules and regulations I know are distributed misinformation set in place in order to calm frail human sensibilities. Don't you dare tell me that I've been willfully consuming falsehoods my entire life. How irresponsible for romance authors to get their information off Wikipedia instead of doing the *right* thing and seeking out the supernatural community directly.

Huffing, I refuse to ask any questions. Questions will prompt the dialogue exposition that infodumps me into the fantasy aspect of this world. The story gods will never get *me* to follow their outline. I only follow my own.

And my own says someone better *and it was all a dream* trope me this instant.

My skin feels weird, and I hate everything.

I'm not suited for this. I'm just not.

When it comes down to it, *I want my cat back*. My itty bitty boy. My sweet fluffy stinky butt. Mew mew. Meowcifin. Bebe.

The names I have called this *full-grown man* are too many to record. How humiliating.

For one of us.

Uncertain who at the moment.

I *really* need to wake up now. Everything needs to go back to normal *now*. Or…or I don't know what I'll do.

"What's done is done," he says, softly. "You can't spite the powers that be into undoing time by keeping yourself in the dark. You'll just anger the readers because you're willfully enabling the miscommunication trope."

Arms crossed, I give him my *most* bombastic side eye. "Can vampires read minds?"

"Not word for word, and only under specific circumstances."

"Explain."

"It requires an exchange of blood and some emotional connection for accuracy. Thoughts, as I'm sure you know, run rampant. More often than not, minds are a jumble of nonsense scrambled with emotion." The toaster pops, so he goes about buttering the bread and bringing it to my plate before topping it with the eggs he had on the stove. "I am capable of picking up sensations from people I forge bonds with. Decoding those sensations accurately is like playing

Sherlock without an author making sure my speculations are correct in the end."

An exchange of...

My eye twitches. "Have *we* exchanged blood?"

He has the nerve to blush. Red tints his bone-pale skin, darkening his cheeks, stretching out to the slight points of his ears. "As of last night, there's been an exchange, yes."

Last night.

Memories shoot through my head like tequila, blazing, strong, hazy.

"Shh." He combs his fingers through my hair. "Calm, starlight. Everythin—"

I grip his wrist, bury my nails as deep as they'll go, and force his hand away from me. "If you say *everything's fine* one more time, we will have a physical altercation."

"I might not be opposed to resolving this conflict through..." He catches my eye and clears his throat. "I understand." Slipping out of my grip, he slides into the seat across from me and clasps his hands in front of him on the table. "Last night, a situation arose."

"A situation?" I ask, numbly aware we're referring to the *crap hits the fan* moment. The sickness twisting in my gut makes the scent of the food in front of me stale, and it doesn't escape me that this man knows my favorite breakfast, the plate I use specifically for breakfast, or the only acceptable breakfast bread...

I like things to be a certain way. It's important to me that I have a routine because breaking my routines renders me immobile for multiple business days.

So the fact that I have several kinds of bread in my house right now—all homemade, obviously—only *one* of them is correct for breakfast...and that's the one he's chosen...

It's disturbing.

Disturbing in what literature might frame as an *oh, that's so sweet, he* knows *her* kind of way.

Well. I reject that sentiment. It's not *sweet* unless such attention is *invited*. I passed out no invitations.

In other words, I am sitting across from a textbook stalker, and I shall not perpetuate an idea that it's okay.

His wounded eyes watch me. "You were attacked."

Numb tingles gather at the base of my spine.

Attacked.

I can barely remember anything.

Last night exists in flashes of the man in front of me, hovering over me, shining eyes backdropped by stars. He kissed me. Several times. I have no idea what else he did. Only that I was wearing different clothes before I woke up this morning.

A beat passes, and I am desperate to wake up again. Into a world where things are back to normal. None of this fantasy garbage. I crave quiet, certain days. My soul longs for blissful nothing. Whoever decided peace was boring should evaluate their trauma.

Covering my mouth, I nudge the plate in front of me into the center of the table. Time to get the *big question* out of the way. "Did you…"

A frantic edge grips the vampire's voice as he half stands, palms planted on the table. "No. *No*, starlight. I didn't do anything like that to you. I swear."

Strange.

For the first time, heavy nerves lace that hypnotic voice of his, and for the first time I'm inclined to believe him. I fight down the free falling sensation and nod. "Why was I attacked?"

A beat passes, then he says, "You're mine."

Disgust twists my expression.

"It's simply true."

"No. It's not."

"Yes, it is. I adopted you."

My eyes narrow. "If you really are Lord Keres, Master of Mischief and Darkness, *I* adopted *you*."

Offense overwhelms his expression as he scoffs and flutters a hand. "Well, obviously not. Humans don't adopt cats. Never have, never will."

"Why? Are they all secretly like *you*?"

"Only some of the ones that scratch and bite. If you've ever met a cat that doesn't scratch or bite, you can be almost positive they're not *like me*."

The scratches. I look at my arms, discover the most recent scratches I had have mysteriously disappeared. I blink at my flawless skin. "You little…" I slam my hands down on the table. "Every time you scratched me was a deliberate decision!"

He clears his throat, daring to look sheepish. "I try not to succumb to my base instincts very often, but…it's difficult sometimes. Around you."

Before nausea can hit me again, I stand. "I want a different plot!" I yell at my ceiling. "Give me something *normal*. At least. *Please*. Can I go on an uneventful tale of self-discovery? I will discover the heck out of myself. You will not *believe* the trauma I am capable of unpackin—"

"Starlight…"

Whipping around, I stab my finger at not my cat. "Silence, you…you…*not my cat*. I don't want this. I don't want you." I reference myself, and his eyes sweep down, get stuck. His throat bobs, and my flesh heats. I stammer, "Do you see this underwhelming stature? It belongs in cozy air-conditioned corners, soaking up sunshine, reading about teenagers who are somehow humanity's last hope or adults who are involved in grotesquely unrealistic romances." I jab myself in the chest. "I was born to eat snacks and make sarcastic comments!" My voice pitches. "I do *not* do well in life or death environments! Do you know what happens when you take a fish out of water? *It dies.* Furthermore, a *ton* of fish don't even need to be *taken out of water* to die. I cannot thrive under the duress of these pH levels."

Not my cat rises and braces my shoulders the second I can't hold back my tears. I hate crying. Tears come so unexpectedly. They don't make sense. I can never tell if I'm sad, angry, some mixture of both, or something else entirely. All I know is that crying makes me look pathetic. And it makes people think they have a right to not take me seriously.

I don't need comfort or to be told I'm hysterical.

I need a less overwhelming world.

Barring that, revenge on whoever or whatever has made me cry.

Not my cat's mesmerizing voice cossets. "You're in shock. This accident won't happen again. You have my protection now. You really are *mine* now."

Pressing my hands to my face, I attempt to get my emotions under control. I hate them. They're too much. My body feels like it'll break beneath them. I can't take this. My words are garbled and damp when I speak. "I recoil at the concept of being owned."

His shoulders droop. "I know. I had hoped to have your consent before taking this step. But I couldn't lose you, and I knew one way I could heal you, so…"

My consent?

This *step*?

My eyes snap open, and my arms fall, heavy. No. My head begins shaking as another bout of nausea riots in my stomach. "Am I… Did you…" My breaths turn reedy, and I can barely exhale the words. "Have you *turned* me?"

"Not…exactly."

"What do you mean *not exactly*?"

He wets his lips. "I haven't turned you into a vampire. I've…" His gaze skitters off me.

"You've *what*?"

His cheeks heat, turning deeper shades of crimson.

I grip the apron he's wearing—*my* apron—and drag his face down to mine. "*What did you do to me?*" I hiss through bared teeth.

His long lashes lower. Cheeks still infuriatingly pink, he says, "I made you my thrall."

Chapter 2

~~~~~~~~~~

Main characters are insane.

Thrall.

A slave or captive.

According to not my cat, becoming a vampire's thrall is an honor. It means retaining humanity in exchange for binding my life to his. I don't have to deal with any *unfortunate side effects* that come with being a vampire. I get to *belong* to him, thus taking advantage of being under his full protection constantly.

He's being delicate in his explanations, painting every word in shimmering lights.

I've checked out of the conversation.

Sprawled on my couch, I stare across my living room at the bookcases lining the walls around my entertainment center.

I own some vampire romances. They're tucked neatly in the paranormal section of my shelves.

A grand total of zero depict healthy relationships.

Dragging a hand to my throat, I swallow.

Why me?

Was my life *too* boring? *Too* predictable? *Too* calm?

Did some great force peer upon my peaceful existence, shake its head, and decree that I required something to balance my life and make it at least as stupid as other peoples'? Am I being punished for being unproblematic?

"Starlight…" not my cat's silken voice interrupts the buzz of my thoughts.

I blink absently toward where he's perched on the front window seat. Lord Keres used to cuddle with me in that very spot.

Freaking pervert.

"My name is Willow."

"Starlight is my pet name for you."

My lip curls into a weak sneer. I can't believe it. I'm out of disgust. I've lost my ability to sass. The world has hefted too much insanity upon my plate, and I yearn for the sanctity of my sleep slab.

Alas. It is barely noon.

"What's your name?" I mumble.

"Zylus Myrkur."

Of course it's something exotic. Real keyboard mash, that one.

Letting my eyes close, I rely on one of my best qualities—dissecting myself from my emotions when they become too overwhelming. The skill earned me the title of *mature for my age* when I was growing up. Funny that I outgrew those words almost as quickly as I came into them. In all honesty, panic takes way too much energy. Case in point, I raised my voice earlier, and now I could sleep for a decade.

Unless, of course, this sheer exhaustion is a result of my body rewiring itself as *Zylus's* thrall. I almost died last night. Maybe the whole raising my voice thing isn't exactly what sapped all my energy.

"Please talk to me," Zylus says.

"Why?" I mumble. "Because *communication is key to a healthy relationship*?"

"Yes?"

"We're not in a relationship, healthy or otherwise, and, for the record, your communication skills during the past *five years* consisted of *meow*." I spread my arms wide. "I lie here, waiting for the storymakers to realize their most grievous mistake. *What were we thinking? Willow isn't a female lead. She's barely a functional human. She once sobbed for two hours because she ran out of popcorn for movie night, which is Thursday. Because it's always Thursday. She's chronically allergic to change. The revelation that mythical beings exist will unravel the spaghetti that is her brain and cause her to have a mental break. Oh look. There she goes. Having one now."*

Zylus sighs. "Darling, logically you know that you're not going to be okay until you understand what's going on."

"Logically I know it's creepy for you to know that." Shoving myself upright, I narrow my eyes on him. "You've been pretending to be my cat for five years."

"I'd hardly say I was pretending."

My spine goes rigid as blood rushes from my face. "I've *showered* with you in the bathroom."

Red highlights his cheeks, and he drags his slender fingers across his lips. "*Technically*, you've closed the door on me, trapping me in a prison of non-consensual seduction."

"I've changed in front of you!"

"Again." His eyes close. "One moment, I'm spending quality time with my darling. The next, the door is closed and she's strip-teasing."

"Last—" I swear. "—night. I was lying in the snow, bleeding. This morning, I'm clean and in fresh clothes. *Explain.*"

Pain ripples across his expression, and his fist clenches, trembling subtly.

I could scream if I weren't fresh out of energy. Bracing my elbows against my knees, I either release a deep breath or my soul into the abyss. I've been conned. For five entire years, I have been conned into loving a tiny black purring monster. "You eat kibble," I croak. "I buy you nice kibble. And you eat it."

"Have you ever seen me eat it?"

"It disappears."

"I take it and use it as bait."

I don't want to know. I don't want to know. I don't... I glance at him. "...bait?"

"For when I hunt." Realization dawns on him, and his arms fold as he has the audacity to look both perturbed and hurt. "Speaking of, you never like my gifts. I've protected your garden from so many moles and kept this place mice and rat free, but do I get a *good boy* for my efforts? No. I get *what a poor thing; I'm so sorry I live with a little murderer.* You have no idea how many times those *poor things* were caught red-pawed eating your lettuce. Since we've finally opened communication, I have to say it leaves me feeling very underappreciated."

I cover my mouth, close my eyes, and count down from ten—because it's supposed to help. It doesn't. "I hate everything about this."

"It's okay. You're still processing this shift. Remember that conversation you had with Alice?"

Alice? Who's *Alice*? I stare blankly at Zylus.

He hums. "That's right. You're terrible at remembering names when you don't deem them as pertinent information. Alice works at the bookstore."

My *conversation with Alice* comes back to haunt me, and I shrink.

"Yep." He points. "That."

"Was there or wasn't there a tone? Do you think she hates me?"

"No, I don't think she hates you. But afterward you spent a week staring dismally out the windows, sighing, and berating yourself over the interaction. You only listened to depressing music, and if I remember correctly, you were sprawled in the center of your bedroom floor, asking Athena if you could ever go back. At two a.m."

"Stalker," I hiss.

"We're roommates."

"I never agreed to become roommates."

"You invited me in, bought me food and toys, and—" He directs a slender finger toward the corner, at the cat tower I built from scratch.

I jolt to my feet, get dizzy, and teeter.

He catches me in his arms before I fall, and I whack the broad expanse of his chest. "You *intentionally* ignored all my efforts in favor of the *cardboard box* some of my supplies came in. You *monster*."

Something in his expression shatters, and a stabbing sensation rips through my gut. Slowly, he settles me back down onto the couch and crouches in front of me. He searches my eyes. "It's beautiful, and I don't want to ruin it. You made it for me. I treasure it entirely." His cool fingers skim my cheek, fall away. "I treasure you entirely, starlight. I'm sorry. This is all my fault. I accept responsibility for everything."

"I just want my normal life back."

His lips part, but his gaze falls. Gathering my hands, he presses his face to my fingers. "Things are different now. They don't have to be bad."

"Don't have to be bad?" My voice pitches. "My cat is a man who drinks blood and gives off sketch obsessed vibes. Something tried to kill me yesterday. I know my genre expectations. These kinds of stories aren't the comforting ones where the main character is allowed to sip tea on her porch."

Zylus's shoulders droop. "What attacked you was a boogeyman, or the physical embodiment of fear. Generally, such creatures are unable to physically interact with humans. They denote sadistic pleasure from cultivating fear and hide in bedroom shadows." Pulling away from me, he sits back, crosses his legs, and clutches his fists against his thighs. "I had been hunting it for a few days and left last night to get rid of it once and for all. I didn't realize…" His fingers plunge into his hair, tousling the perfect strands until they hang in a mess against his cheeks. "When I left, it discovered it could interact with you. I will never be able to erase the sound of your scream from the back of my thoughts."

A thin layer of ice stretches across my skin. "*See?*" My breath quakes. "*That* isn't the life I want." I swear. "*Boogeymen?* I didn't want to know those existed. What *else* exists?"

Pained, his eyes latch onto mine, and he remains silent.

I press my fist against my mouth to keep from retching again. "Why don't people know about these things?"

"People do. *You* do. I didn't need to tell you what I was because you already know. I don't need to go into detail about what a boogeyman is because you already know. The information might be convoluted, and some creatures might be known by a hundred different names, but when it comes to their existence, people are aware. They just mark off what they can't understand as fantasy. Human belief is powerful. Dismissive airs rob life from beings born of malice. Things like fear and hate can, after all, only exist when they are fed."

"How come it could attack me? I haven't believed in fantasy monsters for decades."

"I suspect it is because you have a higher concentration of fae blood than most humans."

I blink. My brain breaks. "I'm sorry. *What?*"

If someone had told me five years ago that this is where

my life would lead, I'd have suspected I was missing a vital social cue. Then they'd probably have gotten mad at me for staring too long.

"It's not a massive revelation," Zylus says as though he's not just told me I have magical ancestors. "The fae can be…" He rests back on his palms and stares absently at the ceiling. "I'm going to say *promiscuous*, because it's a *kinder* term than some others, and they can also be vengeful. Lots of humans have muddied ancestries and don't realize it because faeries are very good at being forgotten. Which is problematic for their half-human descendants at times seeing as it makes their memory remarkably selective."

I search his eyes. "Explain."

"Everything in your house is in a specific location, because if it weren't you'd forget it exists. Your object permanence is poor, and your short-term memory is unexceptional at best. That said, fae are passionate, obsessive, and particular. They collect what they love like crows and fixate on details, never forgetting what's important to them. They have a strong sense of justice and pay back what's due, harboring grudges for their entire lives. Dishonesty makes you uncomfortable. Fae are incapable of bearing mistruths." He lies down on the carpet and tucks his hands beneath his head. "Once upon a time when humans believed a little more in these sorts of things, people like you were called changelings, the theory being that the *good human children* had been stolen and replaced with creatures that didn't quite fit in. As a society, humans outgrew that mindset, but the…isolating response almost always remains."

My head's spinning. Curling up, I lie on my side and stare at the vampire in the middle of my living room. This is crazy. I'm losing my mind.

"The faeries that make up your history and the blood that's strongest dictates what traits present most completely in each individual. You have some pixie in you, which is likely why you have some trouble processing emotions and situations."

"How do you know?" My voice is wrong in my own ears, and that whole *trouble processing emotions* thing feels a little too correct. I don't know what I'm feeling. It's all static in my head. Something *wrong*. Vaguely itchy.

"Pixies can only manage one emotion well at a time. Human emotions are more complicated. It takes more effort for you to decode how you're feeling because parts of you are only meant to feel one thing in each instant."

I swear.

"It's why you adapt to routine in order to feel most secure. It takes less energy if you know what to anticipate at a given time."

I swear, louder, draw my legs up to my face, and try to focus on my breaths.

"Malicious creatures are notorious for exploiting humans with higher concentrations of fae blood because malicious creatures rest on the outskirts of humanity's physical bounds. It's extremely rare for humans with fae blood to present any abilities that could protect them, and even if they do present the possibility, they'll lack the knowledge to utilize their potential."

"Stop," I whisper.

Zylus does. Several moments pass while my thoughts run over one another in a jumble I can't make out.

I flinch when I recognize movement beyond my cocoon and peek out to find Zylus sitting up, mismatched eyes intent on me. I look away from them because they make me uncomfortable. They're familiar because they belong to Lord Keres, my kitty, my little boy.

I have been wholly and utterly duped.

And now…

Now I know why I've never felt like I've belonged anywhere. I…

Tears collect and rim my lashes.

I now know why.

I have *not like other girls* energy. My ancestors were faeries. I'm a hybrid creature. *Of course* I don't fit in.

My chest hurts. How dare the story gods burden me with such a hated concept. Might as well let out a breath I don't know I'm holding and pick the lame option in a love triangle, too. Heaven help me. If a love triangle appears, I shall simply enter my room and never leave.

In the most awful ways this makes too much sense. I don't fit in because I'm not entirely human. This is insane. I said I wanted self discovery *instead* of a vampire in my house, not on top of it. Mercy. Did no one hear Zylus just now? My optimal functioning parameters cap at *one* emotion.

This plot's too complex.

I'll never manage.

Part fae. Vampire cat. Boogeyman attacks.

I need three to five business years of nothing going wrong at all in order to cope—and, yes, I mean *nothing going wrong* in a sense of *there better be popcorn every Thursday.*

I will riot if one more scrap of distress befalls me.

The worst part is I want my cat. I want to squish little paws and feel sandpaper tongues. But I can't. Because that is so very weird now.

Every time I think my stomach might settle I remember something else disconcerting. Like the fact *he's licked me*. My hands, fingers, arms. Even my neck and chin and cheeks. "Pervert," I whisper. "How old are you?"

"Seventeen...hundred...ish."

I roll over and groan as I sink my face into the back cushions. Reaching lamely, I tug down my white, fluffy throw and wrap myself up. "What in the world is wrong with you? I'm not even five to you. I'm barely a day old by comparison."

"Technically, I was turned at thirty-four, so my mental and physical age isn't that much older than yours."

I spear my finger into the air. "That is *still* a sizable age gap."

"I respect your opinion."

Talk about a diplomatic shut down. But of course he knows how to be diplomatic. He's *seventeen hundred-ish.* Someone said *power imbalance? Love it,* and mashed the key.

Nothing will ever be okay again. *Nothing.*

"Starlight..."

"Don't *starlight* me. You're an ancient pervert who tricks young women into doing your bidding. I don't want anything to do with you. Let me mourn the loss of my cat in peace."

Silence responds, stretches. By the time it makes my skin crawl, I dare to look behind me.

Though I didn't hear him leave, I'm alone, just like I asked.

For some reason—probably the revelation that *freaking boogeymen exist*—this information is just south of comforting...

Chapter 3

Priorities, people. Priorities.

I awake on the couch, eyes crusted from the tears that put me to sleep, and it is alarming how I can both feel terrible and better at once. Scrubbing at my eyes, I fight the sensation of staleness in my mouth and hobble to the bathroom with my throw wrapped around my shoulders like a cape.

After brushing my teeth and washing my face, I locate a sliver of my will to live.

Naps are miracles.

Life isn't weird.

Life is just *life*.

Stuff happens sometimes.

All I have to do is maintain my usual existence.

As long as I am *okay* right *now*, no problem.

She says, convincingly...

This is no different than having a disastrous conversation at the bookstore. Sure, it might haunt me for the rest of my days and leave me grappling with a sense of self-loathing for all eternity, *but* did it keep me from going back to the bookstore?

Absolutely not.

Now more than ever I require the mental release books provide.

If my brain is *literally* wired to handle one emotion at a time, I'm going to live my life one moment at a time. This moment is okay. I take a deep breath and decide the next one is as well.

Whatever problems might arise, they are not *now*. So I'm going to live as though they are *never*.

I call it *professional disregard for crucial issues*.

Out of sight, out of mind.

Seeing blood on the doorstep but still walking into the haunted house...

Willfully blind. It's my new identity.

There is no vampire cat. There is only dinner. I deserve recreational baking. I have lemons. I should make a pie. Excellent. Now I have a perfectly calm and orderly plan.

Step one: get dressed, because it's long past time to do so, and my skin is starting to feel weird in my pajamas.

Step two: make dinner, because I didn't eat breakfast or lunch.

Step three: bake a pie.

I should probably check on my chickens at some point, too, since I didn't check on them this morning...

Pausing in my room, I discover darkness beyond the window and shudder. My hair prickles, but I shake my head. "You're not scared of the dark," I mutter. "If things have been lurking in it before, they've left you alone. Until last night. But last night was an outlier. Last night should not be counted." Robotically, I choose a black dress with a layered waterfall skirt. While I handle the lace-up back, I try not to think about Lord Keres sitting on my bed and watching me change. If he ever did.

I seem to remember him, on multiple occasions, burying himself so deeply under the covers he couldn't find his way out on his own. His pitiful cries echo in my memory, and it's difficult to consolidate the image of my kitty goon with a tall, dark, and hypnotic man.

A tall, dark, and hypnotic man who I've spent the past five years unknowingly cuddling.

Are there magical committees set in place for instances like this? Some form of government? Witch lawyers who protect poor part human girls who have been housing freeloading pervert vampires unknowingly?

If there are, the chance that they're benevolent is nil.

First rule of literature: the governments are always evil. If they aren't completely evil, the male lead is probably the head of the government and the aspect of it that's out of his control is evil. Get ready for five hundred pages of overthrowing that part and establishing a new regime solely based around Mister Love Interest, which will totally not become problematic in other ways that result in a seven book series.

Authority cannot be trusted.

Long live anarchy.

My sarcastic, ever-present narrative gets me all the way to my kitchen tiles before I look up and scream.

Zylus whirls away from the stove, eyes massive. "Star—"

"What are you doing here?" I blurt. My gaze slashes to the pot of water he's just put down. "What are you making?"

"It's…dinner time. I'm making you dinner."

"*Why?* I told you to go away."

"You told me to let you mourn in peace. So I did."

I rake in a breath, let it out slowly. I am *calm*. I will not freak out again. I can't keep freaking out and sleeping and freaking out and sleeping. That's no way to live. Where would I squeeze reading in? "Did you miss the part where I said I wanted nothing to do with you?"

"No. I've been replaying it in my head for the past five hours." A wounded smile overcomes him. "It still hurts. Every time."

My lips purse, and I glance at the ingredients on the

counter. A box of pasta and a defrosting tupperware of homemade gravy. It's an acceptable dinner. Let's pick our battles, Willow. Our goal right now is figuring out how to pretend yesterday didn't happen. Trailing to the kitchen nook, I take my usual seat and clasp my hands together on the table. "What do you expect to come of this?"

Opening a cabinet, he gets the salt out. "I have no expectations."

I hate his voice. It muddles my mind, tells me his every word is law. "I don't believe you."

"Because you don't believe anything positive. You assume only bad things can be trusted because only bad things don't serve a purpose of lulling you into a false sense of security." He shakes some salt into the water, puts it away, and looks at me.

His *I know you* reflects so deeply in his eyes I don't think he suspects at all that it's unnerving. I shift in my seat. "What am I? Food? A toy?"

"I'm capable of feeding myself."

"Then why have you been scratching me for the past five years?"

"Poor impulse management."

I free a low whistle. "The reddest flag today. How long do I have before the withdrawals set in and you pounce on me like I'm prey?"

His expression hardens. Closing his eyes, he collects himself for a short while. When he has, he stalks toward me.

My heart leaps when his fingers lock beneath my chin, stretch my neck upward, and force me to look into his face as he lowers his head. "Sweetheart, please pay express attention to what I'm about to say." His thumb swipes along my jaw. "I love you. Immensely. You saved my life the moment we met. I have lived ages, experienced dalliances, grown tired of weak romantic connections. Never in all my years has anyone so perfectly enthralled my senses from appearance, to manner, to *scent*. You are dear to me. I am slave to your words and wishes so long as they preserve your wellbeing. Command me in any way you desire. Confine me to the form you're familiar with, for I would never speak again if my voice is all I must trade to remain by your side." His lips touch my forehead. "You are not food even if your blood is an aphrodisiac. You are not a toy or some passing obsession that I intend to amuse myself with until I get bored. I crave you. Every moment of you. Existence with you is enough."

Heat rushes beneath my skin, crawling up my neck to flood my face.

Zylus draws his face back—looking half-drunk on the sight. His lips part. "Do you understand?"

Stiff, I nod once.

Nodding back, he touches his forehead to mine, lingers a moment, then lets my chin slip from his fingers.

I love you. Immensely.

Blood pounds in my ears. I wrestle for sense.

Am I truly the kind of woman who swoons over sweet nothings?

Disappointment. I'm supposed to be stronger than that. *Hates everything but books* archetype, remember? I'm so "hashtag relatable," annotation girlies be sketching #same into the margins every other page.

The mere notion that *someone might love me* isn't meant to tilt the very foundation of my character.

It's a tiny bit hard to breathe.

I can't stop watching the way he moves while he's cooking.

Forcing my attention away from the vampire in my kitchen, I call together a committee of my fraying intellect.

It's his *voice*. He needs to turn the allure off. That's it. I'm getting worked up because he's manipulative, like all vampires—even the "good" ones—tend to be. It's not because I can't remember the last time anyone has ever said *I love you* to me.

Has *anyone* other than my parents and Gram ever said they loved me?

Does it matter?

I'm not interested in getting caught up in an angsty vampire romance where the seventeen-hundred-year-old acts like a questionable stalker teenager whose toxic behavior is excusable due to a lengthy and depressing backstory.

Wait a second.

I've not received even a hint at his depressing backstory.

By every account I can determine, this man cooking in my apron does not display *brooding* qualities, or angst, or torment.

Do the love confessions ever happen this quickly?

Isn't the vampire supposed to struggle for roughly a minimum of three hundred pages over the fact he's a blood-sucking monster? There's drama! Intrigue! Passionate fits where he loses all control, sinks his teeth into her, and comes to his senses at the last second possible!

Then, like an idiot with a death wish, she's all *It's fine, I don't mind, you're still you.*

And like the author expects us to forgive and forget in the face of regret, he's all *Don't look at me. I'm a beast. I don't deserve you.*

Away into the night he goes.

She cries herself to sleep.

They angst in their separate corners for a moment, then either he can't keep himself away (**cough** despite the fact he might literally kill her, wow true love…? **cough**) or something happens where he has to save her. Suddenly either love is stronger than instinct or he's proven that his ability to protect her makes him worthy enough to be with her.

Cue smut.

Zylus sets a bowl of pasta in front of me before I can figure out why the domestic deviance from expectation makes this picture better. Maybe it's because he's not glittering at me and insisting he's got the skin of a killer.

Screw the story gods and their futile attempts at breathing life into an over-saturated genre.

Don't they realize it's going to miss every market if the vampire male lead fails to hit the correct beats?

I poke my food. "So…"

Zylus busies himself putting the leftover ingredients away. "So?"

"You *don't* want to bite me?"

"Want is different from will."

"So you do?"

"Kind of."

"But you won't?"

"I won't. Without permission." He rinses out a washcloth and wipes down the counters.

I take a bite of my food, blindly trusting that it isn't poisoned. It looks correct. I saw him make it. There's no reason I can imagine why he'd want to poison me after five years of this charade… "I'd be able to believe you easier if you turned that thing in your voice off."

"It is off."

"Liar."

"If it were on, you'd be entirely complacent, stuck in the middle of a dream fog, and clinging to me. Shivering."

I force down another bite of my food. "But I can tell

something's not right. It's…hypnotic."

Rinsing the cloth out again, he sets it over the sink divider and stares at it. "Sorry. It's a part of what I am. Vampires are natural narcissists. In order to survive, I must entrance my prey. Everything about me is crafted to incite care in spite of better judgment. Hence why the feline form comes so naturally to many."

He has a point. No matter how many times Lord Keres scratched me, I still played with his little pawsies and told him he was the goodest little boy in the world. Except when he brought me dead things and I had to chide him for being a tiny criminal like a good mother should.

Suffice to say, I have numerous regrets concerning my behavior over the past five years. My brain is presently ripping pages out of my skull and sending them through the shredder.

Focus remaining on the washcloth, Zylus muses, "If it would make you feel any better, I could show you what the contrast is like? It could give you some confidence in the fact you have control enough to reject the implications of my voice right now."

"Oh, sure," I drawl. "Why don't I just invite you into my head like I invited you into my house. That seems like a great idea, and it will have absolutely zero consequences."

"I don't need permission to entrance you. I want to put you at ease."

I stuff a bite of pasta in my mouth and regard him dryly as I chew. "Putting me at ease somehow translates into making me do things against my will? I think you just want me complacent." I shove another bite in my mouth and mumble around it, "And *clinging to you*."

A suave smile softens his lips as he peers lovingly at the dish cloth, and a jolt spears down my spine.

I swallow too early, choke and sputter, leaning over my

bowl, hacking.

He appears beside me with a glass of water, and I take it, shakily forcing gulps down. *"You are not inspiring confidence."*

"I'd rather not pretend to be something I'm not now that we've come this far and you've met my true self." He uses a single finger to draw my hair back over my ear. "I'd delight in the illusion of you wanting me, but I could never bring myself to hurt you like that. Doing something so selfish would mean losing you forever. You would never forgive me, and holding onto you like a mannequin isn't really holding onto you at all. Now is it?" He kisses my cheek, flicks his tongue out.

I launch toward the window and clap my hand to my face. "W-w-w-wh—"

An instant of surprise widens his eyes, and he cups his hand to his mouth. "Ah." He takes a step back. "It seems I'm used to giving and receiving more affection these days... Unfortunately, given recent events, you have decreed to leave me in touch-starved squalor."

For the thousandth time in the past twenty-four hours, I can't believe *this is actually my life.*

Don't freak out. Calm down. Eat your pasta.

It's insultingly good pasta, made exactly the way it's supposed to be. We don't waste food in this household. All scraps go to the chickens. *My chickens.* I twist to look out the window at the darkness. It's a moonless night. Fear scrapes along every bump of my spine, and I don't want to go out there. What if other boogeymen are around? I have a comprehensive knowledge of mythology, story magic, and fantasy things. Who even knows what twisted horrors actually lurk in every shadow?

"It's okay."

My heart thuds. "Says the vampire who's been living

under my roof and lying to me for years."

"I mean that I checked on your chickens earlier, starlight. If you don't believe it's safe out there, you don't have to worry about them. They have food and water, and their heater is working."

"Get out of my head."

"I hardly need to be in your head to recognize the origin of your concern."

"That's worse," I bite out. "You know everything about me, but I know nothing about you. Do you even understand how terrifying this is for me?"

He watches me, unblinking, and it's creepy. It's so *Lord Keres*. Over the course of these past years, every time I looked up, my kitty would be staring, blinking slowly. I smiled at him because I thought it meant he loved me as much as I loved him. And, well, now…

Now everything is different. And I hate it.

"Starlight…" His brows lower, and he lifts a hand, scratches his nape. "…I can smell fear. You're not afraid."

"Excuse me?"

"You're not scared. Of me. The only flickers of fear came just now, when you were looking outside."

What is this freaky vampire man trying to pull? I slap a hand to my chest. "It is a *human right* to be scared."

"You're afraid of very little, all abstract. Change. The unknown. Looming social interaction."

"First of all, it's rude to call me out like that. Second of all, *you're* an unknown."

He smiles, sits, tilts his head. "Am I?"

I hate him. I truly despise him. I cannot stand the idea that we've lived together for this long. Angry, I shove food in my mouth and stare at a being that is definitely not my cat, even though I've seen that head tilt a thousand times.

The way he moves is familiar. He's familiar. The

sensation of him, or something. It's as though on some corporeal level I recognize him as a soul I've spent most of the past five years with. Is that a thing? Do souls know one another, intrinsically?

I curse, look at my food, and commit my energy to shoveling the rest into my face.

This man pinned me in my bathroom, which was understandably disconcerting, but my inner monologue didn't dry up and give way to fear like it was supposed to. I panicked a bit and sarcasmed myself into a disgraced corner.

It stands to reason that *truly afraid people* don't shout at their ceilings and ask for a different plot. They don't fall asleep on their couches or put their backs to threats. And they certainly don't accept food from what they claim to fear.

"You're in my head. You're making me think things are more secure than they are."

He laces his long fingers together. "I'm going to entrance you."

"What? No. Absolutely no—"

"I'm going to entrance you without permission because if I get you to give me permission, you'll always wonder if it parallels being invited into your house." He rises, leaning across the table. "Which, I should add, isn't a strict rule, merely an ingrained sense of etiquette that dates back to my formative years. Younger vampires couldn't care less about what is or isn't proper behavior for a gentleman."

"This is legitimately the strangest *kids these days* I have ever heard."

"I envy the innocuous abandon of the youth."

I press myself against the back rest and stare up at his looming figure. "Why don't we not…?" I whisper. "Just *never?*"

"It's important to me that you trust me as much as I trust you."

My throat tightens. "You trust me?"

"Entirely. With my heart, my life, my body. I would stand in fire if you asked me to."

"I'm asking you not to do this."

"I promise it's painless. It needs to cease being an unknown if we're going to move forward."

Heart lurching, I scramble.

"*Stay.*"

The single word takes hold of my limbs, washes into my mind, caresses my every thought. I stop moving. Tension pours out. What was I...

This is lovely.

I've never felt more safe.

The edges of my mind turn fuzzy and warm. I'm drunk. I'm spinning. I'm floating and flying and light as a feather. Mm. Why was I fighting this? Why was I trying to get away? I've never been better. I could live like this forever, happily. Curled up on the couch in Zylus's arms with a good book...

A giggle escapes, which is odd because I *don't* giggle.

Reality crashes into me, and I gasp, shaking off the drunk sensation as Zylus's power lets me go.

Zylus settles back into his seat, nose scrunched, arms crossed. He looks *pissed*.

Aren't *I* the one supposed to be upset? I told him *no*. He did it anyway. Honestly, now that I know what it's like, I'm more relieved than I want to admit, but I'm also annoyed it was so simple to command me. Even though I knew it was coming, I couldn't fight it at all. If vampires can do *that* without permission, what happens if I encounter another one?

Is that the real villain in this story? The boogeyman is

just an introduction. Later I'll be hunted by another powerful vampire who is less benevolent and would *never* make me breakfast and dinner in one of my frilly aprons? Where's my unsubscribe button? I would *really* like to update my preferences right about now.

"You're thoroughly under my protection." Zylus pouts. "You don't have to worry about anyone else getting in your head. Not even the most powerful of the fae could glamour you while you're my thrall. Becoming *mine* is not a light honor. It provides you with complete and total immunity as well as complete and total immersion. I have claimed you. No one can fool you, use you, or remove you from my senses."

"How many thralls have you had?"

"Only you. I have never before wished to keep a mortal being in my world." His fist clenches around his arm, and he scowls at the tabletop.

I shift my weight slightly forward and peer at him. "You being upset is making it hard for *me* to be upset, which is impolite."

"You *giggled*." His nostrils flare. "You've never *giggled* before. I hate myself."

I scoff.

He points. "See? *That's* how you laugh. Because you're an embittered dark goddess, honed in on the mediocrity of the world. I was looking forward to coaxing a gentler bliss into your life so you could genuinely laugh without ire for the real me. I've been trying very hard to compose myself for your sake, telling myself how I'll make *certain* this mistake leads to more happiness for you than I, as merely a cat, could ever provide. I wanted desperately to hear you laugh *for me* for the first time. Now I've practically gone and ruined my entire year."

Is it just me…or is this my cat?

He's giving *you scolded me for bringing you a dead chipmunk, I am lowly and dejected and will now sit forlornly in the corner* vibes.

Holy heck.

Okay. Weird much, sure. A big *change*, absolutely. Dangerous. Kind of embarrassing... Well, it's embarrassing for both of us, isn't it? This whole man has let me squeeze his toe beans for half a decade.

I force down a deep breath.

I can work with this.

I can make this *normal* again.

The worst thing he can do—taking over my mind—is obvious. He could make me do anything. He could have made me do anything these past five years.

Instead, he hunted rodents, followed me around on errands, lay in sunspots, and snuggled me in a purring, adoring, little black puddle. If this man is my cat, I am just speciest and hate the human body. If this man is my cat, he's basically harmless, a little stupid, and somehow *safe*.

Did I...did I just process this situation?

Is it honestly more traumatic for me when I can't decode the random bookstore clerk's tone of voice? *Seriously?* Rubbing my temple, I sigh.

What even is my brain?

Wait just one second...

Bookstore clerk. Bookstore. *Books*.

My heart pounds, and I glance at Zylus, who is embracing his slouch, melting into the seat in a fit of perturb. "Zylus?"

He perks, anger siphoning away, lips parting in awe.

It's the *she said my name for the first time and I am entranced* trope. Real original. It's not all that exciting. I make a note to *not* react *at all* if he ever calls me *Willow*.

"Yes, starlight?" he asks, tone excruciatingly loving.

I ignore it. "As your thrall, we share the same lifespan, right?"

His expression falters, hesitant. "Yes. We do."

My lips stretch, devious. "So...I'm not going to die for a long while, right?"

"No. You aren't."

Oh no. So sad. The world will go on without me. I'll lose everyone I love (ha, who?). Depressing, depressing, deep and dark and angsty. Blargh.

I grin.

Guess who's going to add books to her TBR with wild abandon, knowing she as *all the time in the world* to read them?

This. Girl.

Crossing my arms, I relax against the booth. "Okay," I comment, conversationally. "On, what, twenty-eighth thought? I think I can actually work with this."

His eyes ignite with unrestrained hope, and his fangs catch the overhead light when he grins.

Chapter 4

A cat's still a cat's still a cat.

Life is absolutely marvelous.

It's been a week since *The New Incident*, which turns out to have been less dramatic than stabbing Christie in kindergarten, go figure. My life is *normal* again. If a tiny bit *not normal*, but we ignore the not normal, because if you ignore a problem long enough, you forget it exists. Until it causes bigger problems. But that is totally an issue for future Willow to deal with.

Future Willow hates present Willow with the passion of five thousand suns. Present Willow adores future Willow. It's a secret pining, enemies-to-they-stay-enemies tragedy.

Alas, poor present Willow and her unrequited love.

Out of the corner of my eye, the dark cat spot on the couch stretches, turns into shadows, and yawns as a man before rolling over and snuggling a pillow in a dark shirt and pair of jeans. His long bare toes stretch and curl over the edge of the armrest.

The two notable exceptions to my *normal* are sizable. First, Zylus switches between cat and human forms with no rhyme or reason now. Second, he's no longer welcome in my room.

He appears to be taking the second point better than I am.

Whenever I let myself dwell on it, I *really* miss my cat. We'd been together for years, and we had a routine, and I...

Well, I loved him. *Immensely* and all that.

His presence filled something inside me that let me feel right.

So I really miss thinking about my cat like he's a *cat*.

No more *pspsps*. No more singing to him and dancing around the living room. No more playing with toe beans. No more cuddles.

Eyes still closed, Zylus murmurs, "I welcome all treating me like a kitty behavior."

"Get out of my brain."

"These sensations are new to me. I'm not consciously prying. You're just so *present* now." A little breath leaves him. "I love it. The way everything *you* works is so…so miraculous. I'm quite near addicted to the feeling of your existence on the edge of mine."

My organs respond to the concept of those words in some kind of way. A little too hot. A little too tight.

While I'm trying to unzip the file and spread whatever I'm feeling out in a discernible way, Zylus rolls over again, tumbling off the couch with a graceful *thump*. Blinking up from the floor, he hugs the pillow he's still clutching and stares at the sofa cushions as though they've betrayed him. "As I was saying…I'm open to all humiliating kitty treatment." He smiles at me—from the floor, as though he didn't just fall off the couch like an idiot—and puts his fangs on display. "Especially when I look like this."

I should threaten to toss him out if he doesn't stop flirting with me.

But, *oh my word*, not my cat is so non-threatening ninety-five percent of the time. It's debilitating. Tossing him out brings up images of big, pitiful eyes, cloudy skies, and pouring rain. Sad music. *Donate now* scrolling across the screen. He *needs* me.

Even though I know he totally doesn't.

With utter abandon, he makes a little half-cooing half-purring sound as he snuggles the pillow on the floor and resumes his sleepy time.

I flip the page in my book, absently watching him.

Illegal.

He should be illegal.

"I wanted to mention something," he murmurs. "I've been figuring out the changes that have taken place, and it seems that while the sensation of you and your thoughts relies somewhat on proximity, I can hear you whenever you call me no matter how far apart we are."

I fix my gaze on the lines of words in my lap, no longer reading them. "Typical bond stuff. It's just drama foreshadowing for when I'm fleeing danger and scream your name while tripping to my death so you can arrive last minute looking like you belong in the cover of Vogue. Disgusting and also rejected. I do not run. I will not run. Screaming hurts my throat and makes me tired."

"I guess it's a good thing you don't have to scream for me to hear you, and reaching you takes only a moment."

"Hm?" I offer, dully.

He evaporates into the ground, and I gape, eyes wide on the spot where he vanished. In the next instant, he spills out of my shadow, bracing himself over me on all fours. Bonking his head into mine, he meows.

I clutch my book to my chest and swear.

"We share a shadow." He laughs, fangs glinting in the morning light streaming through the front window.

"*Off.*" It's the same tone I used whenever this little butt nugget jumped on my kitchen counters.

In proper form, the butt nugget doesn't listen. Cocking his head like I'm speaking another language, he peers at me. "I desire a molecule of affection."

"Denied." I'd throw him off like I did whenever he refused to get off the counter, but I am physically incapable of throwing a person of his size.

"Please?" While maintaining his smile, he manages to look pitiful, pretty eyes all large and weepy.

The sad commercial music plays.

"I miss you," he says.

"Were you always this needy?"

"Yes."

That checks out. From the moment we met, we've barely been apart. Except, I guess, whenever he went off to hunt either the poor woodland creatures or the terrible woodland monsters.

"I'm wasting away," he complains, lowering his head and pressing it to my hand.

"Could you speed up the process?" I snip, shoving him back so I can plant my attention back on my book. I'm still not reading.

His head intercepts the space between my eyes and the pages. "One pet?"

Running my fingers through his silky, dark hair is tempting, especially if it's as soft as his fur, but I refuse. On matter of principle.

"Begging for attention is less annoying when you're a cat," I mutter.

Shrugging, he dissolves into a black puddle that flops in my lap. I bite my cheek as he rubs his head against my wrist and vibrates with purrs. The urge to cuddle him intensifies, but I squash it deep down. I will not pet the vampire masquerading as a cat. I won't do it.

That's definitely illegal.

I clutch my book and ignore the compulsion. What is it about humans and cute things and the desire to squish them? I am stronger than this.

His ears flick, all cuddly evil gone when he lifts his head.

My heart thuds in response to the sudden change in demeanor.

Spilling off my lap, he strides toward the front door.

"Wait a second. Where are you going?" Clamping my book shut, I kick my legs off the pink plush of the window seat and march after him.

He looks behind himself, at me, then tucks out the pet door I installed shortly after I decided to keep him. Worst decision ever, by the way.

I jerk the door open. "*Zylus.*"

The chickens cluck. A chilly breeze sweeps up under my black skirt. I shy back into the warmth of my home and search the yard. Icy and brown—the dead of winter. No cat.

My hair stands on end. "Zylus?" How fast is he? What did he hear? Didn't he learn his lesson before when he left me alone? I almost *died.*

Arms close around me from behind, and I scream, jabbing my elbow back into hard stomach.

Twisting, I find Zylus folded over, clutching his midsection.

"You...*you idiot!* What do you think you're doing?"

Expression pained, he smiles weakly at me. "Being cute?"

My eye twitches.

"I didn't expect you to panic."

He didn't expect me to— Raking in a breath, I let it out slowly, march past him, and plop back into my seat. I snatch my book and put my back to him. "I hate you. Go away. See if I care."

"Ow..." he whispers, and I sense his physical suffering someplace deep in my chest. It's uncomfortable. Unnerving. Exactly how deeply are we linked? Soft and pitiful, he murmurs, "You don't play with me anymore. If it were only affecting me, I'd endure, but you're hurting, too, starlight. And I can't bear that."

"I'm fine." The lie rests bitter on my tongue, so I remind myself that *all* humans say *I'm fine*, regardless of whether they're fine or not. It's not a lie; it's a social rule. I clench my jaw, hard, and wonder if the awful way I want to blurt all my secrets all the time is because of my faerie blood.

And here I thought the tendency to vomit my life story was due to traumatic neglect and too much dopamine appearing whenever I perceive that someone is willing to listen to me.

Oop. Nope. Just magic blood in my veins.

Silly me.

"You miss me," he says.

"*You* miss *me*."

"I do. Terribly."

Ha. Sucks to suck.

"Starlight."

I don't reply.

"*Starlight*."

The longer I refuse to acknowledge him, the more wounded each rendition of the nickname gets. It carries the same emotion as him meowing to be let in or out of rooms. As I'm well aware, he does not know when to give up. My nerves pinch, and I whip around. "*What?*"

He bonks me in the forehead with his head. "I love you. I'm sorry I scared you. You are so precious."

My irritation falters.

"There's a thing happening tonight."

I tense, suspicious. "A…thing?"

He nods, sitting cross-legged in front of the window seat. "I'd like to take you with me."

"A thing," I repeat.

"It's a party. Of sorts."

My nose scrunches.

He lifts his hand. "Come with me."

It's the most outlandish statement I've heard since he started speaking. *Me* go to *a party*? Is he for real? Why don't I start wearing t-shirts and volunteering at daycare, too? Lifting my hand, I press my fingers to his forehead.

His eyes glaze as his lids lower, and he presses into my touch like I've granted him a blessing of the highest order.

Adoration of such massive proportion freaks me out a little. What am I even…supposed to *do* with it?

Drowsy, he says, "I don't have a fever."

"Are you feeling unwell?"

"I feel wonderful." His fingers close around my wrist, holding my hand steady against him. "I'm going to tell you things you'll likely deny, but that won't make them any less true, okay?"

What's he talking about? I am a beacon of truth. So long as something's correct, regardless of my emotions concerning it, I don't deny—

"You're lonely."

"*I am not.*"

He kisses my wrist, and the flesh his lips graze burns. "You're stubborn and set in your ways. You've made your loneliness a part of your identity." His mouth skims higher, toward my elbow. "You lash out at love because you don't trust it. You distance yourself from everyone to avoid getting hurt." His nose presses to the crook of my elbow. His eyes close.

I watch him breathe, utterly entranced by the sight.

"You seek solace and human connection from letters strangers write and worlds strangers craft, because at least if ink and paper hurt you, you were never the fool." His eyes open, find me, see into the soul he's claimed. "There's an entire world out there made for *us*. You've never touched it before. You don't know what it means to be welcomed somewhere."

The laugh I try to force out gets stuck in my throat. "*Welcomed?* Into your world with dangerous magical beings? Are you serious? I'm mostly human. I know how the stories go. There's rejection in both places. One just ignores you while the other toys with you until you come apart." My teeth bare. "I'm still deciding which is which."

He nods, lips and nose brushing my skin. "Of course. And as you know from literature, vampires are supposed to burn up in sunlight, evaporate in churches, and die from garlic." Daring thickens his alluring tone, and I don't appreciate it.

"I've never seen you in a church or eating anything."

"I eat."

"Blood?"

"Blood is a supplement and a drug. I can function with less than average, which does tend to lead to circulation and stamina issues that are worsened through prolonged standing or heat. It's easier to manage when I'm a cat." He kisses. "I still require food. More water and electrolytes than an average body requires help. And since my 'condition' isn't a mutation or illness, the antibiotic properties of garlic have no effect."

Well, dang. The more you know. "What do you eat if not the kibble I've given you?"

"Mostly the leftovers you forget exist."

"Why don't you eat with me?"

Bliss fills his eyes, and his smile stretches. "You've never invited me to before."

Sorry, I thought you only ate blood and you were fed nice kibble (that you, apparently, have been chucking at squirrels) up until just last week. My mistake. Do forgive my breach of courtesy.

I regard him dully and hope every word of that snark reached him loud and clear before I mutter, "We're off topic. Parties are gross. I'll be outcast."

"Trust me."

"L-O-L. I will not be doing that. That's how all the nice —cough, idiots, cough—main characters in stories wind up in bad places. They trust pretty eyes and dangerous smiles and..." I come to my senses concerning the fact I've been letting him touch me. I pull away. "And I will not be subscribing to brain damage."

He hums. "You won't be outcast. Promise."

"A faerie will threaten to give me a pig head and send the werewolves after me for giggles."

Zylus laughs. "Only my powers can work on you now, and...the only 'werewolf' in this area..." He laughs again. "Oh, darling. I want to teach you so many things. You'll love them. If you let yourself."

"Thanks for the warning."

He smiles. "Starlight."

"*What?*" I drone, less annoyed than I want to admit. It's nice to have someone to talk to. For a man who can physically vanish into shadows, he's so cheerful. And I'm too calm. Is it because of that residue in his voice? Or have I fully attained que sera sera?

My cat's a blood-sucking person. Okay, whatever. It is what it is. Life goes on.

He combs his fingers through my hair, kneels, and brings his mouth within an inch of mine. His breath traces over my lips as he cups my cheek in his palm. "Come with me."

"N...no."

"You're not even living in your comfort zone, my love. You're in total isolation."

My body swells with warmth. Lifting my hand, I latch

onto his wrist. "I am not. You're here."

"I want more for you than just me."

Well, there's a concept that doesn't align with this genre's standard at all. He's supposed to want me all to himself, ownership of my every waking thought, a hand in each dream and nightmare. Complete obsession met with complete possession.

Wanting more for me is almost a healthy concept. I could have sworn paranormal romances said, *uh-uh, we don't do that here*

I have never done well in groups. I've never been to a party that hasn't ended horribly. I'm scared. I'm more scared of the idea of a *party* than I am of Zylus's mouth hovering near mine. It's tempting to suggest that I'll kiss him if he drops it. More tempting than I want to admit. Does he already know?

His swear runs across my lips. "Yes. But I won't accept. My care for you runs a lot deeper than a moment of lust."

I swallow, hard. "I'm not…"

"Mhm."

"It's your own fault. You're too…close."

"Perhaps."

I don't know if either of us know what the other is trying to say.

"Parties suck." I sound pathetic to my own ears. Whiny. Embarrassed.

"I'm sure that's true of every party you've gone to. But you have never been to one like this."

Of course I haven't been to the kind of party an ancient creature might attend. No doubt other vampires and their thralls will be there, pressed in the corners, doing the kinds of things I only read about because being that close to someone…being *this* close to someone has always felt too raw.

I don't desire connections like these. I never have. I've never understood them.

Once upon a time, I longed to be known.

Now I'm so ashamed of myself the notion that anyone might know me makes me want to hide.

It's too late with Zylus. He knows more about me than I do. He's seen five long years of me being myself without ever realizing someone was looking.

Struggling for air, I turn my face away from him at the last second. "Stop." I shudder. "Please."

He pulls his fingers from my hair and his wrist from my grasp as he sits back on his heels.

I hug myself and can't look his way. I'm stronger than this. I'm not desperate. I'm *not* lonely.

I will not fall prey to the same wiles that have claimed countless fictional lassies. "It sounds like an awful idea."

"If you don't like it, we'll come straight back home."

"Unlike the fae, you're able to lie, so…"

"Not to you."

"Because I'm your thrall."

He chuckles, rises, and kisses my forehead. "I'm in love. The choice is yours. If you don't want to go, just know I'm one word away if you need me."

Snuggling into my window seat, I mutter, "Is that supposed to be comforting?"

"I don't know. Is it?"

Instead of lying, I raise my book and put one hundred percent of my energy into ignoring him. Unfortunately, I don't manage to read a single line until all six-foot-something of him turns back into black cat, trots to the abandoned pillow in the middle of the living room floor, and curls up on it in a perfect little circle.

A party with magical creatures.

A million things could go wrong.

Parties are plot devices. Places to introduce other characters. Moments to hint at political intrigue and delicate balances about to break.

Going to one of *those* is an awful idea that directly contradicts my intentions of finding normalcy.

I absolutely will not so much as entertain the thought.

Chapter 5

If anyone asks, I'm still the introvertiest introvert.

I was supposed to have more brain cells.

Pulling on thigh-high platform shoes, I tighten each buckle before rising and scanning myself in my full-length bedroom mirror. The long black drop sleeves of my dress fall nearly to my ankles in tattered ripples. The reaper hood covers most of my hair. I've painted my lips and eyelids pitch, deepening the contrast between what I'm wearing and my fair skin.

I feel dangerous and unapproachable.

The unsettling feeling that mythical creatures would take one look at me, see through the façade to my numerous insecurities, and exploit them puts me on edge.

That's it.

I'm not going.

Zylus isn't *forcing* me to go. I just won't. Forget it. This was a ludicrous break of character. My willpower is stronger than this.

How dare I be curious about a magic party? Am I trying to get myself killed? Have I partaken of the liquid stupid? What was I even thinking?

"Starlight, I can feel you having second thoughts in there."

"I'm a Tim Burton nightmare, and the other vampires will make fun of me!"

Zylus steps into my bedroom, and my heart stammers at the sight. He's traded his usual dark shirt and jeans for a sweeping cloak with a high collar, heavy boots, and gloves. He adjusts one glove as he scans me, slowly, from head to toe. Smiling, he swears.

Red invades my cheeks, ruining my monochrome, and I shift my weight. "Where did you get those clothes? Where do you get *any* of your clothes?"

He lifts his hand, and shadows gather in his palm. They twist and writhe, leaving a black thorny choker with one large rose behind. "May I?"

Lowering my hood and my eyes, I don't object as he steps up to me and pushes my hair aside, leaving strands and his fingers to tickle my nape. He clasps the ornament around my neck. It's light as air, barely a whisper of presence. I trace a petal just to make sure it really exists on some level and find the softest material I've ever felt. "So you're literally wearing shadows?"

"Master of Mischief and Darkness, no?"

"Doesn't that make you kind of naked?" I pull my hood back on.

"No comment."

This should make me more uncomfortable than it does. Am I actually already used to the oddities? Will that assist me at this party?

When Zylus offers his arm, I stare at the appendage. "Are we in the eighteen hundreds?"

"Lovely time. We got bicycles."

I scoff. "*That's* what you, a person who lived through that period, chooses to remember?"

"Bicycles are fun."

With half a wry smile tugging on one corner of my mouth, I slip my hand into the crook of his arm. "You don't say."

He glides me outside into the bitterly cold night, and my breath clouds in front of me as I shiver. Thank goodness

I opted for my lined black tights. Without them, I would become an icicle. Which may very well be the least of my worries.

Zylus whistles, low, and I arch a brow seconds before the darkness clinging to the walkway in front of us turns *alive*. The shadows take a great big breath, pour from every crack, and materialize as my deepest fantasies.

Dark as dripping oil, two perfect skeletal horses take the helm of a hovering coach.

My mouth falls open, and the icy night air freezes my saliva.

Zylus—now a certified *jerk*—tucks a single finger beneath my chin and closes my mouth. "Shall we?"

"*Shall we?*" I echo, livid. "What in the world is *this*? Necromancy?"

"Necromancy isn't a thing."

"It isn't?" I ask, and my voice feels as though it might crack at any moment. Pardon me. I'm having trouble keeping track of what is and isn't *a thing* these days. I'm already reaching my limit of what I can process in a given day, and we haven't so much as made it to the party yet. I have a feeling after tonight, I'm going to need a month's recovery time.

"Contrary to the depictions in popular fiction, the bounds between life and death are not the sort created beings may cross." He opens the door for me, letting me into a lush black cabin.

"Ah," I whisper. "Is that so?" Stepping inside, I ground myself in the plush. It's stable. Secure. It matches my makeup and nail polish and clothes. I blend right into it along with him, only our pale skin standing out against the pitch. This kind of excitement isn't bad, right? A gothic coach is the sort of thing I like. I cross my ankles, fold my hands in my lap, fidget.

Zylus snaps, and the thing *flies*.

Throwing my arms out, I brace myself as trees slash past the murky windows. Breaths rake through my lungs. I count them. No big deal. We're just flying.

People aren't supposed to fly.

"Starlight?"

"What?" I snap.

"You okay?"

"I have regrets."

"Do you want to go back home?"

I swallow rising bile. "I decided I was going to see the party. I can't unplan that plan until I see the party."

He crosses the cabin, sits beside me, and wraps an arm around my shoulders, letting me ground myself in his body. "You're okay."

"Repeat that."

He presses his lips to my ear, murmuring through my hood, "You're okay, starlight. Look." He directs my attention to the sky. Moon-slivered. Star-filled. Stunning.

Massive celestial bodies no larger than specks glitter in the ebony expanse. The sight steals my breath and quiets my heart. I watch the endlessness pass, side by side with a vampire.

Some moments sift away, gone before they have a chance to begin. A lot of my childhood feels like that, empty or hollow. My youth is a collection of snapshots depicting the worst times.

Unlike those blurry memories, this moment feels evergreen. In the years to come, I'll be able to reach it, thumb through it, draw it back in vivid black and silver. I'll remember the threads of panic as they siphoned away. The sturdy, ethereal being beside me, holding me. His lilting, melodic voice, reassuring me. His heat.

My brows knit. "Zylus?"

"Yes?"

"You're warm."

His cheek tilts against my head, and I didn't realize it was there until now. "Yes?"

Turning to him, I touch his chest and ignore the fact he's wearing shadow. Technically, we're riding in shadow, so if it's strong enough to keep us from plummeting to our death, I suppose it's good enough to use as clothes.

All the same, crimson erupts in his cheeks.

I find the pulse in his throat, and it hammers. Fast, fast, fast. He's a vampire. According to everything I know, he isn't supposed to be so *alive*.

"You have a heartbeat?" I ask.

Tense, he whispers, "Yes. An overactive one, at that."

"It's clear I still know nothing about what you are."

His hand covers mine. "I'll teach you."

"I'd prefer a comprehensive pamphlet. Something with an outline." Lips pursing, I say, "I'd joyfully accept a PowerPoint."

"I'll teach you," he echos, drawing my hand up his throat, to his mouth. He kisses my palm, gaze half-lidded and all entranced on me.

I don't know how to feel, so I push his face away and angle my body toward the window. My palm tickles. I dig my nails into the flesh. "Are there any rules I should know so I don't accidentally sell my soul to another vampire?"

"You don't own your soul anymore. There isn't a singular thing you can do to harm yourself, so just be yourself."

"I'm not sure which part of what you just said is more concerning. Things don't go well when *I'm myself*. I don't even make it through the grocery store without someone insulting my clothing choices."

"Appearance is such a small-minded thing to fixate on.

Maybe they're jealous?"

"Doubtful."

"You're so beautiful I don't think humans know what to do with you. They are notorious for ridiculing what they don't understand and envying what they wish they did."

I cross my arms. "Flattery will get you nowhere because compliments make me uncomfortable."

"Seventeen hundred years, and no one has crippled my soul in the way you have, starlight. These words are more fact than compliment."

"Facts aren't subjective."

Slipping his hand into mine and breaking the connection between my nails and my flesh, Zylus sighs. "You know being particular about words is a fae thing. You're going to fit right in."

The coach begins to lower while my mind replays that statement. The second we touch down, it clicks. I turn toward him. "This isn't a vampire party?"

He draws me to my feet, and the shadows disperse around us, dropping us lightly in the middle of a forest, on the edge of a clearing. At first glance, the stars have come to earth. At second, they have wings.

This is not a vampire party.

In the center of the clearing, a fountain of bubbling pink rushes throughout the air. No basin. No physics.

I stare at it, afraid to let the rest of the scene come into focus. Already, nothing makes sense. I *need* things to make sense.

Zylus thought I'd enjoy this? Maybe he doesn't know me at all? Or maybe I am just like all the main characters I read about—a little stupid with a lot of plot armor.

Do I have plot armor?

Is that the reason I've survived so long when, statistically, people who need weeks of mental preparation in order to go shopping *shouldn't* make it past high school graduation?

"Oh my light." One of the tiny gleaming beings zips up to us. In a flash of blinding rays, she touches down on the pine needles in front of me, several inches shorter, gossamer wings flitting, purple eyes massive in a dark-skinned face, long ears shooting back on either side of a silver updo covered in red berries. "Zy. Is this her?" The young woman's fingers lock together, and I notice they're too long by an entire knuckle, the dark skin tipped in a speckling of violet hues.

I'm a *her*. I'm a known being. Do I greet this faerie? Do I wait for Zylus to introduce me? Do I pray for a comet to take me out?

The woman grabs my hand, lifts it, and shakes my arm, letting the billowing fabric of my sleeve play in the breeze. "Oooh."

Zylus swats her off me. "Lesta."

Lesta's wings pin. "Oh. I'm sorry." The woman's beautiful face twists, and she searches me. "Does touch bother you?"

My eyes lock on Zylus, pleading for answers or direction.

Instead, he gives me a textbook explanation. "Some humans struggle to regulate the fact their fae blood calls constantly to the world around them. It can make things like touch overwhelming. In others the opposite occurs, whereby a sense of underwhelm plagues them almost constantly. Pixies find it difficult to employ empathy, so since Lesta errs on the side of underwhelm, she can't imagine what it's like to be at the other end."

Lesta laughs, her voice musical. "It's true."

"Just so you know, Lesta, my darling has quite a bit of dryad in her, so do be considerate of her calm nature."

I bristle. Why am I only learning that *now*?

Lesta's lips form a perfect "O." In a flash of light she returns to no bigger than my thumb. Pointing across the clearing, she cheers, "There!" and she's gone before I know what *there* is meant to refer to.

Zylus wraps an arm around my waist, leading me onward into the scene.

I hiss, "You said I was pixie."

"Some pixie. Mostly dryad."

"Tree people?"

"Keepers of nature. Gentle spirits. Some of the fae you're about to meet."

I scoff. *Natural* is not the vibe people get when they look at me by any means.

Zylus cuts a glance my way as we slip past beings with animal hooves, children with worn, elderly faces, monsters with delicate butterfly wings. Some of the trees walk. Several groups of people rest in puddles of silk pillows, laughing together, picking tiny cakes off golden plates.

A number of the creatures in the whirlwind around me appear drunk.

Music plays, but I don't know from where, and it seems to change depending on who's dancing closest to me.

Beyond the thickest revelry, several women lounge in a patch of grass overburdened with flowers. A tiny chihuahua with big, big ears sits on one's lap, eyes empty, tongue lolling.

My heart brightens at the sight.

There's a puppy.

Maybe tonight won't be terrible.

Those derpy eyes turn toward us, and the little thing yips, shaking like a leaf. The tan and white bundle is so cute I lose my emotional support inhibitions. I love him. Before I can think, I say, "I like your dog."

The woman holding him giggles.

Its tail wags.

"May I pet him?"

The woman's green eyes flick toward Zylus, and her plump lips curl. Something soft and indecipherable enters her tone when she says, "Sure."

As though fully aware, the little guy stands up and looks at me. Its tongue flicks out, hanging like a limp noodle.

Zylus wraps his arm tighter around my waist and refuses to let me crouch. With a chilling smile on his face, he says, "I will—" Expletives. "—if you even think about —" Expletives. "Okay?"

Slowly, I twist, fixing a look of horror on not my cat. Is he dogcist or something? I get that he can turn into a cat, and there's an ancient rivalry between dogs and cats, but who does he think he is?

"Notice I could have tucked my tail and whimpered, and she would have hated you forever." The smooth, rich tone of voice strikes me as masculine, despite the fact there's only a group of oak-skinned dryads in simple emerald gowns behind me. "I didn't do that."

"Appreciated," Zylus notes.

Chewing my cheek, I face the puppy, who is—of course —now a man with spots of white splattered across his tan skin. Sandy, wild hair falls over round ears, and his neck stretches as the dryad woman whose lap he's occupying scratches him beneath the chin.

Zylus's hold on me eases. "Darling, meet Doliver, the 'werewolf'."

Doliver the…

I fix my attention on the man as he flops in the dryad's lap, head on her thigh. What I saw moments ago was not a wolf. It was barely a dog.

A second before my legs give out, Zylus settles himself in the grass and draws me onto his lap. Bracing a hand at my back, he rubs a circle around one bump of my spine. "Ollie's my best friend, which makes him think he has the right to be a little—"

"Hey," Ollie interjects. "I'm a delight."

He had one brain cell three seconds ago.

I know I said I didn't want to be in a generic vampire story with teenage angst, but I am also ill-equipped to watch all my fantasy beliefs unravel at the seams. Vampires are clingy cats. Werewolves are derpy dogs. They're best friends. And...and aren't fae supposed to be horrifically powerful, threatening beings that play tricks on people? Behind me, the children with elderly faces giggle and run throughout the streams of sparkling pink, playing tag.

This is too wholesome for paranormal. I almost died last week. Did we miss that part?

There was an attack.

A near-death experience.

I'm seated on the lap of a man who drinks *blood*, for crying out loud.

This genre's not genreing correctly.

"She's cute." Ollie reaches for my dress.

Zylus hisses, scooting me further up his thigh until I'm pressed firmly to his chest. His mismatched eyes flash with foreboding promises.

"Possessive much." Ollie's lips pucker as he plants his elbow on the dryad's thigh and rests his chin in the palm of his hand. His earthy brown eyes settle on me. "How's he treating you? Not too nippy, I hope."

"Ollie," Zylus warns.

"What?" Ollie grins. "We all know you bite."

"You do bite," I confirm, because I don't know what else to say. "Scratch, too."

"Menace." Ollie chuckles, eyes glittering in the literal faerie lights.

Zylus's lips turn down as his hand drops to my hip, cementing me against him.

An odd sensation travels up my spine, but I ignore it as the dryad holding Ollie tugs on my sleeve. "Zy says you keep a garden. I would like to talk about your garden." The woman pushes back the curtain of her dark hair, and her beauty strikes me thoroughly. The sight of her smiling at me, the way her green eyes flick my way a moment before settling on a flower beside her, she's enchanting.

I want her to like me.

I haven't wanted someone to like me for a long time. I gave up on such desires sometime between stabbing Christie with paper-only scissors and entering high school. My parents like to say that my life of crime started young and I came fully into my dark soul about the time I started refusing to wear color, but they didn't understand.

They didn't understand how much I *tried* before I gave up on the possibility I would ever be someone people wanted to have around…someone people wanted to talk to…someone people looked at and thought *I want her to like me.*

Zylus taps me on the back, and I jerk my thoughts out of the nowhere zone they spiraled down, wondering with some small bit of apprehension if he could hear them, feel them, whatever. He looks at the dryad. "Pila, please don't casually reveal how much I talk about her."

Focus remaining on the flower in her palm, which steadily grows larger with her touch, Pila says, "Oh. Was that a secret?"

"A poorly kept one."

Pila laughs, plucks the flower once it's spilling from both her hands, and gives it to me. "We've heard of nothing else for five years."

"Pila," Zylus chides.

She covers her mouth. "Oh. We weren't joking?" Conspiring, she hugs Ollie around the chest and leans closer to me. "Zy's tone is always so pleasant. It's hard to tell what he's thinking, isn't it?"

"Is it hypnotic for you, too?" I ask, because I'm deeply curious, and maybe it's because this group of women radiates peace, but I don't even feel like I'm at a party. The chaos behind me is a blur of bad decisions I won't make, but I'm sitting in the book club corner, chatting about Anne Rice.

Pila nods. "I'm a sprout. Perhaps some of the older fae wouldn't notice." Her voice drops, barely a whispering breeze. "But I'm barely thirty."

"Ma'am. I'm barely twenty-six. I have no idea what's going on."

Laughter pours from her, and my heart soars.

Conversation from that point ebbs and flows—strange and peaceful. Pila chats with me as though I belong, asking about my garden, what I'll be planting as soon as winter breaks, when I'll be starting my seeds, if I'd like her to stop by and help. There's no underlying tension. No overwhelm from the surrounding chaos, which feels secluded elsewhere. At one point, a man with deer hooves stops by, offering us flutes of some sparkling drink, and Zylus covers my eyes because he's only wearing a single scrap of fur around his waist.

The event strikes me funny.

So I snort, pull his hand away, and smirk at him. His cheeks blister beneath wide eyes, so he tugs my hood down over my face and hugs me a little closer.

I'm delirious, confused, drunk on the scent of faerie wine.

It's too much and too little all at once, so I ignore the pinching in my chest as it builds and builds until Zylus excuses us from the revel. The vampire and werewolf and dryads exchange parting pleasantries, vaguely mention future visits or other parties, then we're back in the flying coach.

Zylus's arms around me.

My face pressed tight to his chest.

With sobs I don't understand tearing me apart.

Chapter 6

My brain runs on Internet Explorer.

Dearest Athena…

I know you don't exist, but I require assistance from someone wiser than I, and I feel bad bothering a deity that does exist with my utter stupidity.

Arms spread, I lie on the floor in my bedroom and stare at my ceiling fan.

You see, I went to a party roughly a week and a half ago, I think. I've lost track of the days since. Anyway, it was lovely. Which was unprecedented, I know. To be completely honest, getting sold to an elf might have hit closer to my expectations.

Speaking of expectations, consider mine destroyed forever. The faeries were nice, polite, friendly in an *I'm not going to trick you into trading me your firstborn* kind of way. They were perfectly frank, which made conversation easy.

I met a werechihuahua.

And that's something you probably don't hear every day.

Or any day.

Because you don't exist.

But, right now, it doesn't feel like I exist, either, so you are in good company.

As I was saying, the party was fun. Welcoming. Filled with a sense of belonging I don't think I've ever experienced before.

So, naturally, I sobbed into a vampire's arms the entire way back home.

My jaw locks, and I turn my head, taking in the large blossom resting in my palm. It's the flower Pila gave me. I crushed it a bit while I was sobbing on the trip back. (Oops.) But, hey, it's not so much as begun to wilt.

In contrast, the choker Zylus gave me turned into mist shortly after I took it off. I'd be lying if I said I wasn't disappointed. It was pretty. I liked it.

I'm getting distracted.

Athena, Greek goddess of wisdom and war strategy, I have but one meager question to ask.

What is wrong with me?

Is the fae blood in my veins messing me up something fierce? Am I built neither for inconvenience nor convenience? Do my mutt genetics condemn me to excessive recovery times after every event, positive or negative?

The weariness in my bones takes me back to my childhood.

Every day after school, like clockwork, I collapsed. Every morning—still exhausted—I forced myself to repeat the cycle so I wouldn't cause trouble for my parents. I spent the weekends doing mindless gardening or rewatching reruns of whatever brought comfort.

For a long time, I could recite entire episodes of *Teen Titans*. Word for word. And when school was entirely too much, I played the show in my head in the back of the classroom. My grades sucked because I was too busy surviving to pay attention. Teachers ignored me. Children bullied me relentlessly.

Nowhere felt safe.

Society beat the angry outbursts that led to Christie stabbings out of me, leaving me defenseless.

If it weren't for my grandmother leaving me everything, I don't think I would have made it this long.

Now, I've seen monsters, magic, and skeleton horses that fly. I live with a vampire cat, whose motives I continue to question despite the fact I've snotted in his shadow clothes. I've smelled faerie wine. I've discussed square-foot gardening with a dryad. A boogeyman nearly killed me.

In spite of everything new swirling around me, humans scare me more.

In spite of everything, if given the choice between this or going back to *school*, I'd put my socks on inside out, wear my clothes backward, and walk blindly into the woods, never to be heard from again...

A knock sounds on my door, so I hiss, drawing my flower in closer and curling around it.

In this world of chaos, the twelve-inch bloom is all that brings me peace.

Her name is Deidra. And I love her.

"I thought hissing was my thing," Zylus provides as he opens my bedroom door. "May I come in, starlight?"

"No."

"Please?"

I grunt, and I guess he takes that as permission because he steps into my room, scans me in my Victorian mansion ghost gown longer than necessary, and frees a little sigh. "We're steadily running out of food."

"*I'm* steadily running out of food. You've got plenty hiding in the woods."

He crouches near me, braces his elbows on his knees, and cups his cheeks in his hands. "I need more than blood to survive."

"Eat a whole rat. I bet the bones are crunchy."

"I'd feel bad dragging so many out of their nests in the

dead of winter to sustain me. Wouldn't you?"

I bury my nose in Deidra's soft petals. "I can honestly say I have never once had a reason to think about it."

"Lucky."

"Leave me alone to perish."

"No can do. I'm attached to you."

I mutter, "Literally or emotionally? As your thrall, does the life bond thing go both ways?"

"Being my thrall means you are under my complete protection. My death would only see to restart your clock where currently it has been paused. The extent of your duties is to remain by my side."

"Delightful."

He grazes his fingers through my hair. "Only in my most dreadful fantasies…" His touch traces the shell of my ear before pulling away. "Come on, starlight. It's time to rise and shine."

"I do, occasionally, rise to care for my chickens and eat a cookie. I *never* shine. And so long as I have a choice, I don't want to listen to you. Ever."

"We're out of cookies."

"Hence the reason I soon perish." I flail a hand at my attire. "Why do you think I'm wearing this? I want to be a cool ghost."

"Ghosts don't exist."

Just another thing to ruin my day…

Zylus's brows dip before he lies beside me, fingers laced atop his midsection. "You should know that if I don't medicate, I get hangry."

I close my eyes. "If you're saying that if you don't maintain blood intake, you turn into the feral vampire tween angst expectation…please don't use modern slang."

His voice lowers. "I'm saying that if we lie here together long enough, I might try to bite."

I glare dully at him.

He whispers, "I'm not me when I'm hungry."

"That's it." I huff, roll over, and put my back to him. Which…I shouldn't do. And especially not when he's teasing about drinking my blood. But. Whatever. "You've got legs. There's money in my purse. Bye."

"You can't lie on the floor forever."

"Can. Will. Bye."

"Starlight."

"If you don't like it, *fix me*. Use that pretty voice of yours and make my brain function correctly." Although my tone is scathing, tears well in my eyes, and my throat closes. I don't want to cry again. Not in front of him. He's seen enough of my fragile moments. He has all my secrets and brokenness tucked away in his head already. This is why I live alone in the woods. I'm not made to be around people.

Good or bad, I can't handle interactions.

"Your brain isn't wrong. It's just different." His tone hardens, firm and impenetrable. "Also, it's only been fed cookies for days. That can't be good for it."

"Who made you a doctor?"

"Harvard. I was bored for a decade."

I shoot a glance over my shoulder, find Zylus's severe, mismatched eyes. Now I know why vampire slayers exist. Vampires are remarkably stabbable. I kind of want to stab him.

"I'd let you."

"Let me what?"

"Stab me." He folds his arms beneath his head, an innocent. "The thought came so crystal clear, you must really want to, and who am I to stand in the way of your dreams?"

"I yearn for the abyss. A world where my cat isn't a

vampire who reads minds. That's my dream. Get out the way of it."

"You'd be lonely."

I would be so lonely. Giving my head a firm shake, I tell myself that little thought was a consequence of his mesmerizing voice and roll my eyes. "Just go to the store. And get more cookies."

"I'll get protein bars."

"You must hate me."

Lifting his hand, he coils a lock of my hair around his fingers, draws it across the slice of carpet between us, and presses his lips to the white and black strands. "Could I but hate you I'd suffer far less." My hair slips from his fingers, and I assume that when he gets up, he's going to grab the money from my purse and get the most disgusting protein bars he can find in order to prove a point. Instead, he sweeps down and scoops me up off the carpet.

I scree in distress as Deidra tumbles from my fingers, and I scramble for her. "Hey!"

Zylus jostles me, rocking my weight against his chest. "We're going to the store."

"I'm not wearing shoes. Are you going to *carry* me through the store?"

"I'm thinking about it. I just don't know if I have the stamina." The tiny indent between his brows clues me in to the fact he's telling the truth.

"Zylus!"

He lowers me, and my skin turns electric. I'm pressed tight to his body, every inch firm beyond the wisping fabric of my gown. My toes hit the floor, but I remain settled against his heat.

Warmth spreads before I can stop it.

Whoa. No, no, no.

I yank myself away, and the warmth in my chest floods

to my face.

We're not toying with attraction again. Bad idea. Worse idea than going to a party. This man was made to enchant poor, unprotected women, and I want nothing to do with it.

"Starlight," he murmurs, and a tingle that didn't get my most recent memo erupts in my chest.

I cut a glance at him, trying my best to look upset even though my eyes are still watery with tears and there's a high chance I'm flushed. "What?"

"Put some shoes on. We're going out."

Trailing my fingers down my skirt, I mutter, "If I refuse, are you going to make me?"

"Through sheer force of constant nagging, yes."

That might be worse than hypnotism.

With a heavy sigh, I make sure Deidra is comfortable on my dresser and get ready to leave.

Sunlight slices through the chilled air as I step out into the yard with Zylus at my side. The light immediately hones in on my pale gray eyes and stabs through my retinas. I don't want to people. I don't have the energy to people. I'm not doing this.

Turning on my heel, I find myself making a full circle as Zylus spins me forward again. "One foot in front of the other, darling."

"I despise you," I mutter, but I take my first step down the stairs to the stone path and flinch at the way my chest twinges. "Are you going to punish me whenever I say something you don't like?"

"I would never punish you."

"You just made my chest hurt because I said I didn't like you, and it's not the first time."

Surprise stills every muscle in him for a moment. His eyes search mine, and—not for the first time—his effortless beauty strikes me. "My apologies," he says at last. "I wasn't aware the link between our souls could allow you to sense my pain, too." His lashes lower. "I care deeply for you. I miss existing in your adoration. When you say you hate me, I feel gutted, and it must spill over into you."

"You tricked me into adoring you."

"I existed. And I've already told you I would return to that form at your word."

I drag my attention off him before he can get deeper in my head. Gathering my coat tighter around my chest, I march past him.

"Would I have your word?" he calls, and the phrasing feels oh so fae-like. When I ignore him, his presence seems to skate just behind my back, raking apprehension and threat down my spine. "Command me so I might become whatever most suits you, starlight."

I whirl, inches from him. I have to tilt my head way back to meet his blue and green eyes. "Quit it."

"I long to serve you."

"I said *stop*."

Reserve refines his expression as he tucks his fingers into the pockets of his coat and watches me down the bridge of his regal nose. He doesn't make another sound. He just stares, his dual-colored eyes catching dappled rays.

Breath shivers through my lungs, pouring into the cold late afternoon. "Telling you what you can be is wrong."

"More or less wrong than invading your life under the guise of being a cat and putting you beneath my power against your will?"

"*Wrong* is *wrong*. There's no more or less."

"How fae of you."

I bite my cheek and taste iron.

Zylus's eyes focus, pupils swallowing colored irises. He swallows. I watch his throat move.

The vivid image of him kissing me and sweeping his

tongue into my mouth to catch the blood off my wound forces me back a step.

"I would never—"

"You already did," I snap. Wind hits my back, freezing it as though I'm beneath him in the snow-spotted yard again. His lips on mine. Addiction in his every inch. Fear and pain and confusion coalescing into a beast of my very own.

Recognition widens his eyes. "Starlight…that night…I didn't. I *wouldn't*. I was breathing for you."

"What?" I whisper.

He covers his mouth. "That night… That wasn't a kiss. I was breathing for you. You stopped breathing during the transition, and I panicked. Has that bothered you all this time?"

"I've tried not to think about it."

"I'm so sorry."

It's the regret. The remorse. The brokenness.

I believe him. I believe he is wholly repentant. Not just for the kiss, either.

He's ashamed of the entire situation, that I was harmed while in his care, that he almost lost me, that it had to come to this, and that saving me had other consequences.

Looking at him right now, I feel the sensation of his arms wrapped around me in the coach on the way back from the party and the hush of his words as he told me—voice breaking—that I was all right while I sobbed.

I love you. Immensely.

No one loves me. No one other than Gram has ever *really* loved me. I was even too much for my parents. They were glad to see me leave. They're disappointed I'm doing little more than existing every time they call, but there's this undertone of indifference, too.

Like they expected as much of me, their failure of a

daughter.

Zylus takes a step forward, closing the distance between us. His hand lifts, and I should be more nervous when his cold fingers meet my cold cheek, caressing and gentle. But I'm not. Earnest, he says, "I truly love you."

"Why?" My voice isn't my own. With another stiff breeze, it could blow away. "Because I stopped a couple brats from bullying you years ago?"

"Because you are mine."

"A recent and regrettable affliction."

His head shakes, and his fingers coast down to rest at my neck, thumb to pulse. "The moment I saw you, the moment I heard you, the moment I tasted you, the moment I touched you, every part that makes you up from form to thought to action... It's as though you were born for me, Willow."

My lips part, and I don't know how to respond. The desperate edge in his voice as he says my name—for the first time—leaves me shaken to my very core. I told myself I wouldn't react if it happened, and I guess I'm keeping my promises. I can hardly so much as breathe.

If soulmates are a thing, wouldn't this obsessive attraction and concept of perfection go both ways? Does it? Have I been fighting it because of what he is and my futile wish to not wind up in a situation I already know I can't handle?

If the storymakers wrote me into an instalove soulmate romance, I'm throwing a tantrum. I loved my *cat*, but loving an animal is different from loving a person, and this person is largely a stranger to me. Although the compulsion to admire him remains on the outskirts of my will, I've never liked when authors interpret physical appeal as love. Physical attraction isn't love. And I don't even know how deep it goes between us. He doesn't repulse me like many other men do, but I'm not *craving* anything either. When he gets too close, I feel *something*, but I don't know what it is, and it's definitely not demanding anything like what I sometimes read about in the kinds of books with creatures like him.

I wait a few seconds for the enamored way he's looking at me to materialize in my own heart, but it doesn't. Which is a relief.

Isn't it?

Maybe a stupid, fragile part of me wished—just a little bit—that the kind of certainty that keeps me coming back to those sappy instaloves might infiltrate my reality.

It's nice to believe in a benevolent fate.

It's nice to believe that the universe itself demands someone love you throughout every cell of their being. No matter what happens, what you do, what anyone else says.

No doubt someone bitter like me doesn't deserve a destiny like that. After all, this man saved my life, and I haven't so much as thanked him.

I've kicked him out of all the places he's spent the last five years considering home. I've told him I don't want anything to do with him. I've told him to leave me alone.

Even though "home" wouldn't be the same without him. Even though he has an entire world of friends and people who know him. Even though I'm the one who's lonely.

I tell him to go away as though he's the one without anyone else to go to.

Clenching my fist, I drop my gaze. "Truce."

"Pardon?"

"Truce. I'm calling a truce. I'll forgive you for all the scratches and the lies of omission if you forgive me for being ungrateful." Extending my hand, I lift my chin. "You saved my life. I haven't even thanked you."

"I poorly repaid a debt. There's nothing to forgive nor thank."

I arch a brow. "So you don't want a truce?"

He clasps my hand, pulls me a step closer, and bumps his forehead to mine. "I don't want you to think we have ever been at war." With that, he steps around me and pulls me through the remainder of the woods and into town.

Chapter 7

Is this the real life...

"We need boundaries. A roommate agreement," I say as I peruse the bakery section of Martyn's. I'm out of cookies, and I don't have the energy to make anything more elaborate than box mac and cheese. In other words, yes, I should get all the cinnamon rolls. With a side of cupcakes. And there was a pie that never got made two weeks ago, wasn't there?

"How Sheldon Cooper of you," Zylus murmurs, hands linked behind his back.

I don't know what manner of magic he's using, but no one's staring at him. Or commenting on the gentle way both his ears end in points. In fact, no one's staring at me either. Given my clothing choices, I've grown used to snide looks wherever I go. Needless to say, this reprieve is welcome.

If his whole *thrall protection program* extends to social protection, I might be warming up to the idea.

"Let's go back and forth proposing points of interest." Shifting the store's shopping basket to the crook of my arm, since I forgot *my* shopping basket, I pull my phone out of the purse I didn't forget. No missed calls from any known numbers and sufficient charge. Lovely. "I'll keep track in my notes app and write up the official document later."

"Fancy."

"First things first, no more flirting."

He picks up a package of blueberry muffins. "Where

you're concerned, flirting is my primary means of communication and thereby nonnegotiable; however, I can promise to always act with utmost respect and apologize if I ever overstep. I propose daily cuddles."

My nose scrunches, and I don't want to suggest that I've missed kitty cuddles, but I think I might die of touch starvation if something doesn't change. "We can tentatively reintroduce *cat* cuddles, and they stop the moment anything gets weird. Fair?"

He nods, a brilliant smile overtaking him, so I tap the rule out.

"Next matter of business: stop bringing me dead things."

His eyes widen, and he sets the package of blueberry muffins back down. "You really do hate my gifts."

I look up off my phone. "Flowers are gifts. Dead mice are a health code violation."

Expression darkening, he mutters, "You prefer Pila's gift to mine, and you only just met her."

"Yep." I tap out *no more carcasses inside the house.*

He whacks the blueberry muffins off the display table, and they skid across the speckled tile. I stare at them.

"Did you just…"

Folding his arms, he refuses to make eye contact with me.

Bemoaning the tomfoolery that is my life, I pick the package up, put it back, and take a breath, letting it out slowly. "I need you to know that I'm only suggesting cohabitation because our souls are linked, and I don't like the idea that boogeymen can drag me out of bed and attack me in my front yard."

His fist clenches against his arm.

"At no point do I see our relationship developing romantically, regardless of the close proximity." The *forced* proximity, if you will. Seriously. What are with these tropes? It's a good thing we aren't *fake dating*, because then this list of rules would become a checklist.

His sharp, two-tone gaze cuts to me, challenging.

"Don't give me that look. This isn't a happily ever after in the making. This is me figuring out how to reclaim my peaceful existence despite the fact my cat is sometimes six feet tall." I present a single finger. "My never-ending TBR pile is the *only* reason I'm not more upset."

"If regaining your love takes eternity, so be it. We have time."

"And, as stated, I'll be spending that time reading."

"With your precious kitty snuggled up on your lap."

My eyes narrow. "In a purely platonic fashion." He lifts his hand, but I grab it before he slaps a pie to the ground. "Stop it."

"I'm expressing myself in a healthy way."

"Destruction of property isn't a healthy way to express yourself."

His lips turn down in a nasty frown. "Repression."

I bark a laugh, and his frown softens as his eyes widen, curious and intent. Shoving the white strands of my hair over my shoulder, I shake my head. "Oh, this is insane," I mutter, decidedly turning away from the incredibly slappable bakery section. It's out of growing season, but I've got plenty of freezer bags of produce and canned goods. I'm missing staples like dairy, things it takes fields to grow like grains, and stuff I can't quite make as unhealthily as processing plants do like snacks.

Obviously, I order everything from most important to least and head to the chip aisle next.

"Okay," I begin as I lift my phone again. "Chores. If we're going to be living together, we should start sharing the workload."

"We have been."

Sour cream and onion or cheddar? Both? Cool. Since I have my notes open, should I put down the other things I need? Probably. Cheese…and… I've already forgotten. Did Zylus just say something? Looking up, I meet his eyes. "What?"

"We are sharing the workload. Shortly after you fall asleep, I normally get myself dinner and tidy up before rejoining you for the rest of the night." He plucks a package of corn chips off the shelf, turning it over and skimming the ingredients.

I stare at him. "You mean…all those times I couldn't be bothered to do the dishes then woke up and assumed I forgot I did them…"

"You're welcome."

How quiet can he… Wait a second. I *have* woken up to him making noise before. I called it zoomies, scooped him up, and toted him back to bed.

This revelation deserves more chips, so I grab a package of barbecue. "You make yourself dinner." Something in my brain—possibly common sense? potentially self preservation?—tells me not to ask the vampire about food, but if the man needs more than the blood he drains out of woodland creatures to live, he's been existing off my leftovers for five years. I'd go mad in his shoes. "We should start making shopping lists, so you can get things you like, too." I offer my basket, since he's yet to release the corn chips. "We can even have dedicated shopping days. If you're relying on the groceries, too, it will be easier for me not to put off until the last second when my kitchen is barren and full of moths."

He sets the bag in the overflowing basket, and it occurs to me I probably could have gotten a cart. Since I forgot my own basket at home, I'll have to suffer through plastic bags anyway, and there are two of us to handle the load.

He's spoken.

I heard nothing.

Again.

I might still be recovering from the general shutdown of the past week.

My brow furrows as I say, "Huh?"

"That's an excellent idea."

I nod. "Great." This is going well, actually. I tap the decision out in the notes app, which is looking more like a wall of text than an organized list. Why must my incompetence constantly thwart my dreams of order? "I can make a chore chart, too."

"You don't have to."

"Having accountability helps me finish tasks." See example: my chickens survive in spite of my recent catatonic state.

Zylus's hand settles beneath my chin, lifting my gaze to meet his.

It's an intimate action.

Too intimate for aisle nine.

"You'll burn out if there are too many things you have to do each day. We've been fine so far where sometimes you do a little more and sometimes I do. Being in a relationship is all about showing up whenever the other person can't."

"We're not in a relationship," I remind him.

"Romantic or otherwise, we are in a relationship. An unbreakable one. In claiming you, I am duty-bound to take care of you. And that means not letting you create a schedule that will guilt you into doing the dishes on certain days regardless of whether you have the energy to or not." His forehead touches mine, and his eyes close.

Again. Way too intimate for aisle nine.

"Whatever you can or can't do each day is enough. I'll handle the rest."

Someone coughs. "PDA."

My heart leaps as the unexpected voice sends me jerking back into the wall of chips. The pillow of bags crunches behind me as I find Ollie with an open bag of cheetos. Face and fingers orange, he munches.

I blink at him.

Where in the world did he come from?

Zylus smiles. "I was wondering when you'd sniff us out."

"I was going to wait until you stopped flirting, but I figured the sun might super nova first." Ollie offers his bag to Zylus, who takes a handful.

"Did you pay for that?" I ask, attempting to regulate my heart rate.

"Not yet. My human will take care of it later."

His...human?

He snorts and nudges Zylus in the arm. "Get this. She still thinks I'm in her purse."

Ollie has a *human*? How many mythical creatures form symbiotic relationships with unsuspecting humans? Lord Keres always came with me to the store. Did he enchant me into thinking he was always right on my heels when he was actually wandering around, eating chips?

"How is your human?" Zylus asks, licking cheese dust off his finger.

I ignore the way heat spreads in the pit of my stomach and turn back to the chips. Yes, my basket is overflowing. But, no, I don't think I have enough snacks to last me until the next time I drag myself to the store. How often should we plan to come? Do I designate by day or date?

Squinting at my notes app, I weigh the options, try to organize it some—at the least put the ramble of a shopping list at the bottom and the rules at the top. It's the best I can do to keep my mind from wandering to the way Zylus's tongue slipped up his finger, catching cheeto residue on the way.

"...you know how it is." The solemn tone of Ollie's voice draws me back to the conversation.

Neither cat nor dog are smiling now.

"My condolences," Zylus murmurs.

Ollie shrugs, stuffing another cheeto in his mouth. "It happens. Such is the life of a mateless runt." His brown eyes land on me, beautiful, deep, earthy. In my head, they're crossing in a chihuahua's derpy face, which makes it difficult to appreciate the fact he's handsome. His teeth bare in an animalistic grin. "Speaking of mates, how're things going with yours, Zy?"

"Wonderful." Zylus positions a cheeto in front of my lips.

I contemplate whether or not smacking things is, in fact, a *healthy form of expression* before shoving his hand away. Like an adult. He just finished licking his fingers, so I won't be eating from them, thanks. "We're not mates."

"Of course you are." Ollie crunches. "Good, polite vampires don't enthrall anyone else. Or so I'm told."

"We might be soul-linked, but we're not soulmates. I've already tested the soulmate theory, and I'm not burdened by the inexplicable desires that mark such a thing."

Zylus's brows rise. "You've test—"

"So. You don't feel an uncanny sense of calm around him, in spite of the fact he's a natural-born killer?" Ollie arches a brow, munching.

Zylus interjects, "I'm sorry. How did you t—"

"He already told me that everything about him is manufactured to incite care in spite of better judgment. So, sure, there's a moment or two where I comprehend his appeal, but I'm not at risk of throwing myself at him."

Ollie nods. "Right, of course. Throwing yourself at someone is the mark of true soulmates. Because real connection is purely at a physical level."

"I don't like your tone, chihuahua man."

"Sorry. Excuse me. I'd really li—"

Ollie laughs. "*Chihuahua man?*"

"I said what I said." I drop my phone back into my purse. "You're a chihuahua man. He's a cat man. It's all very well and good. I know my soulmate trope, and I'm pretty sure it feels more like when Zylus entranced me that one time."

Ollie gasps and covers his mouth, warm eyes twinkling with mischief. "He *entranced* you?"

"Yes. To show me the difference between unavoidable voice allure and intentional voice allure. I'm bitter about it, but I'm not above admitting the merit."

"And here I thought I was the dog."

Zylus deflates. "It was for a brief *innocent* demonstration. As I was saying—"

"You're his mate." Ollie cuts Zylus off and gestures toward me with his cheeto bag.

"I am not."

"It's not really up for debate."

I sneer. "It is so."

"Is not. You are what you are. Zy's too good a guy to enthrall anyone else. Even though his freaky vampire voice allows him to perform the soul bind with anyone, he wouldn't. He's been waiting for you so long he practically gave up on the possibility of his soul having a pair. If you can't see how unbelievably precious you are to him—"

Zylus hisses, and my heart jumps as both Ollie and I turn toward him. He regards us each dryly before clasping his hands together and smiling at me. "Starlight, what do you mean you *tested* it?"

I arch a brow. "I asked myself if I loved you, even though I know nothing about you. The answer was no. Well, the answer was actually *I loved my cat, but this man lacks the toe beans required to win my affection.*"

Ollie chokes on his laugh, and a cheeto.

Zylus closes his eyes.

"What?" I snap. "That's how the soulmate trope works. Cosmic forces cackle deviously and shove two people together whether they want to be in love or not. It's all destiny and tension. Insert some lame excuse on why they must fight the force drawing them together. Like, I don't know, he killed her brother, but he didn't really. It was a misunderstanding. Around the third book, you discover that actually, okay, yes, he *did* kill her brother in a sense that her brother would still be alive if he didn't exist, but he's not directly responsible for his death, and— Stop laughing!"

Ollie's chest shakes as muted snickers fizzle past his cheeto-stained lips.

Brows dipping, Zylus fixes me with a patient, albeit patronizing, smile. "Darling, that's fantasy. This is real life."

"Ah." My lips purse as I drone, "Right. How foolish of me to get the two mixed up. We're soulmates then? Totally realistic, cosmically-decreed soulmates? That's why you're obsessed? I had assumed brain damage or Stockholm."

The blue and green hues in Zylus's eyes deepen, darkening. "Would you *really* like to test it?"

Would I like some manner of magic to confirm that I don't have a choice on where my relationship with this person ends up?

I'd rather lie in my bed sheets while wearing outdoor clothes. "Nope." Turning on my heel, I march. "What types of cheese should we get? We may need another basket.

Ollie? Can you make yourself useful and get another basket? Thanks."

Ollie tuts. "Shame your soul is under Zy's protection. You never ought to thank the fae, lest you lose yourself to their whims."

"You're a werewolf," I remind him.

"I'm a werecanine, first of all." He hums, walking backward out of the aisle. The last thing I hear before he turns is, "And, second, Pila is a dryad."

Chapter 8

Now I want to slap baked goods.

"Please don't be mad." Zylus sits on the floor in my kitchen while I angry-beat eggs in a large bowl. His weepy eyes fix up on me. "Please."

He cowers when I scowl. "Vampires are faeries. You're a *faerie*."

"And?"

"And you didn't tell me you were a *faerie*."

"I suspected the idea that I could lie might comfort you some." He wets his lips. "Also, such a revelation muddies the genre expectations. You like clarity."

I grit my teeth and curse him. I *do* like knowing exactly what I'm getting into. Ugh. If this whole event were a book, it wouldn't sell at all. For starters, would you market it as paranormal or fantasy? Technically, paranormal falls under fantasy, but the vibes are completely different. If anything, this is a *cozy paranormal comedy*, and where's the market for *that*? People read about vampires for the drama and intrigue. The "sexy" take on anemia.

Derpy chihuahuas, needy cats, and assault chickens don't fit in anything other than comedy.

I'm living in a comedy.

I should have known.

"So you can't lie." I toss vegetables into the bowl of fluffy eggs, folding them all together.

"I cannot speak lies." He clears his throat and rests his head back against the cabinet. "However, vampires do contain the power to speak truth into being."

I glance at him.

"The range of what words I can make law is broader than many average fae. Lies shrivel into ash on the back of a fae's tongue, but my powers allow me to control other beings…"

"So you can change reality, manipulate emotions, actions, thoughts. Make your words true whether they were before you spoke them or not."

He nods, gaze impassible and pinned on me. "I told you. I'm a natural narcissist. And I can take gaslighting to a whole new level."

Fighting a shudder, I pour my mixture into a skillet and ground myself in the sizzle. "At the beginning of all this, you told me *everything is fine*. Everything is still not fine, so you either lied or there's a huge delay on when your words become truth sometimes."

"Everything *is* fine." He wets his lips, flushing faintly. "*Fine* is just a terrible adjective to use when describing anything. Fine, all right, okay…are any of those words an indication of something that attains the realm of decency or merely of something that exists?"

Semantics have never left me feeling more depressed.

Wincing, I mutter, "I'm not even okay."

"You are, though." Kneeling, he peeks over the edge of the counter while I scramble the veggie mixture. He watches me toss the ingredients together in the pan. "You're still breathing. That means you're okay."

The bar is so low.

I nudge him in the side of the head with my elbow as I get the salt. "You're in my way."

Big, mismatched eyes peer up at me, and he—without moving out of my way—points a pale, slender finger at the food. "That's a lot. Are you making some for me?"

"No."

"Is that your human blood talking?"

My lips pinch, and I lower the heat. "Maybe."

His smile warms as he lays an elbow on the counter and rests his cheek in the crook, staring.

The expression does things to my chest—unnecessary, unwanted things. Fluttery, *fuzzy* things.

What Ollie said about soulmates has rested in the forefront of my mind ever since he casually brought the concept up. It's left me questioning whether or not I'm completely...and utterly...and majestically...

Screwed.

If we're soulmates, I might as well bid farewell to free will right where I stand. Fighting the "natural pull" between us would literally be me appeasing those rotten story gods and creating the content they need.

Jerks. Pricks. A-holes.

The longer I fight, the more my story turns into a trilogy. Which is no doubt what they want. I bet whatever powers designed this crap storm of a plot twist in my life are industry-level monsters, doing everything *for the content*. They wear suits to bed and never kiss their kids goodnight.

Curses.

I am against falling into an outline set before me by cosmic hands.

All I want to do is read books and grow vegetables.

Is that so wrong?

Answer: no.

In fact, one could say it's what humans were put on this planet to accomplish.

Turning the heat off completely, I move the skillet to a cold burner and get two plates out of a cabinet, setting them side by side on the counter.

A week and a half ago I learned that vampires need both food and blood to survive. Promptly after, I went out of commission and survived off the cookies and snacks I hoarded in my bedroom.

This will be the first time I share a meal with someone resembling a person inside this house since my grandmother left me.

Maybe it would be a bigger deal if the someone resembling a person I'm sharing the meal with couldn't also have *me* for dinner, but whatever.

I dish out the food, barely managing to do so without Zylus's nose getting stuck in it. He's so feline, it's annoying. "Just so you know, these cat quirks of yours aren't cute even when you're a cat. I merely tolerated them because I figured you were a stupid baby and didn't know any better."

"Please do not do irreparable damage to my feelings." Palms flat like a wee beggar, he holds up his hands, and I bestow his plate upon them. He settles in on the floor with his back against the counter cabinets and smiles stupidly at his food. "I'm a sensitive creature."

He was right a few minutes ago; I do wish he could lie. The idea of him being *sensitive* is almost as concerning as the concept he is—irrefutably—*a creature.*

All the same, when he takes his first bite without moving from the floor, something in my chest sinks hard enough to mute the idiotic bliss marring his expression. "Starlight, what's wrong?"

I slip to the floor and lean against the cabinets across from him. "Nothing."

Eyes wide, he watches me, and heat runs into his cheeks.

"This means *nothing*." I stab my fork at him before shoving a bite in my mouth. I had no idea regret could hit so hard. Why am I so frail? I've been alone almost ten years now. I should be over the inane desire to be with living things who have enough brain capacity to not crap in the same water they drink.

"I'm sorry."

My attention snaps to Zylus.

"I let my own emotions distract me from yours."

Who doesn't? "Well, you are a natural narcissist."

His head shakes. "And you are the most important person in my life. I am the only one who can tend to the things you don't have the strength to say."

Dramatic, much? "I'm fine. It's fine."

Rising, he smiles down at me. "You deserve a better adjective." He extends his hand for me, and emotions I can't identify get stuck in a tangle that knots up my chest when I let him pull me to my feet.

It's just a meal together.

That's all.

It's not a big deal.

We sit across from one another at the table.

It's just a meal together.

A tear rolls down my cheek.

Zylus plants his palms on the blue surface between us, leans over our food, and catches the drop on his tongue.

Wetly, I ask, "What do you think you're doing?"

He kisses my cheek. "Hush." Instead of *you're okay*, he says, "I'm here," and my chest twists painfully.

When I was a child, I yearned for those simple words. I wanted a friend to grab my chubby hand and stay at my side no matter what. I wanted to be someone's favorite. I wanted to be enough for just one person. I wanted a friendship like the ones I saw on TV. Something unbreakable and stable and safe.

Instead, I found myself on the sidelines, looking in on a

collage of faces that smiled at one another and either didn't see me or filled with disgust the second I gained their attention.

It was cold. Isolating. Lonely.

I was a problem student. A problem daughter. A problem. My parents' friends looked at me and laughed and said it was good I was an only child.

At one point in my life, I stopped speaking for months on end. The people around me treated it like a relief.

Fae or not, words have power. And the words I heard growing up still work their awful magic.

"The food's getting cold," I whisper, pretending I can't hear my heart shattering, bit by bit, one fragment at a time.

Zylus settles back into his seat, watches me a moment, then picks up his plate. In the next breath, he's scooted into the place beside me.

I scrub my cheek and move closer to the window. "What are you doing?"

His thigh presses to mine, sturdy and warm. Too close. Not close enough.

I can't help but think I should be incomprehensibly, ravenously attracted to the pressure and the nearness. But… instead…the feelings his closeness incites go deeper than what every soulmate instalove story I've read has prepared me for.

I don't want to kiss him, rip off his clothes, or ease some undefinable ache that's been plaguing me for the past two hundred pages. I just want to sit here. Utterly aware that I'm not sitting here alone.

Minutes must pass before I realize he's continued eating without answering my question.

By the time I lift my own fork to my mouth, the top of my pile's gone cold and I have to toss the still-scalding underneath over it to make it edible again.

My shoulder brushes his as I take bites.

We're both right-handed.

He blows on his food longer than I do, and he's spread it out over his plate, as though he wants it to to go cold. He uses more salt. He separates the eggs as best he can from the vegetables.

I don't know why I'm noticing any details about him.

I don't know why I hide them away to keep them safe.

I don't know why, when we've finished eating, neither one of us moves until the sun has set entirely, leaving a blanket of cold dark to glaze the window. Stars wink above the shady outlines of the trees.

My heart settles until the pain in my chest feels more manageable.

"Thank you," Zylus says when I'm at peace, and I look at the handsome profile of his face.

"Why are…"

"Thank you." Solemn, his eyes meet mine, almost shy. "And only ever you."

My face warms as another thing Ollie said earlier highlights in my brain.

Thanking a faerie is the same as entrusting them with your soul.

"You shouldn't…" I begin.

He shrugs the shoulder near me, and his muscular arm slides against mine.

"I'm not even…"

"You are." Lifting his hand, he cups my cheek, swipes his thumb across my skin. "You are more than enough."

It hurts to swallow. I force out, "That's cheating. You're inside my head. You're saying what I want to hea…"

He doesn't have to remind me he can't lie. The realization eases into my skull and cradles all the terrified parts. I've never had a friend last. The ones who stuck around the longest were using me. They all lied to my face and laughed behind my back.

Lowering my head, I whisper, "Is a faerie's truth relative or all-knowing? Can you speak only what is fact or also what you believe?"

Sighing, he settles his forehead to mine. "Graciously, I am allowed my beliefs until I am aware of the facts, but, my darling, in this instant, my words appease both fact and belief. You are enough. Whether others have realized that truth or not is negligible." His nose skates along the bridge of mine, purely tender. "You are enough. You have always been enough. You will always be enough."

The concept is too foreign.

I hardly know how to respond.

Accepting what he's saying feels fundamentally wrong.

The past decades of rejection feel like proof. They scream in my ears that he *must* be lying. He *must* have a touch of human left in him as well, something that lets him whisper deceit. After all, he said he was turned at thirty-four, didn't he?

That means he was human once. Some part of that humanity must remain.

I can't be what he's telling me. Not when he's the first person to ever have treated me like it's true.

But, then again, maybe truth isn't defined by what the masses *believe*. Maybe truth isn't a belief at its core. Even if he's graciously allowed to speak in accordance with his beliefs, the second fact appears, his beliefs shrivel away.

Like ash.

Popular beliefs aren't facts.

No matter how I've been treated, no matter how many people in the past have rejected me, *I am enough*.

Swearing, I let myself crumple against Zylus once again and hope I might soon run out of tears.

Chapter 9

Everything is totally *fine*.

I'm struggling.

It's not a glorious statement. In most fantasy books, it's neither spoken clearly nor directly. The main characters are *always* struggling. It's a baseline standard that they never exactly turn toward the camera and announce. When they break down, it's so some friend or future lover can pick up the pieces and remind them what they're fighting for.

It's my personal belief that fantasy and reality are one in the same, with subtle differences.

In both worlds, people fight for the right *to stop fighting*.

In the real world, people are tired without the addition of grandiose adventures, sword fights, or all-consuming romances. Because they have taxes. And, honestly, that's enough.

The real world might be a bottomless chasm of despair, but at least it tends to have a low-stakes plot. Right?

Wrong.

In a fantasy novel, the main character's choices may bring about the salvation or doom of the entire world. In reality, the main character's choices may bring about the salvation or doom of *their* entire world. It's the same thing. A moral code that implies an entire world is more important than a single person's is, at its core, flawed.

Pain is pain.

The whole world's so big that no one without actual

cosmic powers is going to come close to saving it on their own. Even in my fantasy novels, *salvation* isn't perfect. It merely means the villain is conquered and the masses no longer worry about enslavement to a dictatorship.

Saving the world is impossible.

Saving *someone's* world might not be.

Maybe I'm not the main character in my own life.

Sprawled on the couch after having cried myself out at dinner, I listen to Zylus's purrs and wonder why this is the calmest I've been since the numb environment I crafted around myself turned over.

Basically, existence equals hard.

Being *okay* is a feat, even if all it equates to is continued breathing.

Sometimes, taking that next breath is the hardest thing someone can do.

I'm struggling.

My world is on fire.

Purring Zylus on my stomach helps more than I want to admit while knowing I'm petting an entire man's head.

It's the whole *hero started the problem but is determined to fix it* plot line. It's his fault things ended up like this. Now he's picking up the pieces.

I'm really not the main character in this story at all. I may be the *female* lead, but it's told from *his* point of view.

And maybe that takes the pressure off playing an adequate role.

He flops, liquid, a cuddly oil spill, and I glance down at his closed-eye bliss. He licks my hand, nuzzling against my palm, kneading air.

It's rude that he's this cute.

How much baby talk have I made him endure?

Have I ever said a logical word to him in my life?

Furthermore, he just let me be an idiot for five whole

years.

Wrapping my arms around him, I give in to the cute malice and crush. He squirms, melts into shadows, and reforms over me, palms planted on the armrest behind my head. "Why?"

I leave my arms crossed over my chest, like I'm in a coffin. "Why what?"

"Why are you trying to kill me?"

"I am not trying to kill you."

"You're angry."

"I'm frustrated."

"Why?"

I roll my eyes off him. Because. It's oh so poetic. The very thing that kills me makes me stronger. The issue is the solution. I should *get over this change* and let him put out the fire. It's useless to fight it. My lifelong plans need adjustment to include a lovey-dovey happily ever after alongside growing carrots and reading books.

I should just accept the bite bite, make babies, bite bite some more.

What is free will but the option to refuse to make dinner, take a shower, or get a job anyway? What is free will but the bane of all existence?

I sigh and admit the truth to myself: I would thrive in a villainous dictatorship.

Tell me what to do, what to wear, where to go. Provide my puny lifespan with some modicum of purpose. Clearly, I was born in the wrong genre. Female lead? Ha. I'm a lackey at best.

Zylus curls a finger in a lock of my hair, drawing me out of my thoughts, which he's no doubt privy to on some level. I wonder what it's like—being on the outskirts and watching a person's descent into madness.

Catching my eye, he presses the silken, white strands to

his lips.

My heart protests at the sight. "What did I say this afternoon at the store when we agreed on reintroducing cuddles?"

"How is this weird?"

I open my mouth to reply, but the butt nugget cuts me off.

"Apart from the fact you are notoriously unaccustomed to being cherished."

I flinch. "That's…playing dirty."

He lets my hair flutter from his grasp and kisses my nose. He whispers a swear. "I love you." Air fills his chest. "Oh—" He swears. "I love you."

Doubt creeps into the cracks in my mind, and I don't understand *how* someone could ever love me, much less someone who's seen me at my rawest, most uninhibited self. Every quiet moment here, with his cat eyes on me, when I thought I was alone…

Love must be like *okay,* or *fine,* or *all right.* It just doesn't mean what I've always thought. It's less intense, nowhere near as earth-shattering a concept as I've come to believe. Especially in English, *love* is frail.

He loves me like I love fries.

With a sigh, he murmurs gibberish.

"What?"

Taking my hand, he presses the back to his cheek and continues uttering as he kisses, as his teeth—his fangs—graze my flesh.

I ignite. I burn. And my world isn't the only thing on fire anymore. "What are you saying?" My heart beats in a new, frantic rhythm. "Are you casting a spell?"

His chuckle breaks through the murmurs. "Other languages have better words for *love*. I know them. So I'm making sure you understand that when I say *I love you*, I mean my existence relies on your breath to fill my lungs." He nips. "Don't doubt me. And don't use me to doubt yourself."

"G…" I throw my free arm over my face. "Get out of my head."

"It's my favorite place."

"It's not public domain."

His breath skims over my wrist. Hot. Damp. "Such beautiful, trembling thoughts and emotions, tangled up in concerns about *me*." He shushes, tone melodic and warm. "Darling…"

His mouth opens. His teeth—

"*Stop!*" Jerking my hand back, I lift my knee, shove it into his chest. Above me, Zylus's fangs glint in the overhead light, wide eyes deeply black, barely ringed in color.

He swallows, closes his mouth, licks his lips. Clearing his throat, he mutters a curse and gets off the couch. "Forgive me."

"You almost…"

"Mm."

I try to temper the heat welling in my chest. I can't regulate it. I can barely function. If I tried to stand, I'd faint. "Are you hungry for blood? Do you need to go hunt or something? You said you didn't do stuff like that unless you were hungry?"

"Actually…" he begins in a tone that leaves me less than confident, "…I said blood was a drug and if I lie with you too long…I get nippy." He lifts his hands, fingers spread. "Don't worry."

"Don't *worry*? You almost *bit* me."

"Well, it wouldn't have been the first time." Fondly, he glances at his pale bare feet. "I've given you many love bites. You've praised me for them on occasion, saying *I love you, too.*"

Yeah, I've praised him for his little kitty love bites, saying *I love you, too,* and *good boy* and *be gentle*—moments before wild took hold of his eyes and he drew blood. This purring monster. "You're an—" I curse.

He winces. "Starlight."

Sitting up, I clench my fists. "Even if you can't lie, you're *fantastic* at manipulation." I swear again. "You don't even try to hide it. You're a narcissist. You know how to gaslight and manipulate for your benefit. You're so good at it you don't *have* to hide the truth."

"Starlight, I *stopped*. It's not like in the storybooks where I can't control myself and I go into a trance and I put you in danger. I can and will stop when you ask."

"So? You'll just try again later until I'm worn down and don't stop you. Right?"

His lips part; I watch the lies turn to ash on his tongue.

"That's what I thought." Rising, I skirt around him and head toward my bedroom. "Next time, stay a cat or—"

Something thundering sounds outside, ending with the shriek of shattering glass.

The penitence in Zylus's eyes hardens. His pupils narrow into slits, and he's in front of me before I understand what's happening. My hand was nearly on my doorknob. Now, I'm almost certain that sound came from *in there*, that my window's broken, that *something* is waiting beyond the wooden slab of my bedroom door.

What was that? feels like giving life to a wholly unnecessary question. *Don't you dare open that door!* seems a touch too dramatic given the fact Zylus has been around since medieval times and probably knows how to take care of himself. Supernatural powers aside, he's sturdy. Large.

No doubt I'm being robbed by a perfectly normal

burglar. A perfectly *human* burglar. He missed the fact the light is on in the living room, so he's not too bright, and I'm almost positive Zylus is faster than a bullet, so even if he has a gun—

Zylus turns the knob, and despite all my fantastic reasoning, I grip my fists in the back of his shirt and peer around his towering chest as he eases the door open.

Moonlight highlights my bedroom, my bed's gauzy canopy, my dresser, the full-length mirror.

It doesn't limn any broken glass.

Zylus swears before I can relax. "Sweetheart?" he murmurs, the word laced with sheer malice and lethal promise. "I'm sorry."

"Huh?"

"I'm sorry I almost bit you. You mean so much more to me than that. I will not do it again until you ask me to."

"Is this really the time to continue that conversation, Zylus?" My heart lunges up my throat. "Are you trying to make things right before you go off to battle something freaky?"

"I'm trying to assure you that I'm not just here because you're a meal." He turns his back on whatever is or isn't in my room. Cradling my face in his hands, he says, "I was in the wrong. I let my desire rule for a moment because I am desperately attracted to you. I can hardly begin to explain how badly I want you in every way that exists. That doesn't mean I will ever force you to bear my selfishness."

Despite how earnestly he appears to be imploring me, I don't know if I can—or should—trust him. "Can you make me hear things?"

"I can. I have not."

"Then what was that noise? Is there something in my room?"

"Willow."

Every cell in my body freezes. I meet Zylus's eyes.

He swipes his thumbs across my cheekbones, smiling faintly. "Sleep now, my love. I'll take care of everything."

My mind hazes, turning foggy, and it's like the first night in the snow. I fight to lift my hand and grasp his wrist, but I run out of strength. "Zy…you…" I mutter a curse as he catches me in his arms, cradles me against his heartbeat.

It's racing.

I struggle to stay awake, but inevitably I lose myself to the pull of his command.

Chapter 10

~~~~~~~~~~

Dandelion tea is pretty good, ngl.

"That f—" I jolt upright in the softest puddle, disoriented, aware only that Zylus knocked me out in my last moments of consciousness. My eyes lock on Pila, sitting beside me on what appears to be a toadstool, and I correct myself. "—reaking jerk." I take a breath, force a shaky smile. "Hi, Pila. Didn't see you there. Um. What's going on?"

She laughs. "Good morning."

Pressing my lips together, I search for confirmation that it is morning and find a cylinder of wood carved out around me. My bed, as it turns out, is a flower petal. Several, actually. Stacked high, plush. And Pila's chair? Yeah, it's an actual mushroom. It along with several others grow right out of the knotted wood floor.

A narrow passage that looks suspiciously like a hollow branch pours sunlight into the room from near the top of the ceiling, where vines covered in tiny flowers shower down. Notches in the wall create a spiraling staircase up to that exit…and…

Okay.

Okay, fine.

I'll admit it.

This is cool. Perfect. What I want my cottage to look like as soon as I tire of elegant soft pinks, whites, and blues. Maybe I should build and theme a gazebo like this?

I just know I need more of whatever this is in my life.

Still, I don't know how I wound up here. And I would

be remiss to ignore the fact *I don't know how tall I am.*

"*Good morning,*" Pila repeats before I spiral deeper, and I straighten.

"Good morning. I'm sorry. Where…am I?"

"My home." She smiles pleasantly and rises, heading to a kitchen nook with bark cabinets and little acorn jars labeled with little painted leaf letters.

I need it. Copy and paste. It's my new kitchen.

"Dandelion tea?" she asks.

You can make tea out of dandelions?

Somehow I must convince her to like me and teach me her ways…

"That would be great." Stopping myself from thanking her, I smooth my hands against the flower petal blanket covering me. It's peach, soft, warm, clashing starkly with the gothic lace of my dress. At least this time I'm waking in the same clothes I was wearing before?

Is that *character development* on Zylus's part? Dare I say, *a major improvement*?

I really need to reevaluate my standards.

"Where's Zylus?" The question escapes before I realize, and my lack of ire surprises me. The man knocked me out and dropped me off in a place with impending social interaction. By all accounts, he should be dead to me. Instead, I might be worried. Something's knotting in my gut, and I don't like it.

"He's taking care of something."

Something. How ominously vague. "What?" I ask as Pila sets a wooden cup in my hands and returns to her toadstool with her own.

The warm, sweet aroma rises around me, soothing. So soothing I nearly miss when she says, "It could be anything. He asked me to watch over you, and I nearly teased him about owing me a debt for the favor, but he

117

wasn't quite himself, so I abstained." She giggles into her cup. "Just imagine. An ancient vampire owing a sprout of a dryad a debt."

Prickles of unease run over my skin, turning my flesh inside out. "What do you mean he wasn't quite himself?"

She hums, sipping her tea. "Had I teased him, he may have glamoured me. Until near their three hundredth year, being tame is a mark of those who are human-born. For the fae who come from human blood, the three hundredth year is when humanity slips away. Instinct takes hold. And instinct is not always gentle."

I don't want to think about what *instinct* might be for a vampire. In literature, it's *feed*, and seeing as I'm the primary blood bag in his vicinity, it isn't a topic I want to explore in any depth.

"Is he going to be all right?" I ask, then I shake my head. Stupid words and their paltry meaning. "I mean, is he going to come back soon, uninjured?"

"I would assume as much. I have never seen him injured, and he's been caring for these woods longer than I and my sisters combined." The softness of her smile fades. "I have only heard stories of it from my eldest sister, but, once, he took down a wendigo alone."

"A wendigo?"

"It's human-born, but a human that has lost all sense of humanity. Worse, perhaps, a human that has given humanity up."

I chew my lip and tuck the concept that humans can mutate into *other things* away to process later. "Is a wendigo stronger or weaker than a boogeyman?"

Pila laughs. "Much, much stro—" Realization lights in her eyes, and the words seem to die in her mouth. "Well…I wonder. Generally, much stronger. Boogeymen are concepts of fear that exist in that frail place between wake and rest. Emotion fuels them, and they hide in the shadows to feed on it. They are the faces you might see in the corners of your vision. The feeling of being watched. The sounds you think you hear. The memories better forgotten." She takes a sip of her tea. "I've only ever known one boogeyman I liked, and I suppose now he isn't truly categorized under that name."

My eyes widen. "Sorry. What? You've met an entity of fear that you *liked*?"

Mischief curls her lips, and her eyes spark without lifting from her teacup. "The world is so vast, sapling. I've barely grazed the surface of it. But one thing best learned early is the fact nothing comes in black and white."

A noise from the hollow branch above sends a shudder skittering down my spine. I look up just in time to find a black cat billowing through the air. He lands perfectly on all fours, just beside Pila.

She beams. "Welcome back, Zy. Did everything go well?"

His dual-colored eyes flick to her and hold long enough for the knot in my gut to twist.

Moving his gaze to me, he shifts into his human form and doesn't answer her question. "I appreciate you looking after her, Pila."

"Can I have a fa—"

"No."

Pila shrinks.

Zylus closes his eyes, composes himself, then smiles gently and beautifully and…unless I'm mistaken…a little falsely toward her. "You already know bargains aren't required among friends."

"They're fun."

"In the minds of the mischievous youth, perhaps."

Pila takes a dainty sip of her tea. "Careful, Zy. Your

sweet mate is younger than I if you see to belittle youthfulness."

"My darling must already know that I revere her among the ones who hung the stars in the sky and set the tides in motion. How she would assume it possible for me to insult her I would not understand."

"All is well?" Pila asks.

Zylus's pause doesn't inspire much confidence, but he finally says, "For the moment."

When concern ripples in Pila's eyes, I sense on some level the response means about as much as *okay* in fae terms. Hopefully I'm wrong. It wouldn't be the first time I failed to read the hidden meanings in someone's words, but the fae speak blatantly. Their language has clear rules that they toy with at a literal and logical level.

It's easier for me. It's consistent.

The hidden meanings are already within the text, not layered beneath social constructs, body language, or tone.

Words means what words mean.

And in that sense…a moment equates to nothing.

Eyes narrow, I scowl at Zylus when he offers me his hand.

He doesn't so much as sigh. "If you would spare my pride and save your distaste until we are back home, I would be grateful."

"You'll answer my questions when we get back?"

"Indeed."

I lift my chin. "I want a more direct answer."

His smile warms. "Yes, starlight. I will answer your questions when we get back home."

Ignoring his hand, I slip out of the petal bed, finish my tea, and offer Pila the empty cup. "This was good. I'd like to know how to make it."

"I'll stop by sometime and show you."

We exchange a smile, then I brave the precarious stairs with Zylus at my side. At the top, I find myself on the edge of a cut tree limb, looking out at a vast, massive forest. When a frigid breeze collides with me, I clutch Zylus's clothes, twist my hand in the fabric, and tell myself the air isn't thinner up here. I'm not *actually* high up. It's just that I'm…two inches tall.

Why am I two inches tall?

How am I two inches tall??

"I don't like this freaky magic stuff." My voice breaks as I fight back burning tears.

"You get used to it," Zylus says, seconds before sweeping me into his arms and *jumping*.

My stomach soars through my chest to catch in my throat. I open my mouth to scream, but the solid sound of his boots hitting the ground comes before I get the chance. Clutching him around the neck, I dare squint into the daylight and find the branch he just leaped from right behind his head.

It makes no sense.

None.

Then again, it makes about as much sense as the skeletal horses and coach materializing in front of us when I look forward.

Everything is…chaos. It's just chaos now. A different sort than the kind that permeates human societies. This chaos isn't masquerading as order. I'm not *supposed* to know all the details. Everyone is so different and bright and open. It's wild and free enough that no one can condemn anyone else without condemning themselves.

In some ways, this is better, isn't it? After all, if *everything* is chaos, I don't have to worry about the chaos inside me. I'm not a *problem*.

Problems are the games that fae play on the weekends.

I am wholly, completely, and entirely an acceptable being within the bounds of the fae world's rules.

Or so I hope.

I have been wrong before.

The ride back in Zylus's coach is quiet. I feel my mind slipping, but I think I can catch myself before I'm talking to Athena and eating Famous Amos on my bedroom floor again. Identifying a harmful cycle is the first step to breaking it, right?

My stomach hurts.

History marks humans as notoriously adaptable creatures. I wonder if the same can be said about fae-human hybrids, who may or may not need another ten years to contemplate that fact alone.

The second I enter my cottage, I scan the living room for distress, a battle, proof that *something* less-than-palatable occurred on the premises. Finding nothing, I plant my hands on my hips and face Zylus.

He looks…tired.

Closing the door behind him, he sinks into the front window seat and watches me, patiently waiting.

Every question I mulled over during the ride back flits off. I find myself opening my mouth to ask if he's okay, then searching for a better term, and landing on the one Pila used, "Are you well?"

His eyes close, and he releases a sigh. "Well enough."

Okay, that's still a useless answer. But I don't know how to get a better one, and maybe there isn't any way to get a better one. Maybe words that address relative, emotional ideas at an acceptable level don't exist. "What happened?"

"I almost lost you once. I didn't want to take any chances this time. I'm sorry that I was rough with you." His mouth opens, hangs there for a moment, fangs on display and limned in sunlight. He wets his lips, pressing them together. Agony sweeps across his face. His fist clenches, and his gaze meets mine, tormented. "The sensation of feeding air into your lungs haunts my waking thoughts. It would take ages to more perfectly describe how important you are to me. Your pain terrifies me. Your sadness carves out my heart. Your anger leaves me feeling hopeless and lost. You are dear." His eyes close again, and he buries his face in his hands. "You are so dear, starlight."

My eyes roll. "If I'm so *dear*, why have you been scratch happy these past five years?"

"Addiction mixed with an innate knowledge of what I could too easily get away with."

"Do you need a support group?"

"Probably."

He's too tired.

I don't like this.

The sight of him like this leaves me feeling imbalanced. I shift my weight from one foot to the other and drop my arms. "Are we safe here?"

"For now."

"How long is *for now*?"

His chest fills, and he cuts his fingers back into his hair. "Until the next time we are not."

That is by no means reassuring.

"What was in my room?" I ask.

"I'd rather not say."

"You said you'd answer my questions."

A frail smile lifts one corner of his mouth. "Darling, that is an answer."

I could skin him alive. "You tricked me."

"Charmingly fae of me, no?"

Charming is not the adjective I'd use. The adjective I'd use would up the rating of my inner monologue from PG-

13 to R. Therefore, I refrain.

That knot in my gut hasn't lessened. It's beginning to make me sick, and it probably means I'm hungry, so while talking to Zylus feels like a lost cause, I turn on my heel. "I'm making breakfast. Any requests?"

"You."

I bristle and peer at him over my shoulder, half expecting to find him looming an inch away, fangs and eyes glinting with horrid promise. In stark contempt of genre standard, he has instead harmlessly melted into an ink spot and curled up in the sunlight, tail wrapped snugly around his furry body.

Does he need blood? Is this lethargy a side effect of not being…"medicated"?

So long as I'm not volunteering myself, the best I could do is see if I have any mouse traps lying around. Even then, mice are nocturnal, so it would probably go off in the middle of the night, and I don't know if he needs his "medication" sooner than that.

While I throw together some oatmeal, I contemplate sacrificing my rooster, and after I'm done, I learn I'm more nauseous than hungry, so I set a bowl of oatmeal beside my sleeping kitty and gather what I need to take a shower—AKA the next thing on my *I feel wrong, that might help* list.

You are dear.

What an outrageous concept.

He wasn't kidding when he said I was unaccustomed to being cherished.

In fact, it makes me itchy.

So I scrub, and scrub, and scrub until my skin feels raw and I've somewhat offset the sensation of unease stirring in my gut. It's probably because I spent the night being two inches tall, honestly. That's bound to make anyone who isn't regularly two inches tall feel a bit off.

If I'm part pixie and mostly dryad, where does this frustrating desire to make sense of the world come from? As far as I can tell from my brief encounter with Lesta, she couldn't care less if things made sense, and from what I've seen of Pila, she exudes calm entirely unconcerned with the *why*.

Does their world already make sense to them?

Or is this the human in me fighting for purchase?

There should really be more scientific studies based around these topics.

How many humans struggle in painful ignorance without a clue as to why they can't seem to find a place to belong among what seem to be their "peers"? Someone needs to be there for them, tell them the truth, *help* them when they're so lost and alone and sad that they just—

I freeze in the middle of getting dressed, fingers wrapped around the laces of my corset, and find my reflection in the steamed bathroom mirror. My pale gray eyes watch me.

My chest aches.

Someone needs to help the people who are so lost and alone and sad that they just…don't want to be here anymore.

Not everyone like me is lucky enough to inherit a safe —lonely—place from their grandmother and enough money to manage. Not everyone like me can thrive in *lonely* environments. Not everyone like me figures out enough on their own in order to cope with the untethered feelings of confusion and isolation.

Not everyone responds to having had *enough* with sarcasm, cookies, and mental letters to Athena.

Some people don't want to be here anymore more than they want to read another good book.

Firmly shaking my head, I march out of the bathroom,

get my shopping basket, and find Zylus curled up around his now empty breakfast bowl. Hugging it with his entire body.

Someone dear…

Does he have people who tell him he's someone dear?

Or, if I'm his cosmic chosen one on some level, is that supposed to be *my* job?

Lazily, his weary eyes open.

I wish I had more information about what he did all night, what he fought, if he got rid of it, if I'm a target for the boogeymen and the wendigos and the other monsters now on account of *being his*. It's clear he's high up on the hierarchy of faerie beings. He no doubt has more enemies than friends. In stories, other faeries would target him for clout alone.

Which is so dumb because he's obviously just a floppy kitty whose current emotional state relies entirely on the fact I made him a bowl of oatmeal.

Anyone who attacks him is dumb. I've battled tights that pose more threat.

Extending my basket, I say, "I'm going to the bookstore."

I don't know why I'm going to the bookstore. I went to town *yesterday*. I had a conversation *this morning*. It's chilly outside, even though it's sunny. Despite what may or may not have happened in my room, my house still seems safer than wandering through the woods to reach town.

All the same, an odd pressure in my lungs compels me to move. Get out. See something that retains my definition of normal.

Normal sorts of things happen in sweet small town Mountain Vale, Virginia. And the only bearable place in sweet small town Mountain Vale, Virginia is the bookstore.

So I have to go to the bookstore.

Zylus slinks into my basket while I'm dissecting the reasons behind my impulses, and the familiar weight settles something primitive within me.

As I march outside, Ollie's comment from yesterday rings loud and clear.

So. You don't feel an uncanny sense of calm around him, in spite of the fact he's a natural-born killer?

Okay.

Fine.

I'll admit it.

I do.

Chapter 11

Avoid the problem until it goes away.

The scent of paper and ink surrounds me while I peruse the YA fantasy shelves at Page Turner, also known as our small town's *ye olde bookstore*. It's a quaint place, cozy, organized by genre not author—which is ideal and lovely and a blessing. Since I neglected to stop in yesterday and I hadn't left my house for a few weeks prior, there are a few new titles.

So far in the "new" category, we've got *he's a knight; she's a princess; can they ever be together?*

And other highly original tales.

On second thought, maybe there isn't anything new since the last time I was here.

But maybe I don't care.

Maybe my new and improved lifespan has given me the awful permission to guiltlessly read the same beautiful story, as told in different fonts, for the eternal remainder of my days. Hehehe. (I put the book in my basket beside a very sleepy kitty.)

Speaking of *the eternal remainder of my days*, am I going to have to move periodically in the future to avoid becoming a government experiment?

Embracing the rumors that I'm a witch will end in fire.

Was that whole fiasco in Salem a result of real witches? *Are* witches real? Are they good? Bad…? Terribly misunderstood on account of their preference for bold makeup, mildly archaic clothing, corsets over torture devices (AKA bras), and monochromatic stylings?

If people here only saw the pink, white, and blue accents in my house's decor, they'd change their minds about starting up another Crucible.

Yep.

Nothing witchy about me. Apart from my love of creepy crawlies. And the way I dress. My poliosis. The makeup. The fact they'll turn eighty while I'm still rocking Victorian mansion garb in my mid-twenties.

Okay, I'm beginning to see the issues.

Zylus yawns, rolling over in my basket so his little face presses against the cover of my newest book.

Several weeks ago, I would have taken a picture.

Now that seems like exploitation without consent. I need him to sign a waiver that allows me to videotape and photograph his toe beans. Just in case there are faerie lawyers. At least they'd be honest, but—alas—honesty doesn't help when you're guilty. And I would be *so* guilty.

Half my phone's photo memory belongs to this furball.

I squint at him.

Wait just one second.

Is he... Is this a naked man?

His eyes open, slow and judgy, so I look away, muttering, "Out of my head."

He snuffs, a cat laugh, and it's so strange to think of him as more than he once was.

I'm used to people becoming less than my initial impressions of them. Often, once I think I've figured someone out, they change. I learn they never liked me. They were being polite. They got tired of pretending. I'm no fun.

Too much. Not enough. Loud. Quiet. Somewhere just north of *wrong* and just south of *right*.

Sighing, I pull another book free and jolt at the sight of

a tiny sleeping figure on the shelf behind it. Like before, the tiny creature is wearing a little grass dress that spills purple-tinted, lanky limbs.

"Lesta?" I whisper.

Zylus coos in my basket, half-rising before giving up with his chin pressed against the woven side at an awkward angle.

Yawning, Lesta lifts her arms in a stretch. Her violet eyes fix on me and her laughter titters before she flits to my cheek, hugging me in her own tiny way. "Oh, my, light! Zy's human! Hello." She snuggles a moment longer then seats herself on my shoulder. "It's so nice to see you again."

"You as well."

She snorts, tumbles back, and kicks her legs in the air. "Funny human half." Gasping, she tugs on my hair. "Ooh, *how are you?*"

Mediocre. Overwhelmed. Startled by her random cameo. Unprepared for more social interaction than checking out my books, which I'm also somewhat unprepared for given the fact *Alice* is at the counter. "Fine. And you?"

Lesta loses it, laughter chiming like a chorus of bells. Kneeling on my shoulder, wings all aflutter, she points a too-long finger at me and says, "Silly fake words. Don't you hate them?"

I inch the book I took out back into place and clear my throat. "I don't understand."

"Humans use templates to communicate. It's funny. They talk themselves in circles. Let's try again." Her head tilts, and she beams, entirely too welcoming, bubbly, a real sunshine character, the antithesis to all that is me. "Hi. I'm super happy to see you again. How are you?"

She can't want the truth. People never want the…

My brow furrows, and I stare at the sparkling creature wrapped in grass with tiny wooden flowers in her silver hair. The realization hits me. *This isn't a human person.* "I am on the verge of a mental breakdown. Which would be the astounding third this month. I don't know how many more I have in me, only that they are exhausting, and I'd like to unsubscribe."

A laugh explodes out of her, then she throws her arms around my neck, burying her entire body beneath locks of my hair. "See? Wasn't that better?"

I...have no idea. It was more honest, and she's not upset, but does that count as *better*? Do I feel lighter for having said the truth out loud? Is it nice to be able to say something to someone and not have them stare blankly back at me as though I've done something wrong?

I just don't know. Not right now. Maybe I will in five to seven business days.

"What's a mental breakdown like?" Lesta inquires. "I don't think I've ever experienced one."

"It's not fun." I pull out another book, make sure a different creature isn't hiding behind it, and glance at the back. Reviews. Ha ha. Watch and see if I don't have my mental breakdown *right here*. "Everything shuts off. I barely remember how to function, and I don't want to do anything."

She gasps, horrified. "Not even the things you like?"

"Not even the things I like. I barely take care of myself and run on autopilot for everything that I can't avoid doing, like taking care of my chickens." Or, until recently, feeding my cat. I glance down at Zylus again and find him pretzeling on his back, toe beans in the air. Picture perfect.

Butt nugget.

He blinks at me, and I look away.

Sniffles sound near my ear a moment before I realize

Lesta is bawling. "That's so sad! Why would you ever do that?"

"I don't know." My mouth goes slightly dry, and I wrestle for the *right* words. "I don't think I have a choice. Something just breaks, and then I'm all out of... everything."

She scrubs at her eyes and cheeks, gasping for air.

One emotion.

Pixies can only handle one emotion at a time.

And I've just sent her careening into sorrow.

A gnawing sensation I'm almost positive is guilt eats away at my gut. I made a tiny, happy thing sob. Am I a monster?

Zylus stretches, tail flicking, and yawns. I look to him for help, but, in the next instant, he swats Lesta off my shoulder.

My mouth drops open.

She flings to the ground in a splatter of purple sparkles.

My heart stops beating.

What?

What?

What is *wrong* with him? Are we *both* monsters?? Swatting muffins is one thing, but *we do not swat people.*

The tiniest, angriest, harshest curse I've ever heard in my life squeaks from the floor, then Lesta darts, swearing, toward Zylus. She pounds her tiny fists against his body as he curls back up and ignores her like he's got a PhD in the art of disinterest.

I would be inclined to separate them if I didn't agree with every high-pitched word escaping her mouth.

She's a pure, itty bitty thing. Honestly, I'm shocked that didn't kill her...

What are pixies made of? Titanium?

A thought enters my head, escaping before I can screen

it—a testament to my overall weariness. I murmur, "Can faeries touch iron?"

Lesta perks up, turning her large eyes on me. Every ounce of anger pours out, and she sits in Zylus's fur, grinning. "Yes, we can! Humans think iron is a symbol of industrial growth, which implies fading magic, but that's not how anything works. Growth *is* magic. Creation, science, that desire and hunger to learn and explore, it's *everything* we thrive on."

It's official. I do not have the rule book for anything. My entire encyclopedia of fantasy beliefs has been a lie. The information was clearly provided by people who know nothing about the creatures they're attempting to represent. "Do I know anything about faeries?"

Her giggle is like music. "Probably. But the truth is mixed up with make believe. That's just life. You never really know anything about anything unless you encounter it for yourself." Her gaze darts past me, and she gasps. "Puppy!"

By the time I find the golden retriever walking on the other side of the street beyond the glass windows of Page Turner's storefront, Lesta has already darted down the aisle and squeezed herself out the mail slot in the door.

Across the road, a faint trail glistens in the sunlight, exploding in a dust puddle against the dog's fur.

I sigh. "Pixies have very limited attention spans…"

"It's understimulation," Zylus murmurs, near my ear.

I jolt, for the second time in the past ten minutes, and swear as I face him. "Could I get a warning before you start *talking*?"

His brows rise. "I assumed you'd notice the weight in your basket had changed."

I narrow my eyes. It's a fair point. But he forgot to consider the fact I'm running on *low power* mode.

He yawns, still feline, and leans a shoulder against the YA fantasy bookshelf. "It takes almost all their magic to fly, leaving their bodies with less than optimal amounts. They're susceptible to getting stuck in that *need to move* feeling you experienced earlier." He rubs one eye, yawns again. "Depending on how pixie blood presents itself in humans, you can oscillate between the extremes, going from jittery to burnt out without much notice."

"Doesn't the dryad blood help with that? Pila and the others at the party were so calm."

"In some ways. But because dryads are linked strongly to the quiet, steady growth of flora, they don't fair well with quick change. Transitioning between situations, emotions, or sensations takes a lot more time. Dryads are naturally quiet, gentle protectors of nature—unless provoked." The corner of his mouth tugs up, and he gazes at me with sleepy eyes. "Then they can get very violent."

"Why does it seem like that amuses you?"

"I bite. Forgive me for finding aggression enticing."

"I won't." I turn on my heel and head toward the contemporary romance section.

Zylus trots after me. "Pardon?"

"I won't forgive you. You can't make me do it." Selecting a pale purple book, I hum.

"Could. Won't."

What reassuring words. Not for the first time, I think I should be more concerned about exactly what Zylus *can* do but *hasn't yet*. I have been living with a vampire cat for five years. And now I've been knowingly living with one for several weeks.

He can control me. Put me to sleep. Relocate my body halfway across the forest *while* I'm asleep. Who knows what else he's capable of.

Garlic, sunlight, crosses, iron...none of the

"precautions" paranormal stories have taught me about work. I am at his mercy. I should at least be unnerved. Is there such a thing as being too tired to care?

At least this time I have something akin to an excuse for my exhaustion?

I'm not just going to school, like everyone else, yet failing miserably to maintain basic human function. I almost died. And now I live with an all-powerful being. Not everyone almost dies in their front yard or lives with a vampire cat. For once in my life, I'm *allowed* to be burnt out without guilt.

Score.

Zylus sits on the floor against the contemporary romance bookshelf, and I look down at him. "What are you doing?"

"Resting."

"If you're still tired, get in the basket." I hold it out for him.

He lets his head cock back against the shelves. "I want to talk with you."

It's such an innocent comment. Paired with him sitting on the floor, long legs stretched across the aisle, smile fixed up at me, and dual-colored eyes bright, it's easy to assume he's as non-threatening as a hamster.

Do I have energy for communication?

The buzz beneath my skin that banished me from my own house faded as soon as I encountered people strolling the sidewalks in town. I regretted my decision the second I saw Alice behind the front desk, but it was too late. For books I braved the outdoors, and for books I told myself I would remain strong.

Why do I always seem to forget the fact I am *not* strong? *Strong female lead* is not my archetype. *Perpetually exhausted pigeon* is.

Nevertheless, I say, "What do you want to talk about?" Crouching, I pull a paperback free and ignore the fact I've unconsciously moved closer to him.

He lifts his hand, traps a few straying strands of my hair behind my ear. "You can say you don't want to talk."

"I've been told on numerous occasions that's rude." Putting the book back, I choose another. "It's not that I care whether or not I'm rude to you. Some things are just ingrained in the writhing amoeba that passes as my brain."

"I don't care whether or not you're rude to me, starlight. I care whether or not you're honest. I want to talk. Do you?"

My attention homes in on a single word on the back of the book I'm holding. I read it four times before it—*cinnamon*—registers as a real thing. Then, almost immediately, it ceases to look like a word. I rub one eye. I'm tired. I'm ready to go home. I don't know why I'm still here. I have plenty of books to read at home and plenty to buy in my basket already. I'm going through my usual motions of perusing every section I enjoy as though something bad might happen if I don't.

Crazy.

I think I've already won the lotto when it comes to *bad things happening*.

"No," I decide at last, "I don't want to talk."

He smiles, warm and beautiful, and closes his eyes.

He's silent the rest of the trip, slinking back into my basket and snuggling with my books as soon as it's time to return home. He's quiet as the sun sets and we eat dinner together at the table. He makes a single, dismissive motion when I realize I need to check on my chickens, then he does it for me.

It's supposed to be weird.

Intentional silence between us is supposed to be

awkward, strained, uncomfortable. It's supposed to feel like wearing a too-tight shirt that has never been washed.

It doesn't.

This is what we've known already—my silent spells, his purring presence, an uncanny sensation that for once in my life another being doesn't mind my existence even when my existence is existing at sub-optimal levels.

To be fair, I assumed that last part was because I was keeping him warm and safe and fed. Although, the same tactics have never worked for any of my roosters.

Ingrates.

It's probably the dryad in me battling the pixie, but new things in the real world have always seemed dangerous. The most *new* and *excitement* I want comes from my books, and even then some of them leave me in week-long processing paralysis.

In weird ways, this new—this *different*—feels like enough of the same. I'm just…okay with it.

Perhaps that's why when I reach chapter five of my newest book, I angle myself away from the front window, murmur, "Zy," and watch him open his eyes.

He's all man, stretched out on my couch with his arms tucked beneath his head. He is starkly handsome. Gloriously so. "Yes, precious?" he asks.

I tap my lap. "Kitty."

Displaying his fangs in an eager smile, he melts into a puddle of darkness and obeys my summon without another word.

Chapter 12

Well, my day is ruined.

A real cat would have scratched me, escaped, and fled under the couch for the foreseeable future. Seeing as Zylus has displayed thoroughly feline traits, it's a miracle he's not given in to those instincts yet again.

As far as I know, I've been curled up on the floor in my kitchen for either ten minutes or four hours.

My chest hurts. I want to cry. I shouldn't cry. It's not worth crying over. My throat hurts. Is it dangerous to hold in tears? Am I holding Zylus too tight? He's a vampire. He can probably handle whatever strength I have. Am I being cat vampire-cist by thinking that?

Am I a horrible, useless person who can't do anything right?

Zylus meows, and I choke back a sob.

Atop my kitchen counter is soup. Not *actual* soup, which would be wholly acceptable. The part that makes it *not* acceptable is that it was supposed to be a pie. But it didn't set, so it's soup.

I've been wanting to make a pie for weeks. I finally found enough energy to try a new recipe. And what does the universe give me for my troubles?

Soup.

Meringue soup.

I don't know what I did wrong.

I don't know why everything in the universe is against me.

I thought I was beginning to handle the *my cat is a vampire and we might be soulmates* thing well. More well than at the start, anyway. At least more well than lying on my bedroom floor, staring at the ceiling, and arguing with mythical deities while asking another mythical deity—who has sworn off love like a genius—for help.

Here I am, though. Once again. On the floor.

To make matters worse, I'm on the floor grappling with things that are arguably less stressful than *hey, your cat self-medicates with blood, which is an addictive drug, because he's a vampire, and you're destined to be fantasy married to him foreverrr.*

Honestly.

What is my life?

Why was I even born?

Zylus's body begins to change into something less wriggly and soft in my arms.

"No," I whisper, frail. "Go away. I'm sorry. I'm sorry... I just want my stupid cat."

He hesitates, stops, and remains as my stupid cat. Stretching, he reaches his paws around my neck in a kitty hug and purrs against my chest.

I can hardly resolve the insanity of him obeying my feeble demand. I'm not kind. No one has ever liked me. Even my parents got sick of me. They never understood why I got all Gram's inheritance, but they were glad it provided an avenue to get me out of their lives.

I'd been a burden on them for too long.

But it's not like *I* asked to be born.

I *hate* how every single person on this planet has to deal with the consequences of another's actions. Honestly, it's no different than finding out my cat's a vampire and the world is full of magic. It's just more plot I didn't have a say in writing myself.

Zylus lifts his head off my shoulder, flicks his ears, and seems to brighten slightly. A moment later, the front door opens and shuts.

"Your garden space is beautiful!" Pila exclaims from the living room, voice drawing closer. "Have you already planned your spring crops? Is anything rooting yet? Can I see?"

Tension fills my limbs, and the tears I was valiantly holding back pour free at the exact moment Pila finds me on the floor in the kitchen. Her smile fades. She looks from me to the soup on the counter beside the stove.

This is going to haunt me for the rest of my life.

She's going to hesitate a moment, take a step back, and suggest she came at a bad time before giving me a tight smile and leaving.

I'll never see her again. Yet again, I'll have lost someone who was almost a friend.

"Lemon meringue?" She sweeps in front of the stove and surveys the disaster.

My heart thumps a horrid rhythm in my head. *You're twenty-six* overlays the pounding drum. I need to get a grip. Adults aren't supposed to have breakdowns or emotions—identifiable or otherwise.

Those are the kinds of things you get out of your system as a child.

Zylus coos, bonking his head into my chin, and I can't help but think maybe he's protesting against my completely accurate thoughts.

His ears pin, and he stretches up to bonk his head into my forehead before he licks a tear cascading down my cheek.

Pila opens my fridge. "I made plant-based jello for a party one time," she begins as she gets my heavy whipping cream out. "All my sisters were coming. I wanted to impress them. So I sourced the pectin myself." Her brown nose scrunches. "Bad idea. I should have tested the spell well in advance, but..." She lifts a shoulder. "It was *spring*, growing season, and I lost track of time." Pulling my standing mixer forward, she adds the cream, turns it on, and heads to my pantry. "I was a bush by the time they arrived."

My brow furrows. "What?"

"I turned into a bush." She searches my pantry for a moment, locates the condensed milk because I keep everything labeled and in plain view...lest I forget it exists. "Aspen, my eldest sister, laughed."

That must have been horrible. My heart sinks, and the overall *wrongness* in my body heightens.

"But she told me something as she was pruning my branches...and I've never forgotten it. Even when jello doesn't set up right, it's still sweet, it's still flavored, it's still something." She scoops the condensed milk into the mixer, adds the mistake of a pie, and turns to face me with a smile. "Nothing is a waste, and it's never the end. Life is like a seed. We plant it with an understanding we will inevitably get out what we put in. A tomato will be a tomato. An apple an apple. A carrot a carrot. We can't control how the stem grows, where the roots go, how the fruit forms. All we can do is nurture the seeds we plant and trust there will be something to harvest."

"But—"

Her head shakes. "No *buts*. Sometimes this world convinces us that *different* means wrong. Other times it tells us that *perfect* is attainable and defined clearly by people we don't even know." Extending her hand, she smiles. "Don't get lost, sapling. You're blooming just fine."

More tears flood, and my heart breaks a little as I lift my shaking hand to hers and let her pull me to my feet. Sobbing, I stand in the middle of my kitchen as the mixer whirs and the dryad hugs me tight, then tighter.

"I don't know why I'm like this," I croak. "I'm sorry."

"Everyone needs to turn into a bush now and again."

I sniffle. "What are you making?"

"Not sure." Letting me go, she stops the mixer and looks in at the pale yellow mass of fluff scattered with graham cracker crumbs. "Looks good though. Zy?"

From the blue and white checkered tile, Zylus looks up and coos.

"Tea."

In the following instant, Zylus shifts and pads barefoot to my pantry, shuffling through my extensive collection of artisan teas. Wordlessly, he begins to make a pot.

Nausea riffles about in my gut. "I— I'm sorry. I'm fine. W-we'll have to make plans later, when I'm more—"

Pila settles a bowl of lemon fluff in my hands. "Do you have a tea parlor?"

Do I have a *tea parlor*? This house is two-feet long. She's seen all of it.

Do I need to construct a tea parlor?

Maybe she should come back once I've built a tea p—

"Starlight." Zylus's tone is an odd mix of stern and tender.

It shocks my system, pulling my full attention to him. He's not smiling at the water he's boiling. The atmosphere around him rests on the side of ethereal. Beauty in the statuistic. He's art. Unwavering, marble art.

"I'll bring the tea to the living room once it's ready." Gliding to the silverware drawer, he retrieves two spoons, then I find myself ushered to the couch, clutching one in my hand like a lifeline.

Pila sits beside me, but before I'm grappling for the *correct* topic of conversation, she's formulating a spoken essay on why I require significantly more fruit trees, how she can help with them, and how we can rope Ollie into digging the holes.

The image of us commanding a tiny, derpy chihuahua to dig holes gets stuck in my head long enough for the revolt under my skin to die down.

I take a bite of the lemon concoction.

It's good.

Not pie.

But good.

Is it illegal to make tiny, derpy chihuahuas dig holes?

"Is that animal cruelty?" I ask, even though Pila's halfway through a list of *which* fruit trees grow best here and how I need *all* of them.

She stops short, takes a bite of her lemon fluff, and cocks her head.

My face warms. "I...I'm sorry." I wasn't listening. I only vaguely registered the last ninety paragraphs. I'm still thinking about forcing tiny dogs to dig pits bigger than them. That has to be against the faerie law. Shouldn't a faerie government be on my case by now?

Where is the *forbidden love* aspect? Is it entirely overshadowed by the *forbidding* love aspect?

Sworn off relationships is also a trope. Even though it normally comes on the tail end of a bitter romance, not from the soul of a plain old bitter person.

Zylus sets the tea tray on the coffee table while I'm spinning down avenues of thought and gaping silently in Pila's direction. Thankfully, she's not looking at me, but she has to know the silence is weird. I don't know what to say. What am I supposed to say?

I just want to be alone in my room where I can dig my own mental pit until it's big enough for me to hide in and never come out.

"Ollie likes digging holes," Zylus says as he pours me a

steaming cup of hazelnut tea, adds the exactly correct amount of sugar and the precisely right amount of cream. "Don't worry about him." He sets my glass, gold-lined cup down on my side of the coffee table, meets my eye, and says, "*Ever.*"

"*Oh.*" Pila laughs while Zylus pours another cup of tea, adding less sugar and no cream. "Yes. Don't worry about Ollie. Doliver Talon will do just about anything gleefully for a chicken foot. And he *does* like digging holes." Trading her lemon fluff for her teacup, she exhales into the steam and lets her eyes close.

"For a…chicken foot…"

"You can buy them at the pet store." Zylus sits behind the coffee table and crosses his legs. Smiling fondly, he notes, "He is entirely uncivilized at times."

"Speaking of uncivilized, you know what we should also grow this spring?" Pila's eyes open, wicked. "Catnip."

Zylus's back straightens, and his smile falls off his lips.

"Guess what vampire has kitty receptors that respond to nepetalactone," Pila sings.

"You wouldn't da—"

Pila grins my way. "Let's do it."

My lips part, close. I swallow and consume myself in scooping another bite of the lemon concoction. "I think I have some moral reservations?" Also, if Zylus gets addicted to kitty crack, what happens the next time a boogeyman attacks?

I perish, that's what.

He rolls around in cat weed, and I bleed out in the yard.

I shudder. Nope. Not giving my not a cat drugs. He's my source of paranormal protection. Which is mildly unsettling. All these years I thought he was the one relying on me. Now, everything has turned upside down.

Yet again, the conversation moves on without my

attention registering. I'm still out of it. When I rein my straying thoughts in, I find Pila and Zylus bantering back and forth about catnip. Pila insists she's going to carpet the yard with the stuff—if she can get permission from me. Zylus claims he'll start a forest fire—if I give permission.

It's all plausible talk, tangled up in strings of requirements that make none of their "threats" worrisome, unless I condone the madness.

I won't.

Smokey Bear taught me better than to toy with the dangers of prompting arson.

The part that gets to me is the fact they're *friends*.

Good friends.

Zylus knows the way she likes her tea just like he knows the way I like mine. Who knows how long they've known each other? Zylus could have been there when she sprouted. He could have carried her around as a child. He could have taught her how to be mischievous and was a prime contributing factor behind putting the glint in her green eyes.

Other people make relationships seem so easy.

Zylus's attention flicks to me, so I jerk mine down to my bowl.

Get out. *Get out, get out, get out.*

Rising, he sidesteps the coffee table, plants his hands on either side of me, and braces his weight against the back cushions. Leaning down, he kisses my forehead. The world slows as his lips graze my skin. "I'll go hunt."

My heart trips.

He's already out the door by the time Pila's eyes widen, and she covers her mouth with her hand. "Did something happen?"

My innards clench. I should have stopped him. Now *I'm* responsible for carrying this conversation. "No," I squeak. My tongue burns. "I-I mean…"

She sips her tea, and she must be judging me. I wish I could get inside her head like Zylus can get inside mine. Maybe that's why it's so easy for him to communicate with people—he knows the right things to say based on information they don't say. But, wait, he can't hear *everyone's* thoughts. Only those from the people he exchanges blood with. And I wouldn't think he'd have exchanged blood with Pila, rig—

"Are you well?"

My thoughts clip. "What?"

"You can tell me to leave if I'm upsetting you."

"*No*." I take a breath, attempt to unweld my jaw. The bones in my skull hurt. "No…I'm sorry. I…" I don't want her to think I don't want her here. I've never had a friend who stops by to see me before. I don't want to ruin this. Tears pool in my eyes again. Head aching, I lift a hand and scrub my face.

She sets her cup down beside where Zylus left mine on the table and gathers me up in her arms. "You had a bad moment. It's not a bad day."

"I'm sorry."

"All will be well." Her fingers sink into my hair. "It's hard. I know it's hard. You're so used to living in a world that isn't yours, but you're home now. And you are nothing like what you've been taught to believe. Your worth is not reliant on anything you do or do not manage to accomplish."

My grip tightens on the bowl, white-knuckling around my spoon. I bury my face against her shoulder and fight to contain myself. "I'm overwhelmed," I whisper. The words come broken, fragile as a butterfly wing beat.

"Do you need space?"

I rock my head. "I like you. I want to be friends. I don't

know how to do that. I'm glad you came to see me. I'm sorry I'm...I'm *like this*."

Bracing her hands at my shoulders, she pushes me away. Her nails dig, and my heart lurches when I find her scowl.

I've messed up. I—

"Do *not* apologize for the parts of yourself that are harmless." She searches my face for several long moments, then she sneers. "If you've a list of names and addresses of the people who have made you feel so small, we can plant brambles in their yards. I'll overrun their houses with blackberries and cross thorns over their windows." Standing, she clenches a fist. "Come, Prince Cael is having court today in Faerie. We'll take this matter there."

"What?"

Baffled, she peers back at me and spreads her hand. "Matters of premeditated large-scale distress against humans must be petitioned before the local reigning head, lest we risk royal punishment."

Sorry. *This* is how the storymakers are introducing me to the faerie government? That's illegal. I'm not supposed to meet the faerie government on benign terms. I'm *also* not supposed to want to do the magic equivalent of egging a person's house. "*What?*"

"I don't understand your reservation."

I don't understand my *lack* of reservation. I'm all for this. I should not be. Going to see the faerie government is the perfect distraction from pie disasters. And I've been left marvelously unsupervised. Chewing my lip, I hesitate, staring. If anything goes wrong, I can just call for Zylus, right? Yeah. Totally.

He's saved me before. He'll probably save me again.

It's not that I trust him; I merely have *facts* that imply his investment in my safety.

I close my hand into a fist. What am I thinking? What happened to the Willow who absolutely did *not* want to be a part of a fantasy story? One bad pie ruins my day and leaves me questioning my existence. I'm not built for actual problems.

I solemnly swear I will not become an idiot protagonist who creates issues.

Step one of not getting stuck in a fae government fiasco is not *going* to see the fae government leader whereby I will inevitably cause a fiasco.

I would simply waste away if Zylus appeared to save me, asked me why I'm there, and I hur-dur-hur say I am on a fruitless mission to petition vengeance against people I haven't seen for over a decade.

Filling Christie's yard with impossible to remove thorny blackberry bushes does call to an evil piece of my dark soul, but I just won't do it.

I refuse.

"We probably shouldn't bother a prince with something like this," I say. Maturely. And non-protagonistically. Suck it, story gods.

"Oh, but we definitely should."

Wish I could say that weren't an airtight argument. Lame by comparison, I offer, "I'm sure he has more important things to take care of." Like security. A boogeyman attacked me and something was in my bedroom the other day. Hopefully, those creatures didn't get their petitions to cause me distress approved. If they did, that probably means Zylus is on the wrong side of this government, and I absolutely should not go cause a war.

Pila insists, "This matter is of equivalent importance to many that he deals with daily."

I crave more information.

If the faerie world is where the people hug me instead

of telling me to *grow up already*, I want to understand it in the same way someone who had the privilege of growing up in it does.

I want to make it *mine*.

And I can't do that if I don't walk blindly into potential danger, hoping vaguely it—like everything else thus far—will be something different than I expect.

Besides, maybe I shouldn't, but I trust that Pila wouldn't try to put me in danger or take me somewhere that her friend Zylus wouldn't approve of.

Curiosity is dreadfully good at prompting rationalization.

"Okay, fine, you've convinced me," I say. "Let's go."

Chapter 13

I am nothing if not moved by bribery.

After confirming that what I'm wearing is fine, Pila leads me through the chilled woods until frost overruns the trees and icicles hang from the bare branches. Sunlight winks through the weeping spears, and every droplet that falls paints a snowflake on the ground.

There's magic in the air. Tiny gleaming creatures draw frozen veins into rough bark. Pine needles shiver in the wake of wing beats above. Below, among the patches of crunching snow, Pila's bare footsteps warm the earth and turn the brown leaves green again.

Once we come upon a sheer rock cliff split down the center with a crack no wider than an inch, I realize I've spent the last thirty minutes of walking in silence. "What are the rules?" I blurt, hoping we're not about to climb the slab of shimmering stone before us. I don't think I could manage. Once again I feel compelled to remind the deities in charge of my story that I was built to harvest green beans, not scale mountains.

Also, hi. I'm in platforms. And if I try to go barefoot like Pila, I will lose my toes to the winter winds.

Pila stops just short of walking directly into the rock and looks at me. "Rules?"

Dread explodes in my chest. "Was I supposed to bring a gift?"

A funny look creases her brows. Looking down, she plucks a dry leaf off the ground. It bursts into burning orange between her fingers as she hands it to me. "There. A gift."

I barely get half a second to compute the fire shades now contrasting my skin before she grabs my free hand and charges into the rock face.

Collision never comes.

Freaking magic.

Toddling after Pila in my knee-high platform shoes as she tugs me through the crevice, I stare way up at the fading light pouring through the rift behind us. Note to self: becoming two inches tall is a recurring dilemma within the fae world.

Do not be alarmed.

Clearly, it's normal.

I release a breath.

It makes more sense than asking a question but not wanting the real answer. It makes more sense than *small talk* about the weather. It makes more sense than a lot of things I've lived with.

Like telling someone who is clearly falling apart to *grow up* instead of giving them a hug.

Finding my resolve, I face forward and hold Pila's hand a little tighter as we traverse the dim, gaping passage. At the farthest end of the tunnel, two sentries stand before a tall door made of glistening silver bark. Rhinoceros beetle helmets cover their faces, shining mandibles piercing upward. A sliver of the bluest eyes I've ever seen cut toward Pila, then toward me.

Not a word passes between them before both pull open the doors.

Breath catches in my chest.

Light and luxury spin before my eyes. The precise instant the doors close behind me—locking me in for the foreseeable future—I realize that unassuming crack in the side of the mountain was the entrance to a *palace*.

Sunlight shines through tall, gilded windows that frame the long room. It caresses chandeliers and crystal. It facilitates shadows across the polished pearl floors.

Craning my head, I fight for a better look past the array of twirling, flying, cascading creatures and decide that maybe—just maybe—that unassuming crack in the side of the mountain was the entrance to another world.

Faerie. If I remember what Pila said earlier. Faerie. The mythical realm of the fae.

The crowd neither parts nor obstructs us as Pila takes me through the center of the room. I'm so distracted by…everything…I register nothing until I'm positioned before a man seated sideways on a crystal throne, legs tossed over one armrest, brilliant trailing wings flung over the other.

His eyes catch hold of me, burnished amber. A pale copper brow that matches the shades in his wings rises as he plants his elbow on the armrest and sets his chin in his palm.

This is it.

The beginning of the end.

The two giant yellow antennae protruding from his brow tilt forward, their hefty feathered plumes fanning. His eyes widen a fraction, and he lifts his chin from his palm. Then?

Then he swears.

Laughter tumbles out of Pila as he stands, wings spread. They're so large they cover his throne entirely until he's marched fully down the two steps and stopped in front of us. His arms fold. He fills his lungs with air, letting it all out in a single, irate puff. "Her name?"

Pila laughs a little harder as she shakes her head. "I have no idea. He calls her *starlight*."

Prince Cael echos the term as though it disgusts him.

Then he splays his fingers over his face and swears softly. Composing himself, he smiles at me—overtly gentle and innately disconcerting on account of it. "How should I address you, miss?"

First of all, I can't believe I didn't realize Zylus never introduced me to anyone. Second of all, I don't think I'm supposed to answer. Telling a faerie your name is bad.

At least that's what my highly-unreliable fantasy stories have taught me.

The prince narrows his eyes. "Is she...shy?"

"She's been inundated with slander about us and likely thinks we are asking to own her name."

He relaxes. "Ah. Poor thing. Those of us here only steal the souls of the ones who have all but lost them anyway. And, even then, it's rare we bother."

"Indeed." Pila beams. "Are we too late to partake of court? We've come to petition mischief."

A spark of interest lights in his gaze. "Oh?"

Excited, Pila nods. "I would encase a dozen or more human homes in thorns and brambles."

"As would I, were it an agreeable action to take against the pitiable beings. Oft they cause their own misfortune without the addition of our help." He sweeps his hand into his mid-length bronze hair. "What, pray tell, has set you off?"

"They have done my friend wrong."

Heat flutters to my cheeks, and I clutch the leaf gift against my chest, wholly unsure when I'm meant to present it. Pila just called me her *friend*. We're *friends*. Is this winning? Have I arrived? A dryad considers me to be *her friend*.

A dryad is willing to destroy private property on my behalf.

Thank you, Athena. Your blessings are numerous, and

Crap.

I might cry again.

While I fight back the sudden burning sensation behind my eyes, the prince's wings droop. "People have done this human wrong?" He peers at Pila wearily. "And *you* are the one seeking to remedy that? Why would they still breathe when she belongs to Zy?"

"I know. The outrage. You should have a talk with him about properly avenging his mate."

Wait.

"I believe you'd do well not to overestimate your relationship with my knight, little one. A mere suggestion that he isn't properly caring for his beloved would lead to my handling paperwork for murder."

Hold on.

"I've known him my whole life. He's only been in your service a fraction of his. You might be the one overestimating your relationship with him, for I am allowed to suggest whatever I wish without fear of repercussion."

Back…back up. Just one—

"*Allowed* is far from *advised*. You should err on the side of caution where the mate bond is concerned. I recognize th…" Prince Cael glances at me, and some color drains from his face. "Miss, are you well?"

"You *know* Zy? He's your…your *knight*?" My eye twitches. "You have to do *paperwork*?"

The picture of frivolous fae governments that I've grown attached to shatters. Yet another debunked expectation. I don't feel well at all. I feel faint, actually. I know less than nothing because I know lies. Also, what the heck, Zylus? Are you an *extrovert*? Why do you know *everyone*?

A deep, resounding sigh pours from behind me, and the

prince tenses, swearing again.

Arms coil around my waist, soldering me to a familiar chest. "You spoke my name, starlight?" His words send a skitter down my spine. "You were supposed to have quiet afternoon tea with your friend. Why are you in Faerie?"

I suppress a shudder. "Because."

"Because, why?"

"You left me unsupervised." I am, therefore, unable to be held accountable for any and all actions I commit. Obviously. That's how it works. Also, I didn't know that *just* the act of saying his name could summon him.

I really wish I had a comprehensive pamphlet explaining these things.

He ignores my stink eye in favor of laughing, and the action vibrates my entire body. "Cael. My mate."

Cael, as in "they're such good friends he doesn't say *prince*" Cael, fits his hands to his narrow hips. "Yes, I gathered that from your scent all over her. Why wasn't I introduced?" The man's amber eyes ripple with hurt that baffles me. A faerie prince is genuinely offended that he wasn't introduced to Zylus's…"mate." Exactly how far up in the social hierarchy is Zylus? I wouldn't assume a knight to have a close relationship with their liege. They stand guard at balls, pine after princesses, and swing swords in courtyards.

Where's Zylus's sword? Does he have a cool helmet like those guards outside?

"Darling, behave," he murmurs in my ear. "Your thoughts are running rampant."

Oh. Well. *Excuse* me.

He kisses my temple, then answers Cael, "She was some overwhelmed by the elves' simple revel. I'd not thought her ready to mingle amongst the nobility."

"You could have told me she had entered our fold."

"And risk you fluttering off to meet her yourself now that no glamour has hope of working on her? Hardly."

"I'd have been discreet."

"You'd have been a twelve-inch Hercules moth clinging to her window screen."

Cael's lips purse. "A *discreet* twelve-inch Hercules moth. Since when do humans pay any mind to moths?"

"If you believe humans wouldn't pay attention to a moth the size of one's head, you are more poorly accustomed to the other realm than I thought."

"You insult me."

Entirely undaunted, Zylus snuggles my shoulder and murmurs, "He is easily distracted by shiny objects and lights. If I had a kingdom for every time I've stopped him from nearly being hit by a car—"

"—you'd have *two* kingdoms." Cael's arms fold. "You're embarrassing me. Stop it."

"Two kingdoms is more than enough," Zylus notes.

"It is strange that it's happened twice," Pila muses.

Red blooms in Cael's cheeks, and he turns his back on us, leaving me to stare at the massive eye spots of his wings. He mutters, "You abuse the high regard I hold you in."

"Only at every feasible opportunity." Zylus finally unravels himself from around me. "Cael."

The prince lowers one forewing so he can glance over his shoulder at us.

Zylus splays his palm against my back, and heat soaks through my dress. "This is Willow, my eternity."

Pila clasps her hands together. "*Willow*. Oh what a lovely name."

Cael's expression softens. "You're content, Zy?"

"Blissful."

"I envy you."

"You will find yours."

Cael's gaze drops, and he twists the topic. "The time for court has long since ended. I've lingered purely out of an affliction of boredom. Have you any cure?"

"Not if you don't stop talking in riddles."

Cael huffs. "I would spend time with you and Willow, partaking of an activity."

I bristle. An *activity*? What kind of activity? And for how long? It's *Thursday*. I have to be home by seven thirty to make popcorn for movie night at eight.

Zylus watches me for several long moments, then—because he's *obsessed* with being in my head—he says, "Movies are an activity."

He can't be suggesting that I allow faerie royalty into my little cottage. That's...crazy.

"We can invite Ollie, too."

No, see, sir, the issue was not insufficient magical creatures in my living room.

"Pila has an amazing brownie recipe."

My spine goes rod straight, and I press my leaf gift close to my chest. "So is everyone okay with coming by at eight and watching an animated film?"

Zylus grins, fangs on display, then claps his hand against Cael's chest. "Tell Ollie seven. Pila can show you the way. We'll see you all there."

Cael brightens. "Most excellent."

Most...something.

That's for sure.

Chapter 14

I really wish my stupid cat would get out of my head.

"You never kept any of the gifts I gave you," Zylus calls from the kitchen while I'm dusting the entertainment center under the leaf that never made it to Cael. Beside it, Deidra—the still-flourishing bloom Pila gave me at the party—sits in royal perfection.

She is a princess. And I still love her.

My leaf needs a name.

A name like Edwin.

"When you say *gifts*, are you talking about dead animals?" I call back.

Holding the broom, he pokes his head into the living room. "You could have had an entire collection of tiny skulls by now. Wouldn't you love that?"

It is disturbing how, under an entirely different context, I would not be opposed to having a collection of little skulls—the context being that they are fake and purely for aesthetic purposes. I could put them up the path in order to ward off straying travelers. "Technically, the leaf was supposed to be a gift for Cael."

Zylus reels back, clutching the broom to his chest. "Why does *Cael* need gifts from *you*?"

"I swore it was proper etiquette to bring a gift when meeting royalty. I suspect a misunderstanding transpired." I hope Pila doesn't mind if I keep Edwin for myself. He's in love with Deidra.

"I know you're not attempting to distress me, but you

are."

"Give better gifts," I say as I move to dust the coffee table. "And finish sweeping the floor."

He scowls but obeys. The shush of the broom against tile underlays his perturbed tone. "Now you are trying to distress me."

A smile curves my lips. "How intuitive an observation, Zy." Putting up the duster, I head into the kitchen to get the popcorn started.

Strange.

I pull the bag of kernels out of the pantry and get the machine out of a lower cabinet.

This feels normal.

Having a vampire, who can shift into a cat, sweeping my kitchen floor feels *normal.*

I know the concept of normality is relative, but I never would have thought it *this* relative.

This seems dangerous while feeling normal.

Next thing I know, I'll be kissing him and baring my throat.

He freezes, staring at the modest mound of dirt on the tile.

"*Out,*" I grit, dumping kernels into the machine and starting it up. "I'm having *private* thoughts. *Stop* listening."

"I'd really like to make sure I heard correctly—"

"*No.* You weren't *supposed* to *hear* anything. Go out of range. You can watch the movie tonight through the window while standing out in the yard."

He clears his throat. "It's just that it was a very vivid picture and—"

The popcorn begins going off like gunshots.

I slap my palms down on the island counter, lean forward, and hiss, "There was no vivid picture. There was *nothing.* It's called an intrusive thought, and I don't want you listening to them." They're awful. He's awful. I hate him.

My chest seizes, and panic slices across his face before the pain cuts abruptly off. The broom falls out of his hands. "Starlight…"

That was worse than the other times I've felt his pain, and I don't want to think about what that might mean. Swearing, I stumble back when he comes closer.

He stops, mismatched eyes wide and hopeless. "I'm sorry."

"You respond to the words in my head more accurately than *picking up sensations*, Zy."

His lips part, but silence prevails, weighing heavy in the space between us. Broken and frail, he says, "I know you. You are mine. I hear you more clearly than anything else. Your thoughts sing into my skull, and I ache with the ones that hurt you. I long for your peace. I beg for your fleeting desire. I…" Torment ripples in his eyes. "I fear that when you reject me you always will. I despise anything that separates me further from you." He lifts his hand, staring at his palm, searching, swallowing, closing his eyes then his fingers. "I was human, once, Willow. A terribly long time ago. Every cell in me has forgotten what it means, but when I look at you, things I haven't felt in ages consume me. I had assumed I'd outgrown this terror of not being enough or of being too much for someone, but I *must* be perfect for you. I just don't know how to be when—had I stayed human—nothing would be different." When his eyes reopen, a tear traces down his cheek to the tip of his chin. "You still wouldn't want me, or, at the very least, not all of me. It is a cruel thing to acknowledge that it is not *what* I am that disturbs you. It is the fact that I *am* at all."

The popping kernels slow to periodic bursts.

I don't know what to make of the scene before me or

the words echoing in my head.

It's finally a hint of the angst I've been waiting for, sure, but it's not the screaming sort layered with desperation and frustration or barely-restrained passion that seems oh so prevalent in my trashy novels. This is pleading. For understanding. Patience. A chance.

It isn't a blazing fire ready to spill through the cracks and turn everything to ash

It's a request to love and be loved, in the rawest sense. Beyond physical. Beyond desire. To the depths of the soul.

"Am I scared?" I ask.

Zylus takes a moment, then he shakes his head.

"What am I feeling?"

Clutching his fists at his sides, he murmurs, "Inadequate. Incapable. Unprepared. You can't fathom what I'm suggesting. You can't fathom being wanted at such staggering depths when no one has ever so much as entertained wanting you at far shallower ones." Wetting his lips, he reads my spirit, the words in my heart that not even I've put into cohesive lines. "'If I'm unlovable skin-deep, soul-deep must be despicable.'"

I mutter a curse, turn to the popcorn machine as the contents start to burn, and unplug. "Get the stuff."

I don't need to elaborate. Zylus goes so far as to get the designated popcorn bowl along with the flavoring. I dump the popcorn in, picking out the worst bits before he takes over dousing it in butter powder.

"Are you sure we're soulmates?" I ask.

"Positive."

"Because it seems like our damage feeds off one another and we're going to implode."

His lips pull into a slight pout. "My love, that is the point."

"What do you mean that's the point?"

"We overcome together, or we burn."

Speaking of burn, I grab a kernel and pop it in my mouth to make sure the burnt taste didn't saturate. Thankfully, it's not that bad. Who knows if it's good enough for royalty, though? Who knows if it's good enough for *Pila*?

I should make another batch.

"Is this a cosmic therapy program?" I ask as I measure out more kernels. "Because I don't love the concept that the universe decided I required non-refundable mental health assistance."

Zylus smiles. "I thought you were pro universal health care."

I snort. "I never would have bundled it with *universal matchmaking*."

He returns to the dirt pile, retrieves the broom, and sweeps it up into the dustpan. "Love cures a lot."

"Anddd we're a Hallmark movie now. Can we please pick a genre lane?"

"Which one would you prefer?"

My mouth opens as the cacophony of popping corn starts up again. I take a moment to give the quandary some thought. "That is an excellent question. How about slice of life?"

"Too episodic. And mundane. Fantasy at least needs to be a subgenre so I can exist."

"Right. Of course. *Fantasy* or *paranormal* needs to be a subgenre, and which one is the question, Mr. I'm a Vampire Fairy."

"I'm a vampire cat, which is a faerie. Think of it like how paranormal rests beneath the fantasy umbrella. I rest beneath the faerie umbrella."

"Clearly, based on the coherency of this conversation, you've been living with me for too long."

"Eternity wouldn't be long enough, starlight."

I hiss, because *what* have I told him about compliments making me uncomfortable? At this point it's just rude.

Still.

If I like the pieces of his world that let me be me without consequence, will I inevitably have to address the fact whatever *we* are is a part of it?

"We don't have to be lovers," he says as he dumps the contents of the dustpan in the trash. "If that's too much, you don't have to assume we'll ever wind up there."

"Right. You said you'd be happy enough just being my cat."

"I want to be near you."

A concept that perplexes me thoroughly. "So you'll stop the PDA?"

His head tilts.

The popcorn stops popping, and this time I turn the machine off before it burns. "Forehead, cheek, and hand kisses. All the hugging and cuddling. Only kitty head pats allowed. And no licking. Because weird."

"That doesn't have to be lover affection." His arms cross.

I regard him dryly as I dump butter flavor all over the popcorn. "So you'd partake of all the aforementioned actions with Ollie?"

"Bold of you to assume I haven't. We're *best friends*."

"Well then. I'm looking forward to third-wheeling tonight," I say, plucking up the non-burnt popcorn bowl and marching out of the room.

Chapter 15

I just want to play Sims.

I have not been watching the movie. Not even a little bit. I have a sneaking suspicion Zylus isn't watching the movie either, not with the entertainment my thoughts no doubt provide.

Cael and Pila sit side-by-side on the floor in front of the coffee table, the dregs of the acceptable popcorn bowl between them. The screen lights reflect in their enraptured eyes, and I'm a thousand percent sure they are oblivious to the scene taking place behind them, where Ollie and Zylus sit on the couch.

Or, rather, where Ollie and Zylus sit partway on the couch and partway on top of each other. They're a tangle of limbs and cuddles. I've caught half a dozen forehead kisses, feeding one another popcorn, playing with each other's hands and hair...

I'm *jealous*.

So. Dang. Jealous.

How does one friendship at this level?

The second Ollie arrived, Zylus grabbed him and shoved him into the bathroom. When they walked out, the werecanine was beneath the vampire cat's arm, and they've not separated since.

This goes beyond Zylus trying to prove a point concerning platonic affection. Ollie finding the very nature of his request acceptable fills me with inexplicable longing. *I* want a friend like derpy chihuahua man who accepts my nonsense without batting an eye.

I don't have an operating system capable of computing this turn of events. The existence of a boogeyman startles me less.

Is this normal?

Are *best friends* generally okay with partaking in PDA upon request? Have I just never had a *best friend* before? Platonic affection at this level equals a thing, bold letters, seven question marks.

My eyes narrow.

Oi. Zylus. Look at me when I'm irritated with you.

His blue and green eyes slip my way, and, holding my gaze, he pecks Ollie's forehead before resting his cheek against the chihuahua's dusky brown hair.

Ollie shifts to get more comfortable and doesn't pay me a gram of mind.

I'm going to cut off their tails and feed them to the woodland monsters.

Zylus's lips turn down, chiding, so I huff, drag my legs up against my chest and look outside. It's a clear winter night filled with frost and mist. I'm not unsettled by the shadows—probably because Pila's here, and a faerie prince. (Mostly Pila.) Right now, this place is untouchable. Safe.

By some cruel twist of fate, the picture behind me reflects in the glass, and it's warm.

Terribly warm.

My breath fogs the image away, but it remains engraved in my mind.

I'm having a movie night with people who could be good friends someday.

This is my house. My living room. My TV. But I'm the odd one out.

They all have decades of history I wasn't a part of.

They know and trust each other. They share memories. They come from the same world.

I'm not even fully fae.

"Starlight."

My heart jumps, and I look back at the couch.

Hand extended, Zylus beckons.

He's got to be kidding. There's no way I'm going over there. It's #cringe enough from where I'm sitting. Any closer, and my eyes might catch fire.

So why am I standing?

Ollie glances at me when I walk in front of him, and he smiles as I take Zylus's hand. Naturally, he unwinds himself from the limb tangle. Unnaturally, he shifts into the derpy spotted chihuahua, circles on the one side of the couch, and settles in, resting his chin against his paws as he peers at the TV screen.

I sit beside Zylus with a huff, whispering, "You're full of garbage."

"Am I?" he whispers back, against my forehead, which he is kissing.

"Heaps."

His fingers flow through my hair. He whispers a curse against the crown of my head. "I love you."

I can't imagine why.

Funny how emotions shift throughout life. Vaguely, I recall a time when I couldn't imagine why people *didn't* like me. Wasn't I nice enough? Pretty enough? Interesting enough? I looked enough like the people around me. I put as much effort as I could into behaving like them. But it didn't work. And I didn't understand.

My wee formative years trained me to anticipate rejection.

Not receiving it now tips me off balance.

When wrong things begin to feel right, right things start

to feel wrong.

It's just a part of life.

Unlearning beliefs takes more energy than I tend to average in a given day.

Compliments cut off my airflow. Affection makes my skin weird.

I want *so badly* to be a part of the kinds of lifelong, magical relationships depicted in movies like the one we're supposed to be watching, but I just can't figure out how to make such a fantasy concept possible.

It's more foreign than the fact a man just turned into a chihuahua on my couch.

It's too late. I'm exhausted. Who knows how long I'll shut down after this? Who knows how many nights I'll spend replaying the reflections in my mind and wondering why—even though I've moved into the picture—I still can't seem to find myself in the glass.

★

"I've figured it out," I say aloud to the cat purring on my stomach.

Hi, yes. Welcome back to my bedroom floor. Lovely place. Five stars.

Zylus coos, rolling over, and I am mature enough to recognize that he's an absolute trooper for putting up with my near-constant collapses. He's a good guy. There. I thought it. Took me a month and a half to understand that a cat man willing to feed me in my comatose states, peer pressure me into taking at least one shower a week, and sit with me for hours without saying a word is a decent being.

"I'm an old computer. Downloading the Sims."

Zylus's head tilts. He's so floppy. Innocent. Certainly didn't try and bring me a wet leaf a few days ago in an effort to cheer me up.

"Every social interaction is a new Sims game I have to

pack inside. We're talking old school. Several CDs. My hard drive is bursting, but I'm persistent because I require the expansion pack, for it will make me happy. The already foreboding *seventeen hour* time frame trips into several days, which coughs into multiple weeks." I take a breath. "By the time I *do* get the whole thing downloaded and started up, I'm running at three frames per second. My character turns out all kinds of wonky. I get frustrated before I can really start playing, give up, and erase it all, hoping I might free some room for something else." Picking Zylus up beneath the armpits, I dangle him and stare into his multicolored eyes. "Problem is: I'm full *without* the addition of these games. The programs that say *feed yourself* and *shower* are nowhere near optimized, so they take up every byte. The developer stopped updating and fixing bugs ages ago. Any attempts at improving function now crash the system, forcing reboot. My hardware isn't compatible with any vital normal stuff people are supposed to grow into. I'm stuck." I shake him. "Do you understand?"

His furry body morphs, and I jerk my hands off him as he kneels around me, pushes back his hair, and says, "I might be the only person who can."

Is it just me, or do we wind up in this position overmuch? Weird. There's a potential I should feel more unnerved. But I don't.

I say, "I want to play the Sims. I just can't."

"You can afford a new computer."

"No, I can't. A new computer would feel wrong. It wouldn't be *my* computer anymore."

He smooths his thumb against my cheekbone. "It would. You would make it your computer."

I scowl. "Impossible."

He taps my forehead. "Darling, this is your computer.

Yes, the programs that you need to survive take up more space than they do for a lot of other people, but you're also holding onto things you don't need."

I cross my arms. "I suppose you would know, seeing as you've hacked into my system and won't get out."

Zylus sighs, tenderly, as though I'm not upsetting in the slightest. "You're plenty. For me. For Pila, and Ollie, and Cael. You can get rid of the programs that claim you have to *become someone specific yet undefined* in order to make people like you. They're useless. You know what Ollie's capable of?"

"Not even remotely."

"Shifting into any canine form."

My brows rise.

"That means the chihuahua is a conscious decision." His fingertip traces my ear. "And Cael? *Prince Cael?* He once flicked a light switch on and off for three hours. He only stopped because I dragged him away. And I'm not saying I left him with the light switch on purpose so I could take care of something else, but yes I did."

"Should you be sharing this personal information about your prince with me? It sounds like he and the light switch were very serious, and he'd prefer to keep his intimate relationships private."

Zylus's lips curl into a dry smirk. "I'm trying to make a point. You are among chihuahuas, bushes, light switch addicts, and strays. We take care of each other. We laugh with each other. We accept the highs and lows. We understand outbursts and overwhelm. You're mine, so you already fit. You don't need programs that center around *trying* to be accepted."

Turning my face away from him, I grumble, "Joke's on you. I gave up trying a long time ago. All I want to do now is exist in peace."

"And play Sims."

"Sims is a luxury I understand I will never enjoy. I don't have the patience. And what grown person can't boil spaghetti without setting their house on fire, anyway?"

He bonks his head to mine, fills his lungs with air, and lets his huff run across my lips. "Oh my darling. Obviously a grown person without a single cooking skill."

That's right. He was around during my most recent Sims phase. I haven't touched my laptop or the modest stack of video games for months, but when I had obsessed over them for about three weeks, he was right there, on my lap, watching. I bought every last character a black cat in his honor. Named them all different endearments I had for Lord Keres.

I swear. "I'm the best owner."

"It's true."

"You're not a bad pet, either."

His smile fades as his eyes open, wide. He peers down at me—shocked.

"What? You're in my skull. You have to already know how I feel about *cat* you."

"I never would have expected you to express such a lack of distaste aloud."

Lifting my hand, I rustle his long dark hair until the strands fall over his shoulders and tickle my neck. "You've not scratched my couch or torn up my carpet. You've never once puked on my bed. Honestly, I should have known you weren't a real cat ages ago."

His eyelids waver as his pupils swallow the color in his irises. He leans into my touch. "I bite."

"Nobody's perfect."

"You just care more about your couch than you do about yourself," he murmurs. "Which…" He lowers his head, flicks his tongue against my cheek, kisses. "…is bad."

It's a nice couch.

Abruptly, he jerks himself away and stands. "I'll make you something to eat."

Tilting my head back against the carpet, I watch him march out the door. Once he's out of sight, I call, "Were you about to bite?"

"Not without permission," he calls back, and I hear a pan clatter in the kitchen, just before a soft swear. "Do you want potatoes?"

What does he take me for? Of course I want potatoes.

By the time I drag myself out of my bedroom, he's peeling a pile of potatoes beside the sink, jaw clenched. I sit at the kitchen nook.

He winces before bracing himself against the counter.

I'm on my feet before I register moving. "Hey, are you all right?"

"Fine," he says, eyes closed, knuckles going Victorian-child-with-cholera pale around the peeler.

"*Are you well?*" I ask, and that question leaves him silent.

"I should do this at the table."

Rounding the island, I slip the peeler from his hand. "Or not at all. Sit down. I'll do this."

He doesn't move.

"Zy."

"Sorry. I need a moment." Eyes unfocused, he stares ahead at the potato peelings scattered across robin-egg blue, then whispers, "I can't see right now."

I curse. "What do you mean you can't see?"

"I stood up too fast. Then I got things from the lower cabinets. The up and down…bad." He closes his eyes again. "Just give me a moment."

The stern, steady tone of his voice tells me,

horrifyingly, this is *normal*. He's used to it. The idea that he can be used to being unable to see even when his eyes are open sends a prickle down my spine. A voice that sounds a lot like mine asks, "Do you need blood?"

His eyes snap open, still distant. His throat bobs. Weakly, he echoes, "Just give me a moment."

So I do. I give him several. At the end of them we've switched places. I'm peeling potatoes, and he's plastered against my kitchen table, arms thrown above his head, muttering a curse every once in a while.

"Have you been taking care of yourself while I've been out of commission?" I rinse the peeled potatoes then dunk them in the water and set them on the stove to boil.

He swears.

"Zy."

His face pinches. "I don't like going far when you're like that."

"You've not 'medicated' for a week?"

"I have." His words soften, muffle, and clump together. "Just not as consistently as perhaps advised. It's less convenient to wait for prey to find me here, especially during this time of year."

"How are you supposed to hunt now that you're like this?"

Blearily, he glares nowhere in particular. "Very carefully."

That answer does not inspire much confidence.

I check the freezer for red meat and come up empty. Because I've been lamenting on my floor for a week, torn between the concept of *wanting friends* and *friends sound exhausting*. There's nothing "bloody" in here.

"Can't be dead blood," he drawls.

I tuck the rule away alongside an understanding that if the blood has to come from something living, it's me or my chickens.

"Or Ollie."

I bristle. "What?"

"Ollie helps me sometimes. So does Cael. But it causes trouble for Cael, and Cael's usually farther away." Zylus heaves a breath. "I'll be well enough soon. No need to worry. Believe it or not, this is all I remember from when I was human."

"I thought this was a vampire thing."

"It is. I was like you, part fae, with no idea how to manage those pieces because I didn't even know they existed. It was a different time. Being a weak male meant you were useless. When the vampire who turned me fully found me and offered to help, I was so tired of being a burden I didn't think twice." A dry laugh escapes him, hollow. "I just wanted to stop hurting. I just wanted the pressure to push through the exhaustion to go away. I only survived as long as I did because my family was wealthy enough to confine me to mundane tasks, like stewardship since I'm good at math…but it was awful, Willow." Shallow breath moves through him. "I can still taste the loneliness and the shame. Even though I don't remember the faces of the people who I once called my family, I can still remember the isolation." Drawing his arms beneath his head in a pillow, he murmurs, "Knowing the truth is a gift many don't receive."

He's right. Yet when I received it, I scorned it.

"Don't think like that." His lips pull into a wry smile. "My love, there's nothing wrong with wishing you didn't have to deal with any of it. Before I understood, all I wanted was to be normal, too."

"And now?"

His gaze lingers on me. "Now, I am home. And I wouldn't trade that for a steady heartbeat in a million years."

My heartbeat trips in response, so I turn toward the stove, check on the potatoes, and pull some veggies out of the freezer to steam. "How did you survive without air conditioning if heat makes it worse?"

He laughs. "Migration. I've spent many summers in places where the sky is a rainbow and the sun doesn't shine."

He migrated. "Can you take other forms like Ollie?"

"And is one of them a bird?"

I clear my throat. "Well, I wasn't going to say that part aloud."

"I am a cat."

"That doesn't sound like a no."

"Many faeries possess the ability to shapeshift within the bounds of what they are. I know some vampire bats. And snakes. The occasional vampire spider. Several crows and ravens. But I am a cat." His eyes close, content and secure in those words. There's a strange peace surrounding the declaration.

I can't help but wonder if, maybe someday, I'll find the confidence to define what I am, too.

Chapter 16

Is this when I break character?

Ollie's human lives in a quaint home several roads past downtown, off Old Old Bridge Lane, not to be confused with Old Bridge Lane farther up. Overgrown bushes frame the front windows and climb pale peach siding while a fireplace glows inside. Smoke pours from the brick chimney, dusting the air with a winter scent even as spring lurks around the very next corner.

I need to get my plants rooting soon. No more breakdowns.

She says.

As though they are a conscious decision.

I stop on the sidewalk beside the waist-high fenced-in yard and shift my basket cat from one arm to the other. "So...do I knock on the door and ask his human if they think their chihuahua is interested in donating blood?"

Zylus's eyes open on me, amused.

"I don't know how this works," I snap.

He slinks out of the basket, shifts in front of me, and leans against the short wooden fence. "With the rumors surrounding you, are you certain asking for a blood offering will go over marvelously?"

Fair point. Counterpoint: now I'm morbidly interested in the reaction.

Before I get a chance to sweep the devious thought under the mental rug, a wee *yip* sounds from inside and spills into a chorus. Next thing I know, a little tan and white chihuahua streaks across the brittle lawn, tongue flapping in the wind. Ollie shifts last second, grips the fence, and lunges over onto the sidewalk before leaning back against the pickets beside Zylus. Warm beauty. He flashes a *No, I don't spend most of my time cross-eyed* smile. "Hey, guys."

"Hi," I say, unsure when I'll get used to watching the derpiest animal in existence explode into a model. Zylus shifting from cat to not cat is one thing. Like he said earlier, the *cat* thing feels extremely correct. He *is* feline. It suits him. Ollie being a chihuahua doesn't match him quite the same.

He scans Zylus, and his dimples fade. "Oh, buddy."

"Sorry." Zylus offers a weak smile. "I mismanaged myself."

Ollie pulls up the sleeve of his cable-knit sweater and gives Zylus his wrist without hesitation. Without suggesting that it's *my job to feed him now*. Without even waiting for Zylus to ask.

I swallow hard when Zylus opens his mouth and sinks his fangs. There's a peacefulness to it that my, ahem, *fine literature* did not prepare me for. One friend helping out another. That simple. There's no obsession, starvation, uncontrollable angst or lust or urge. Every animalistic trait associated with vampires *feeding* is starkly absent.

"Doesn't that hurt?" I ask after assessing that Ollie's levels of chill remain entirely unimpaired in spite of the teeth embedded in his flesh.

Ollie's attention skids toward me, then toward the sky. He lifts a shoulder. "Maybe? I might be used to it."

"This happens often?"

"Usually at least once in summer."

My brows knit. "And you don't mind?"

Ollie's gaze drops, pinning on mine, severe. "Of course not."

My stomach twists. "I'm sorry. I—"

Zylus unlatches and wipes his mouth. "Starlight, he's not upset."

Laughter bubbles out of Ollie before he licks his puncture wounds. "Sorry. Did I sound upset? I'm rarely upset when I look like this. Anger's for the animal, after all. Gotta bottle it up so the beast can yip at strangers." Tugging his sleeve back down, he plants a palm to his heart. "In a human body, you just say *bless your heart* and go on your merry little way, right?"

His grasp on human nuance is impressive.

Ollie continues, "To clarify my statement, you're seeing things through stereotypes where the concept of a vampire feeding is dramatic. When vampires get *really* hungry, they don't turn into vicious, senseless monsters. They get tired. And when they feed, it's not some sensual, sex-sells gimmick. It's about as sexy as an IV bag." Ollie crosses one ankle over the other, bracing his elbows on the top of the fence. "Maybe it'll help if you think of it like fish oil. Not the most palatable, but a necessary supplement if you're lacking in certain vitamins."

Zylus coughs against his clenched fist and watches the sidewalk. "Just so you aren't misinformed, darling…Ollie isn't wrong from a platonic point of view, but between us—if ever such a thing occurs—it wouldn't exactly be so… clinical."

"You don't say?" Ollie's brows rise.

Zylus scowls at him. "Obviously. Anything that involves my mouth near my mate isn't going to be purely medicinal."

"Scandalous."

"Do shut up."

"I was innocent, once," Ollie croons.

Zylus rolls his eyes, but the touch of a smile hooks one

corner of his lips.

His gaze shifts toward me, and his lips part before I realize I'm smiling, too.

Immediately, I scrub the expression off my face and look elsewhere, through the windows into Ollie's human's house. Inside, before the fire on a couch overburdened with crocheted blankets sits an elderly woman with a book in her lap. Her head dips toward her chest as she fights to stay awake.

"Elsie," Ollie supplies. "My human for the past thirteen years."

"She's...your human? Like I'm Zy's?"

A cloud puffs from Ollie's lips, rising into the chilled air as evening deepens the shadows around us. "She's my human, like she feeds me and buys me the quality dog beds. I'm not looking for my mate."

"Why not?"

"That's a personal question, and the answer I want to give isn't the truth, so..." Eyes sticking to Elsie, Ollie presses his lips together. "Have you ever loved someone so much that the idea they might not be constantly and perfectly and blissfully happy knotted up your chest until you couldn't breathe?"

I loved my grandmother. So, so much. She made me feel like myself when no one else could. When I lost her, my chest knotted up and I couldn't breathe for months. Sometimes, when I think about it too much, I still can't. "Maybe."

"Having a mate is like that. You would do *anything* for that one precious being. All you want is for them to be happy. They deserve the world." He grins, something about the expression off balance. "But, well, if you can't give it to them, it's best if you don't put yourself in a position where you'll want to try."

Something in my ancient, outdated, won't-run-Sims brain clicks. "How do you know you can't give it to them?"

"Hm?" He runs his fingers through his hair. "Because. I don't own the world. I don't even own my house. To put things in a manner you'll understand..." He clears his throat, lays the back of his hand against his forehead, and declares, "I've no money and no prospects. I'm already a burden to my human—"

"—and you're frightened." A twisted laugh leaves me. "Yeah." My eyes sting, and I might cry if I'm not careful. "The day Zy chose to follow me home changed my life. No other living thing had ever picked me before. It meant the world to me. You don't know what will mean the world to your mate, but if you weren't able to supply it, I don't think they'd be *your mate*." I glance at Zylus for confirmation, but every thought in my head leaves the moment our eyes lock. My chest tightens at the soft, desperate way he's watching me.

This means nothing.

I think the words as forcefully as possible, over and over, but the warmth in his eyes doesn't falter.

I know I can't read his mind or feel the sensation of him anywhere near the same level as he can with me. The most I've ever felt or sensed has been his pain.

But I do swear he responds with *it means everything*.

Ollie's hand touching the top of my head snaps my attention away from Zylus and back to the werecanine's spotted face. "Who knows?" he says, non-committal while ruffling my hair. Dropping his hand back to his side, he tucks his fingers in his pocket and looks toward Zylus. "You want to wreak some kind of havoc tonight, or are you planning to sleep for seventeen hours?"

"Second option."

"Predictable."

"I prefer the term *on brand*."

Ollie shakes his head. "So on brand." He swings himself back over the fence and into the yard. "Thursdays are movie night, right?"

I straighten with awareness he's talking to me again. "Yes."

"I'll bring a snack. See you next week." With his next step, he's a chihuahua, bounding across the yard.

Chapter 17

And there was only one stupid bed.

I can't sleep.

What I said to Ollie bounces around in my skull, and I can't figure out where the words came from. It must have been some mixture of what Zylus told me about deleting the *trying* programs in favor of just being myself and my attempts to comfort the half-stranger.

Since when do I comfort anyone?

Since when do I care?

Since when do I believe that anyone could possibly be *enough* for anyone else?

And, on that note, since when am *I* an advocate for a relationship that doesn't even exist yet?

Maybe I've been body snatched. Faeries messed with my brain and dropped me back in my little cottage as—shudder—*a romantic*.

I should have high-fived Ollie for his determination to not partake in the universe's mental health care, matchmaking mash up program. We should have banded together against such devious things and petitioned the storymakers to knock it off.

Romance belongs in books!

Viva la revolución!

Well, I do doubt Ollie would have joined me if it meant breaking Zylus's heart.

Tonight proved they've got that high-class brothers bond.

Take my kidney, but don't touch my phone charger energy.

Not that I've seen where they have phones. They should get phones.

Rubbing my eye, I open my bedroom door and step out.

The ground moves beneath my foot; a yowl sends me lurching backward.

Big, big kitty eyes stare into my soul, and my stomach bottoms out.

My child.

I've hurt him.

"I'm so sorry. Momm—" I cover my mouth just short of blubbering in baby kitty speak. I am *not* this full man's mother. Why is he asleep on the cold tile outside my bedroom door? "What the—" I swear, composing myself, and find the strength to look away from his still-massive wounded eyes. Those things can't fool me anymore. He is not baby. He is adult. "What are you doing?"

"You stepped on me."

"Yeah? You kind of blend into the floor. It's the middle of the night. Why aren't you on the couch or something?"

Even as a man, his eyes carry that *you should feel guilt, wallow in guilt* whimpering look when he tips his face back into my line of vision. "I sleep here."

"There's a perfectly good cou—" His eyes bore into me, so I look away again. "Sleeping right outside my door is creepy. You have to know that."

"Given the situation that led to you knowing what I am and the fact it's still…" His voice trails.

My skin prickles. "What? What do you mean *the fact it's still*? What is *still*?"

In the dim moonlight shining through my window, Zylus's jaw clenches. He yawns. "I'm still gathering my senses after finding myself awakened by betrayal."

"Listen here, you overgrown rodent...it wasn't intentional. You are a shadow."

"A shadow with feelings."

"I'm not distracted. Answer me clearly: is the boogeyman *still* around?"

"There are always boogeymen around."

I feel lightheaded. He's avoiding the simple *yes* or *no*. The thing that attacked me before is *still* out there. For all I know the noise in my room *multiple weeks ago* never ended up resolved. "Have I been sleeping with the monster that dragged me outside under my bed or in my closet all this time?"

"No." Zylus crosses his legs and grips his ankles. "I've made sure you're safe."

And what about him? If this is the same creature and it has evaded him for weeks, it has to be more intelligent than at least I assumed it could be. Then again, didn't Pila mention there was one boogeyman she liked? That implies that the species has a touch more sense than a culmination of fear dead-set on hurting people.

"Why are you up, starlight?"

I blink out of my thoughts and find Zylus peering up at me, eyes gleaming and vast, two perfectly crystal colors garbed in the hall's darkness. He's terribly feline. Despite his human form, I want to give him cream and head pats. Instead, I answer his question, "I'm having difficulty sleeping on account of the fact I chose peace this evening when I swore I was loyal to violence."

Zylus's expression melts into a heated smile. "I'm grateful you said what you did."

"I told you it meant nothing."

"Between us, to you, perhaps. But for Ollie?"

My stomach tightens, and I force down a swallow.

"I *hope* it meant something for Ollie."

My skin prickles, and I take a step back, away from this man who makes me envy friendships I doubt I'll ever have. How can a being who survives off leeching express such selflessness for anyone?

His head tilts. Feline. My cat. The prick who consciously screamed me awake some days to fill a bowl with food he never ate. I forgave him every time I dumped his little scoop in and he looked at it before giving a tiny approving nod and walking away without touching it.

I should practice holding more grudges against animals.

PETA has no idea what they think they're protecting.

"Do you need to get by?" Zylus asks.

I shake my head.

"Are you well?"

My chest aches. I'm uneasy. Apparently Zylus has been sleeping outside my door for over a month. Spring is coming. I need to start my seedlings if I want a garden this year. I'm tired. I *still* haven't made a pie. And now I learn that there's still a threat looming in the air. Different, conquerable threats is one thing. But the *same* one? I don't like that at all. "Well enough."

Zylus rises, wraps his arms around me, and pulls me close.

My heart stutters. "What are…" My voice fades as the stability of his body stretches into my skin. His heartbeat rests against my ear as my cheek presses to his chest. While his arms seem capable of holding me together, mine dangle uselessly at my sides. All the tension pours out of my shoulders, and I find myself left with *tired*. Only tired. I could sleep. I should sleep. "Are you doing freaky vampire magic stuff?"

"I'm hugging you."

"And draining my energy through a crazy straw?"

He chuckles, lowers himself, and gathers me in his

arms. "No."

I look up at the definition of his jaw as he walks me to my bed, lays me in the coziness, and combs my hair away from my forehead so he can kiss it. He touches his brow to mine a moment before he whispers, "Sleep well, starlight."

Rising, he turns.

My fingers latch onto his shirt, stopping him in place. I don't know why.

Wait.

What?

I seriously don't know why. What am I doing? Not *this*. Anything but *this*.

Zylus glances over his broad shoulder at me, and my heart trips, stumbles, does a full-blown marathon all around my chest. I stare blankly, horrified, and he remains still.

A voice like mine says, "Are you going to sleep on the floor again?"

"Yes."

"Is what I told Ollie completely true?"

Turning, Zylus settles on his knees at my bedside, lifts my fingers to his lips, and says, "Yes."

A swallow sticks in my throat. "How do you know I'm your...mate?"

"I hear your soul singing to mine."

"Poetic," I mutter.

"The moment you saw me, didn't you feel drawn to me? The idea that I might leave you frightened you completely, didn't it?"

Okay, listen here, you're asking me to remember *five years ago*. I don't even remember if I ate yesterday. The problem is, of course, the idea of living without him still haunts me a little, if I dare let myself think about it. I can't picture an existence without him in it or identify the emotions that rise in response. All I know is that a world where my cat and I aren't together is no longer a world that is correct.

The concept feels vaguely reminiscent of a reading slump. Stuck. Hollow. *Wrong.*

"Feelings aren't facts," I offer.

"True. But feelings are a result of something. Even the ones that seem to come out of nowhere have an origin. They hint at truths or issues. Even if they aren't reliable on their own, you can trace them back to facts. Sometimes the fact is unreliable like a hormone imbalance or trauma trigger. Sometimes the fact is a subconscious intuition." He turns his cheek against my fingers and closes his eyes. "Sometimes the fact is my soul recognized it belonged to yours, and by that recognition I have found myself utterly undone."

That's not concrete enough to inspire much confidence, is it?

I am unused to being cherished. I am unaccustomed to trusting. I am afraid of finding myself reliant, yet again, on a being that can take a step back without me. It happened with everyone I tried to befriend while I was growing up. Then it happened with my grandmother—and how does anyone move on after realizing even the people who *don't* want to leave you…just…*can.*

Pulling my hand from Zylus's touch, I roll over, giving him my back. "Kitty," I mutter into my pillow as I clutch it tight to my face.

Lips.

Lips press through the thin fabric of my nightgown and feed the warm stroke of a breath against my spine. In the next moment, a furry body jumps onto the bed and flops against me. He purrs.

Heat floods beneath my skin.

Evil. *You're evil*, do you hear me?

He coos. Perfectly, flawlessly, unevilly content.

Chapter 18

I blame singular mattresses.

Chapter one: the characters meet. Or something. I guess. The issue those characters are expected to grapple with winds up introduced. Nice. Or, well, I mean, *not* nice. Hints of both internal—oh no, commitment issues—and external—there's a freaking magical world out there, and not all of it is *nice*—conflict finds itself woven between the lines.

The reader's hooked. They may not even know why. Something's relatable. (What's this? Look at us twinning the same insecurities.) Something's dire. (Is the monster still out there?!?) Something's promised. (Hot guy and #actuallymeindisguise *will* end up together, but I must know *how*.)

It's predictable.

It's *romance*.

All it takes is one chapter, then the ending is in view.

Doesn't matter how much one of the main characters resists. Doesn't matter what's standing in their way. It's romance.

Romance practically trademarked *it's the journey, not the destination*. Because we *know* the destination. So long as it really *is* romance. And not, I don't know, *tragedy*.

"We are not going to *Romeo and Juliet*," Zylus tells me as he sits at the kitchen table with me, helping me put all my little seeds to sleep. By the end of the day, there will be a makeshift planter made out of empty plastic cupcake holders on every windowsill.

I decree it.

"You know what?" I tuck the baby tomato seeds in. "I bet Romeo and Juliet didn't think they'd *Romeo and Juliet*, either, but they *did*."

"Romeo and Juliet are fictional characters."

"Did you ever meet Shakespeare?"

Zylus opens his mouth, closes it, and forces his attention down. Taking a plastic spoonful of dirt, he packs up a little cupcake hole. "No."

I frown.

"He was misogynistic and classist and some of his stories directly condone treating women like animals. You really want me to have met him?"

"*No*. I was *hoping* you'd toilet papered one of his shows. Like an ally."

"With what toilet paper?" He lifts a brow.

I tuck some tiny cucumber seeds into their tiny beds. "Have you ever invented something really important and gone into hiding until the world assumed you'd passed on?"

"No."

"Is Keanu Reeves a vampire?"

"Robert Pattinson is."

My mouth drops open.

Zylus grins. "At least he was. In that one film."

I might despise him. But a laugh bursts from me anyway. "You're not going to out anyone?"

"Faeries are masters of being forgotten, which doesn't make for a thriving celebrity career in the human world, now does it? You have to be especially powerful in order to make yourself memorable to humans, and if you've lived that long, you know the dangers. Not only that, many humans are not entirely fond of the fae for reasons similar to why many humans you've met have not been fond of you. We come from vastly different worlds."

Fair points.

"So being a vampire is actually pretty boring."

"I don't think so."

I sigh. "Circling back, how do you know we aren't a tragedy? Or *or* a horror?"

"Cottagecore horror?" Zylus slides a finished tray toward the others awaiting relocation without pulling his gaze off me. "Why can't we be a romance?"

"Because." I nestle a seed in and contemplate the weather to avoid thinking about what I've been avoiding thinking about all morning and afternoon. Sky. Clouds. Sun. Chilly. Spring soon, but not soon enough.

Zylus narrows his eyes. "*Because?*"

Heaving a sigh, I pin him with a look. "What chapter do you think we're on?"

He stares, befuddled.

"At least ten, right? Probably closer to twenty. Heck, depending on what we determine to be our inciting action, we may have slice-of-lifed for several hundred while I still thought you were a cat. You can only slow burn for so long before questioning the existence of a fire." Fire. Winter fires. Moonless nights and fires and cults doing silly dances in the woods. Bad. Bad cults. I hope frogs attack them.

Zylus stares at me as though I've lost my mind.

Maybe I *have*. Maybe I lost my mind entirely in a dream about—clouds and cults and *frogs*. "Don't *sass* me with that look, sir. You know I'm right."

Standing with a couple trays, he slips from the kitchen table. "You read too much fiction."

Mouth gaping, I watch his back retreat into the other room. My mouth is still hanging open by the time he returns. "I can't believe you said that to me." Is this *heartbreak*? "You can't lie either, so you believe those cruel words."

"If you're basing your life around the stories you've read instead of allowing yourself to write your own, it's *too much*."

"Lies!"

Shrugging, he sits, pulling another tray over and burying my carefully-marked seeds with the dexterity of a man who has spent the past five years watching me prep my bitty children each new planting season.

"Stories are reflections of reality," I protest.

"They're also dramatized. And packaged down." A line forms beneath his lower lip, a practical pout. Voice soft, he says, "Please don't cut my chances so short."

"You were the one who said we didn't have to become lovers."

"I never suggested it wasn't my preference. I merely recognized that if it were too much for you to consider, I would choose to stay near you in any capacity." Sunlight winks in his green eye. "Because I love you."

Back kisses. Dreams about back kisses. On replay. All night. *I mean clouds, and sunlight, and I sure hope it doesn't snow again before spring.*

"Back kisses," he echoes.

"*Don't*," I spit between gritted teeth before I snatch a couple trays and flee into the living room. Before I can straighten after setting them down on the window seat, a hand splays over my waist and lips find my shoulder blade.

An incoherent screech gets stuck in my throat as Zylus's mouth singes my flesh. My stomach clenches against his fingers. His nose skates down the bared bumps of my spine until the skin disappears beneath the low-cut dark lace of my dress.

Everything tingles. Everything's warm.

He teases a tie of my corset around his thumb as I melt

into a puddle.

Athena. I was not made for affection. I haven't shaved in two months, for I cannot be bothered. I am not a flawlessly pretty little female lead. My stature is where the likeness ends. I average two showers a week, opting usually for one whenever I can't wrap my head around the task. I'm a gothic nightmare. Nothing about me is—

"You're so—" He swears. "—beautiful I wouldn't hesitate to make you mine the instant your heart tells me you crave such a thing." His heavy exhale hits my neck. "I want you. Terribly."

My heart thunders in my ears.

"But I won't..." His voice trails off.

I can't breathe. I don't dare think. My mind replays his touch, on loop, over and over, until I'm forced to cover my burning face with my hands.

Zylus braces my back against his chest, and his shuddering breath vibrates in my body. His cool fingertips trace from one of my elbows to my wrist. He pulls my hand away from my face, raises it above my head, and lets a damp kiss linger against my pulse. He swears.

He knows.

The pictures of all the things that haunted my dreams last night paint across my mind. Screaming color. Bold as Arial Black. "Stop," I exhale. "Hormones," I utter, explaining everything.

I am *not* lighting sparks. I was not built for the emotional turmoil of a romance plot. I'm *bad* with emotions. I don't want anything to do with them. I'm scared.

I'm *scared.*

This has to be fear. This has to be terror.

It's like I'm on fire, boiling away all the blood in my veins.

Zylus wraps me up in a hug, squeezes, then lets me go. "Hormones."

"*Hormones.*" They make some girls fall in love with *posters*. Music videos. *Celebrities*. Wicked things, hormones. And, yet, how wonderful they are. The perfect scapegoats.

Not that I need a scapegoat. Because last night's dream was absolutely, completely, one hundred percent the result of hormones.

I have not tripped.

This isn't the start of a fall.

Only one bed magic doesn't count unless both participants are in forms resembling something *human*. Obviously. Kitty and I have exhausted the trope. It's basically meaningless now. Unless…unless of course he *weren't* kitty.

That *would* change everything.

But we aren't *going* to change everything, now are we? No. We are *going* to plant little seed babies and read *too much fiction*.

I've been positively slacking on my reading. What, with all the *mental breakdowns* lately.

Turning on my heel, I shriek when I discover Zylus hasn't moved back by even one inch. "What are you doing?"

"Decoding the chaos."

"*No*. Get *out*."

"It's so hypnotic."

I clap my hands to my forehead, as though that will help. I am going to fashion an aluminum foil hat.

Zylus's brows dip, and he bites his lip, muting a smile.

"Please. *Stop*." I can't live with him knowing all my embarrassing thoughts. I don't know *how* to be seen. I am not good or kind at my core. I'm flawed and broken and unwanted. I don't know when some straying idea in my skull will hurt him so badly he'll never forgive me.

And then I'll be all alone again.

"Willow. Nothing could separate you from my love. *Nothing*. You could spend eons rejecting me. Millennia hating me. You could concoct new ways to despise me each evening and put them all into action come morning, but none of it would stop me from adoring you with my every breath."

"How is that fair to you?" My voice shakes. "That sounds horrible. This is the part in soulmate stories that I can't stand. Where's our choice?"

His head tilts. "I choose to love you, just like you choose not to love me. Love is never fair, starlight, because that choice remains whether a soul cries for the other or not." He extends his hand. "In every instance, love meets another person wherever they are, and there is no perfect *middle* to be found."

I want to take his hand. And he knows I want to take his hand. Thankfully, I don't think either of us knows *why*.

"I love every part of you," he says.

"And what about when that's not enough?"

His brows rise. "What else is there?"

I shake my head and march past him as though I can't feel the spread of his fingers against my stomach, the way he squeezed me tight for a moment, the rake of his heat beneath my skin. Whenever I find him watching me, listening in on the chaotic sensations my head gives off, the look in his eyes says anything but *irritated*.

Knowing that others less privy to the constant chaos in my brain have been unwilling to put up with me makes it… puzzling.

I am not interested in a vampire romance.

I do not *swoon*. I *lament*.

There are other more important things to worry about.

"I'm sorry."

At the sound of his voice, I stop a foot from the kitchen table, where the rest of my little babies await nap time.

"I didn't want it to be like this. I didn't want to rush you into anything, emotional or physical. Now that it's come about, ignoring what I sense seems dishonest, but if you'd prefer I make no indication of acknowledgment, I will pretend. Graciously, the fae are allowed their lies of omission."

He's just so *good*. So kind. And open. And understanding. Obsessed, sure, but what male lead isn't a touch obsessed? And, okay, there are random acts of PDA, but when aren't cats demanding head pats? He's a needy creature.

Just like me.

Unlike me, he's bold enough to demand what I'm scared I'll begin to rely on. He's bold enough to ask for what he needs, graceful enough to accept when he's gone too far, and good enough to stop.

I don't want to depend on something I can't control ever again.

I need stability.

I *need* stability.

It goes beyond a craving. It's a requirement. I can't function without reliable footing, clear steps, scripts, patterns, routines. I have been off-kilter from the moment I woke up in my yard when I was supposed to be in bed.

Clenching my jaw, I face him.

He's beautiful and foreign. Familiar but not completely the same. Mine.

Incomprehensibly mine.

In three steps, I'm in front of him. In one motion, I've locked my hands in the collar of his black shirt and pulled him down to my height. Before realization ignites in his eyes, I've melded our mouths together.

My heart jumps.

So does his.

I feel it like an echo, then a pound. His hammering heartbeat rips through my chest, thundering until my bones rattle.

A curse slips into my head, resting suspended in my thoughts. And—it's the strangest thing—I'm not certain it was mine. It almost sounded like his voice.

Zylus snakes his arms around me, fusing our bodies. He tilts his face, deepening the kiss as though he needs it like air. My knees go weak, and so do his. Somehow we wind up kneeling on the kitchen floor, wrapped up in each other.

Head empty.

No thoughts.

Just heat, hands, lips, him, me.

Sensations I can't compute rush into my veins—scalding and desperate. His.

Once I've run out of breath, he buries his face against my neck, kissing trails along my skin. His fingers tangle in my hair, guide my head so I'm bared in the most precarious way.

Not an ounce of concern weighs me down. Clearly, I cannot be bothered to worry about the fact he's a vampire flicking his tongue out against the most cliché location for him to bite.

He laughs against my flesh—the sound hoarse, tight, blissfully happy.

Then a droplet hits my shoulder.

His arms crush me to him, and a shudder moves his chest.

"Zy?" I whisper and discover that my voice is also strained. Interesting. Don't like that. "Are you well?"

"Yes." The word breaks, hitching. "Yes, starlight. I am well."

He doesn't sound like my definition of *well*, but he also physically can't lie, so... "You're crying?"

"A little."

Must be them happy tears that literature told me about. The elusive joyful cry. How strange to find such a thing in the wild. I had assumed crying from happiness was a fantasy element snuggled right beside dragons. And werewolves. And vampires.

Huh.

Maybe it totally is.

Zylus kisses my collarbone, using my body to mute another shaking laugh. "You're so..." He takes a breath. "...perfect."

I'm far from perfect. My skin feels like the sound an Etch-A-Sketch makes when it's shaken. I'm TV static. *Old* TV static. The kind you could feel when you ran your hand against the screen. I don't know how long it's going to take me to process this. Decades? Centuries?

At least I have time?

Zylus pulls back just far enough that I can see into his watery eyes. He wipes away a tear with his knuckle before it can fall, and I get slightly lost in the shimmering jewel tones.

He's ethereal.

"How do I compare to your dream?" he asks.

My face explodes crimson. I press my palms against his chest, cut up the raging memories when they burst forth, and chuck them in the oven. "Do *not*."

"Do I have to try harder?"

I scramble, attempting to free myself from the snare I didn't just *walk* into. I stomped up to, grabbed, and yanked into a kiss. What is wrong with me? "This experiment is *over.* I need to process the consequences of my actions for the foreseeable future now!"

"Experiment?" he muses, reluctant to let me free. Graciously, he does loosen his hold—after several pouting moments.

Like a graceful worm in three layers of skirts and a corset, I wriggle away, push off his thigh, and skid across the floor toward the table.

"What were the results?" He doesn't move from where he's kneeling on the floor, and I can still see where I was snuggled up between his legs, pressed to his shirt, wrinkling it with my grip. He's covered in the residue of what just happened.

I don't know why I did that. What was I thinking? Was I thinking? I specifically think I was *not* thinking because, if I were, he would have known before I…kissed him…and he did not.

I distinctly recall a thread of panic ripple in his eyes before he melted around me.

What *were* the results? No idea. I barely managed high school and didn't go to college. I am not licensed to perform experiments of any kind. With my luck, they'll all wind up…explosive.

I swallow, press my lips together. "Inconclusive."

"If there's insufficient data—"

I jab my finger at him. "*No.*"

"I'm trying to be helpful."

I'm trying to remember what a resting heart rate feels like. I had things to do today. Seedling children to plant and love and nurture and stare at as though the very act of my tucking them into a warm dirt bed and setting them before the window would make them instantaneously sprout.

"Am I scared?" I ask.

Zylus watches me for a moment, tilts his head, then

says, "Mildly disconcerted."

Only mildly?

"Why?"

He glances sidelong away, smooths the wrinkles I caused out of his shirt, and bends one knee up against his chest, wrapping his arms around it. "I'm uncertain you want me to vocalize the reasoning."

I can identify nothing on my own. It's all a hum. He either tells me, or I won't know. "Go on."

"You liked it."

I swear.

"At a physical level, you're entranced. You're buzzing. Hot everywhere. Eager for another taste. Your thoughts are struggling to catch up and sort the sensations, so it's overwhelming. Something about it is too right to ignore, even though you can't place why, and since you've jerked away, something feels very wrong. Not only that, it seems you were able to connect to sensations of me briefly. Since you don't know me as well as I know you, they aren't so simple to decode, and since you struggle enough with your own emotions, the addition of mine is troubling to consider. Hence, you are mildly disconcerted."

Circling my arms around my chest, I shudder. "So what you're saying is...I'm an intimacy addict."

"I...am not saying that at all." He cups his hand to his mouth, hiding a smile. "W-where did you even get that from what I said?"

"No touchy feel wrong."

His eyes close. "Ah."

Scowling, I turn my back on him, flex my fingers, and monitor my breaths. I've never kissed someone before. I have lived a blissful life of isolation. My boyfriends are books. I have many. A harem. My harem of book boyfriends have never made me feel some kind of way.

They inspire toe wiggles during the sweet moments and eye rolls when they decide to play the bedroom Twister as though they are trained contortionists.

Put simply, intimacy confuses me just like everything else that involves other people.

Slowly, I reach behind me.

Silently, Zylus moves close enough to hold my hand. "Are you well, starlight?"

"I am…" Something. He probably knows how *well* I am better than I do.

I don't know how long I sit on the floor, practically beneath the table, with my hand latched around his. All I know is that he remains quiet and stable behind me, pressing nothing, while my brain grapples to sort through my thoughts.

I don't like people. People are rotten at every point. Children are horrible and cruel. Teenagers need no introduction. Young adults are soaked in the righteous meanness of whatever is socially acceptable and trending. Regular adults find themselves stuck in the entitlement of outdated knowledge. The elderly leave you behind.

People are not safe.

They don't make sense.

Relationships are the number one cause of problems.

They aren't fair.

They aren't equal.

They fall apart without any notice the second someone decides they are doing too much.

They're exhausting, and confusing, and I was sick of being the one putting in all the effort only to watch everyone else decide the bare minimum I begged for was too much for them.

All I have ever wanted…is to read books in peace.

With my cat.

Chapter 19

Is this an obligatory plot device?

It's not a date, because dates are those things you see in movies where the people get all dressed up and go out to dinner and maybe see a horror film—where they wind up squished together, touching hands, yada, yada.

It's not a date because *dates* are stupid. They imply that the participating members are *dating*, and Zylus and I absolutely aren't doing that.

Dating is a waste of time.

Dating is where people judge other people within the bounds of a social norm. In what other setting are people *encouraged* to nitpick every facet of another being's personality then grade them publicly among their peers? Oh, you didn't pull out my chair. Minus points. I see we're splitting the bill—minus points. Letting me walk on the outer side of the sidewalk? Oh, ho, ho. Buddy... We will not be seeing one another again.

It's ridiculous.

Dating is *additional* novels of rules laced in the license to mentally list flaws for reiteration and disgrace later. All the while, I hate to break it to you, but the *perfect* people? The ones who *do everything right*? Yeah. They've studied the rule book and want something. They're painting the perfection for you with intent.

I don't trust shiny things.

Smiles are so easy for others to forge.

So, to return to my point, this isn't a date because dates

are horrible.

This is a warm night that the onset of spring has blessed us with.

There are no chairs to pull out, no sidewalks to choose sides for, no tabs to pick up.

There's just a picnic blanket, dozens of candles, the night sky, and my shopping basket overflowing with whatever Zylus was baking all afternoon while I flopped around on my couch, reading and trying not to wish he were curled up on my lap.

I am an expert in the field of denial.

"Zy. This is a date, isn't it?"

Zylus's eyes flick up off the basket, wide, like he's been caught shuffling around beneath the linen napkin he's used to hide the contents. "You don't like dates."

"That doesn't answer my question." After the past few months, I'm practically a master at communicating with the fae. It's easy, really. You just say what you mean, continually, with necessary force, and talk them into corners.

The best manipulators never lie. They speak truths out of context and play implication like a finely-tuned instrument.

A gentle breeze toys with the candle flames positioned all around the blanket, casting a strange glow on Zylus's pale skin.

It's weird that we're out here at night with the recent knowledge a boogeyman is still lurking. Maybe I can ask him about all that. Maybe I can coerce him into giving me a direct answer.

"Zy," I prompt when he still hasn't answered me.

Rather, he's gone unnaturally still, one hand in the basket, eyes unblinking as they focus on the cloth.

The candle flames around us whip, and shadows streak

through the looming woods. Closing in. Children laugh, and—

Oh.

Dang it.

I *said* it wasn't a date. And it isn't. It's a *dream*. Except unlike a certain dream I had, what, two or three nights ago? This one doesn't taste like lips and tongues. Rolling my eyes, I sag back on the blanket and stare at the unfamiliar sky. It's speckled and wrong, the stars tilted in awkward places, the moon a touch too bright.

Lovely. My favorite. I do so adore when my brain ramps up the sensation of *incorrect*.

"Willow." Zylus's voice isn't his. It's not mine. It's barely here at all, like he's going to fade away. The barest hints of that *we need to talk* tone become prevalent in my mind, and pounding fear responds in my chest.

"Yeah, yeah. Are these my trust issues coming to literally haunt me, because that's original, and I'm proud of my mind for choosing that over monsters." Lifting a fist that I can't see, I curse the not-sky. "Just so you guys in storyland know, using dreams as plot devices is *lazy* writing! It's what you do when you have no idea what *else* to do." Puffing a laugh, I try not to wish this setting were real.

After that kiss a few days ago, I'm not sure I'd mind a date. If he asked me on one. If *dating* is something faeries even do.

It's strange how minds work—mixing up truth and lies, familiar and unfamiliar, wishes and horrors. I would love to lie under the stars with Zylus and spend the entire night talking until the sun wakes us in a tangle of limbs.

With stray boogeymen on the loose, though, the outdoors don't quite seem safe when they're coated in shadows.

More children laugh in the distant idea of the woods, and my skin crawls.

I *hate* the sound of children laughing. If my brain could not, I'd so appreciate it.

Actually, you know what's in the real world right now and a hundred times better than creepy laughter? My dear sweet kitty.

So I'm going to wake up now.

Yep.

Here we go.

Problem is, the sky stays put, blurs, and it turns cold. The candle lights leech away. The laughter echoes in the hollow of my skull.

Something dark and horrible shifts in the corners of my vision, dragging the sound of laughter to and from.

Someone swears.

Not me. Not Zylus. Not a voice I know.

It's…it's terrifying.

It's coming closer—creeping from beneath my bed, dragging insecurities and panic to the forefront of my brain.

I will never be good enough. I will never be wanted. I will never find a happily ever after. I will always, always crash and burn. And then everyone will laugh. And I will be all alone.

A face erupts in my vision—unfamiliar, beautiful, *scary*. My mouth gapes in a silent scream, and nails puncture my skin. The unfocused face grits sharp teeth. Its lips move, but I hear the words like a shriek in my mind moments late.

"*Wake up.*"

I gasp, and the starry sky shatters, giving way to the canopy of my bed dressed in the subtle light of dawn.

I'm awake. I'm awake, and it's nearly morning.

Sitting up too fast, I force kitty Zylus on my stomach to

tumble into my lap.

He coos, in perfect peace, and stretches his paws, absently kneading the air.

Silence.

Chickens.

No moving shadows.

No children laughing.

The weight on my lap changes from cat to person, and I twitch.

"Starlight?" Concern saturates Zylus's tone.

"What did I say?" I snap, too harsh, some rattled.

With a pout, he glances elsewhere. "No man in bed."

"*No man in bed.*" My feeble sensibilities simply do not have the means to deal with the mental strain of *man in bed*. There's not enough room, anyway. My daybed is a *twin*, for crying out loud.

Sitting up, Zylus runs his fingers through his long straight hair. "What's wrong?"

The flickering memory of the face I saw enters my brain, and my stomach knots. I think my heart is still pounding. Who or *what* was that? Shaking my head, I say, "I don't know."

I have never meant three words more, and yet my mind won't leave it alone. I have to know. I need to know. Whatever went wrong just now I think it's more than a nightmare.

Zylus searches me, splayed across my bed, hopelessly feline, impossibly attractive. My mind drifts from the darkness in my skull to the way his shirt's pulled taut against his chest, revealing usually hidden muscles.

He's stunning. Radiant. Perfect.

And this is why we have the no man in bed rule. I cannot trust myself with him anymore. Not since I kissed him several days ago, held his hand until I could breathe normally again, and found myself far more at ease with the idea of being a vampire's—*his*—mate. I'm a pitiful touch-deprived creature in desperate need of cuddles.

What an absolute disgrace.

"You had a nightmare?" Zylus asks in a tone that suggests he didn't so much as notice my brain raving about his physical appeal and my lusting desires.

"I had a nightmare." I scooch myself out of bed and away from temptation.

Zylus whispers a curse.

It's a major *uh-oh* that freezes me halfway to my closet. I turn, locate him, grow irritated at the way he looks like a distressed model sprawled across my daybed, one hand clapped to his jaw. Eyes pensive. Body tense.

I fold my arms. "What don't I know about nightmares that are magical and whatever?"

"They're caused by boogeymen."

My heart thuds, and I drop my arms to my sides. Oh. *Oh*. "The…same one?"

"Likely."

"So…" I peer around my room, search for shadows, find light streaking from the window and under my bed. It's all pristine. Perfect pinks and whites and untouched glass decorations. Any creepy thing appearing in this room specifically would look so ironic I might laugh. Dubious, I say, "Is it here?"

"Not anymore."

"But it would have to be close, right? I *just* woke up."

"Not necessarily. It's difficult to track the time between a dream ending and consciousness returning." He swears again, squeezes his eyes shut.

He seems more rattled than I am. Maybe because I've got that funky emotional recognition delay? "Boogeymen feed on fear, right?"

His head bobs.

"Okay, so I can defeat it with sheer hubris, right? I'm good at hubris."

Zylus, still a *man* and still in *bed*, peers at me, brows knit.

"One of the many reasons kids didn't like me in school is because I played with spiders." And snakes. And beetles. And anything I could get my hands on, really. Weren't they cool? The other girls didn't think so. Losers. "I'm not easily rattled."

"Boogeymen are designed to know your fears, whatever they are."

"My nightmare was a candlelit dinner surrounded by children laughing."

Zylus opens his mouth and closes it again.

"Yeah. So. I'm probably capable of overcoming that." Maybe. The concept that children laughing is among my greatest fears says a lot about little Willow. Poor kid. Combing my fingers through my hair, I locate a tangle that ties some white strands to the black and set on working it out. "In most fantasy books, there's search magic. Can we not do a search magic for this thing?"

"Not…exactly."

"Explain?"

Zylus closes his eyes and melts against my comforter, looking all kinds of despondent. He's pulling no stops in the angst department this morning. It should be lightly raining. And where's the forlorn music? My bedroom is not an ideal setting for anything remotely disparaged.

He lays the back of his hand against his forehead. "Starlight…" He sighs, tormented.

The scene is giving rising genius actor, no studio budget.

"It's very hard to concentrate with your thoughts

attacking me like this," he murmurs.

"Attacking? They've been nothing but complimentary. You are lovely."

With my bed sheet loosely wrapped around his bent leg, he looks like a poster. An album cover.

"Add to cart," I say.

That gets a reluctant smile out of him. He sprawls his hand over the edge of my bed, beckoning, and I chew my cheek before obliging to *not* take his hand but to sit beside him, my own hands clasped against my nightgown in my lap.

He says, "Boogeymen are hard to track. Most of them vanish when the sun comes up. Those that manage to feed on a very specific or powerful fear can grow into something else—something truly fae."

"What's that?"

"A dream eater."

I feel as though I'm supposed to shudder, but I don't. "Is that what the one that attacked me has become?"

"I don't know if it's quite there yet, but…the person who could help us…the person who will know how to track down one this evasive…is."

Throwing a hand over my mouth, I gasp, and Zylus's eyes widen on me. I wince. "What? Too dramatic?"

"Unexpected." His lips curl into a soft smile, and he rests one cheek against his hand. "Are you trying to compete with me?"

"Even attempting such a thing would give me an aneurysm."

His arms snake around my waist, and he nuzzles his face against my side. "I love you."

My heart responds, more erratic than it did during my dream. The thick, syrupy taste of fear rests on the back of my tongue, but I force myself not to pull away even as I ignore his confession. "So how do we meet with the dream eater? Say his name three times in a lucid dream? Fall asleep with cookies on my forehead?"

"Your mind is a truly remarkable thing."

"It's a meatball filled with electricity. *Remarkable* doesn't begin to describe it. How do we summon him?"

Lifting his face, he rests his cheek on his bicep and looks up at me. "With any luck, he will be home."

Oh. Of course. How foolish of me. This is *fantasy reality*. All the mythical, helpful, ancient, and powerful beings just live in normal houses that you go to for visits when you need to see them. I hope the story gods are happy. They've made vampires *boring*.

"I prefer *borderline healthy*."

"*Borderline?*"

"The will is strong, but the desire lingers, and I misbehave often…" His face nestles against me again, muffling his next words. "…for the will is rarely strong enough."

Chapter 20

Spooky, scary skeletons…in the closet. Specifically.

I don't know how to feel about the fact Mountain Vale, Virginia is apparently a hotspot for mythical creatures. I had somewhat expected Zylus's coach to take us back to the crack in the mountain where Cael's palace and the distinct aroma of *other world* hung heavy in the air.

Instead, it brought us to the other side of town, beyond the shops on main street, beyond the quaint neighborhood where Ollie and his human live, beyond every place I've bothered going. And directly to an unkempt manor sending *haunted* vibes all over the place.

We're talking wrought iron fence, brick walls covered in winter ivy, two feet of brittle grass, skeletal bushes, and evergreen sprigs. The manor itself is a large chipping Victorian-style sun-paled black. It is positively delightful. I want to return with my ghastly gown and get pictures of me trailing the halls barefoot.

Unfortunately, no one seems to have been home for a long, long while. Fortunately, I think I see a broken window. I could totally crawl inside and get some pictures. I just need to go back for props and reassess my emotions concerning a possibility of glass splinters in my bare feet.

Zylus sighs on the sidewalk beside me as his coach dematerializes behind us. "He's home." His blue eye slants toward me, judging. "And please don't crawl over broken glass in order to achieve anything."

"I was joking."

"No, you weren't."

No, I wasn't.

Frowning, I fold my arms. "So he's home? We're going in there? We're going to pick our way up the broken sidewalk, battle briars, knock on the door, and—what—hope the house itself doesn't swallow us whole? *Without* intending to get *any* pictures? How many ghosts are in there?"

"None. Ghosts don't exist."

Right. He said that once before. I forgot. I'm sad now. Sad enough to march up to the spooky house and fully embrace the possibility of an untimely demise.

"There isn't going to be an untimely demise. Pollux is..." Zylus's brows knit, and it doesn't escape me that he's not made any moves toward pushing open the gate and entering. "Pila knows him."

Shock hits me. Hard. "Wait. Is this the boogeyman she told me once that she liked?"

"It's possible. As far as boogeymen go, and certainly as far as dream eaters go, Pollux is..." he trails off again, like he can't find an honest positive adjective that he believes.

Absolutely reassuring.

"Are you scared?" I ask.

"Pollux deals in fear. Pollux sees fear, weaknesses, insecurities. He can manipulate and gather them as physical things. He keeps a store of terror in his bloodstream at all times."

"He exploits fear?" That doesn't sound like it would lead to Pila liking him.

Zylus releases a tight breath. "Not quite."

"You've been a bit off kilter since my nightmare. Are you going to tell me why?"

Dragging his attention off the looming manor—which seems to ominously swallow up the sunlight around it—he looks at me. Scared. He wets his lips, opens his mouth, and continues watching. "I dislike that it was close enough to affect your dreams while I slept soundly."

"I'm unharmed."

"It toyed with your subconscious. It threatened you. Had it kept you in your nightmare long enough, it could have paralyzed you and entered your room. Then, since you are not human enough to be untouchable, there's no telling what it could have done."

I blink. "Don't tell me… Boogeymen are the cause of sleep paralysis?"

Zylus keeps staring, grimly.

"Wow. The more you know. And to think humans chalk it all up to scientific explanations like stress hallucinations."

"Stress is an avenue that fear exploits." Zylus scrubs his hands over his face and plunges his fingers back into his hair. "I do not love this. Were I not afraid you might come to harm the moment I left you, I'd not bring you here. Being in the presence of Pollux is…unpleasant."

Something about that makes my chest twinge with pain —and it's very likely that pain doesn't belong to me. Extending my hand toward Zylus, I say, "For what it's worth, I'm all for exploring the spooky mansion at a recreational level. So you don't have to be scared. I'm brave enough for both of us."

Shoulders sagging, Zylus reaches for my hand and tangles our fingers. "The implication you want to wander aimlessly around a man's house leaves me some disturbed."

"Would he be opposed to providing a tour?"

"Indeed, I believe he would be."

Well, that's depressing.

After taking another fortifying breath, Zylus finally nudges through the gate. The deity of all screeches rips from the hinges before the pin gives up, and the metal falls out of Zylus's hand with an astounding clatter. I stare at the broken gate until Zylus clears his throat. "I...I'm sure that's fine."

"Obviously it's fine," I note. Nudging Zylus in the side, I point ahead through the suddenly gray atmosphere at the front window. "See?"

The barest outline of tattered drapes falls back in front of the cracked glass an instant after Zylus looks up.

He tenses.

"Clichés," I whisper. "Clichés, everywhere." Sniffing, I tug my poor scared kitty forward. "Honestly, they're the spoopiest part so far. Feels like I'm in a fanfiction. Ten out of ten aesthetic. I should construct a parlor themed after Pila's home and a storeroom themed after this place. Just imagine." I beam back at him. "A little storeroom locked behind overgrown wrought iron fences and brick walls. Gothic. Fake tombstones in the yard. The cupboards are standing coffins with shelves."

"Anything you construct would be adorable."

"Are you trying to get abandoned in the spooky mansion? Because calling me *adorable* is how you get abandoned in the spooky mansion."

His hold on my hand tightens.

Sighing, I stop on the front porch—which is deceptively sturdy in spite of the sun damage mixed with a general sense of disrepair—and lift my hand to the ancient knocker. "I hope there are big spiders," I murmur, then I lift the solid instrument.

It pounds once from my own effort. And echoes thrice over.

Naturally, the door creaks open on its own, presenting a dark chasm of nothingness beyond.

"Okay. What do you want to bet it slams shut behind

us?"

"I would not like to make any bets at this time." Zylus's voice cracks.

Props to the storymakers for managing to perfectly write a haunted house but somehow neglect to create an invincible vampire male lead who has angst for breakfast and has already seen the worst of the world, thereby leaving him emotionally unruffled in every other instance.

Smiles?

What are those…?

I lost the ability to sm-ile back in the war…or…well… *one* of the wars. There have been so many.

"Your penchant for insulting my species in your thoughts is truly a skill."

"I'd thank you, but vampires are faeries. And, yes, I'm still mad about it." Tugging him, I step us inside the black.

The door slams.

A sixteenth century chandelier explodes flames like a fire hazard.

It's stunning. I might shed a tear. Are those *real* spiderwebs in the corners? Marvelous.

Before me, a balcony looms over the marble floors, splitting off into two staircases that frame the room. I peer at the height of each, awaiting the lightning flash that will put the man of the hour at the top of one—even though the window I saw *someone* at earlier was downstairs. Drama trumps consistency. Duh.

Instead, a throat clears from the bottom steps on the left. "Zylus." The gravelly voice runs over my exposed flesh like rusty nails. Blood floods from my head.

Zylus hits the ground, bracing one knee against the dark tile. Clutching my hand, he shakes, pulling deep breaths through his lungs. Sweat lines his blanched brow.

I whip my attention toward the sound of the voice.

"What are you—" Fear strikes me through the heart.

Pollux isn't even standing.

He rests across several steps, huge, built, one long leg outstretched, an entire liquor bottle gripped in one hand. His eyes—pits of black where white should be surrounding bleeding crimson—watch me, read me, rip me to pieces.

My mouth goes dry. "You..."

He lifts his bottle in greeting.

My insides contort, but I raise my chin. "What's going on? What's wrong with Zylus?"

"He's scared."

"I *know* that. But I'm still standing."

"He has heart trouble. Being *scared* for him results in some physical impairment."

Well, that bodes less than well.

"Also—" Pollux takes a swig of the alcohol and leans his head back against the step behind him. "—he has more that renders him terrified." The man's lips tip down. "It's always interesting to me when I find a human who fears the death of others more than their own."

My gut shreds, and I can't stop the half step I take back.

"Maybe that's why I find it...*nice*...to see you again, Willow."

A handsome, terrifying face flashes behind my eyes, reminding me *who or what* woke me this morning. Now I'm shaking, too. "Why were *you* in my dream?"

"What?" Zylus exhales the word.

"Common courtesy. You have the strangest nightmares." Pollux's gaze traces the ceiling as he rolls his liquor bottle against the steps. His chest fills with air. "The youngling would have done better to put you in school."

A swallow sticks in my throat.

"Just school. Changing nothing." He lifts the bottle to his lips again. "You use awareness as a weapon and hide behind a prickly façade the moment anything alerts your pattern recognition that something's wrong. A memory of school without anything amiss for you to catch onto would have rendered you helpless before I could have noticed." Pinching his brow, he huffs a sigh. "So...the good news... this issue of yours is still quite manageable. It's young. Dramatic." His gaze pierces me. "But you're not interested in sympathizing with its youth. You're interested in overcoming it, so you should know one very important detail: it won't kill either of you."

My skin feels inside out. "How do you know that?"

"It's not after the dregs of your fear as you slip from this world, Willow." Pollux lifts a finger, directing it at Zylus. "It's after what the idea of that would do to him."

Zylus's eyes are watering when his wide gaze hits mine.

Pollux continues, "The greatest fear Zylus has right now is losing you. Physically. Emotionally. If this youngling kills either of you, that fear evaporates. It must be aware enough to recognize that if it's sending you nightmares in order to antagonize him. By many accounts, a boogey like it is utterly harmless once you understand the fear itself cannot hurt you without your permission."

I squeeze Zylus's hand as I turn back to Pollux. "How do we handle this? Can *you* take care of it?"

A dry exhale escapes humorlessly. "Dear, I'm useless against things that don't have fears. This creature you're up against neither wants for life nor death. It has no passions, no ambitions to exploit. Not a single relationship. Not a single desire beyond malice. It feeds to get stronger to feed and get stronger. The only thing it cares for is its constant, gnawing hunger."

"Weren't you...one of them?" I whisper.

"Once. But I am born of a pure fear. Selfless in every way. It's quite rare a concept. Because even when one fears losing another, it is not from a place that mourns the other's pain. It is the terror of being without them. Fae born of strong emotions fall easily to negative mutation in their formative years when they are heavily susceptible to becoming whatever belief perceives them as."

My head swims. "Would changing my perception of this boogeyman do something?"

Pollux's eyes look through me, then close. "I do not dislike you half as much as I expected I might. Were it *your* fear, it would have evaporated in the sunlight the morning after it appeared. You have a way of suppressing your terrors and shoving the possibility of them out of your life. As it were, it is hard to be afraid of anything but loneliness in an empty room." His head cocks against the step. "And you solved the issue of loneliness by adding a cat."

Zylus pulls himself to his feet, and it might be my own heart stampeding, but I swear I feel his pulse tearing through his hand, beating at a rate that might kill him if he were human. "Is it mine? Did I create it?"

Pollux doesn't move, staying still as death on the steps. His shoulders sag, and he sits up, bracing the bottle in both hands between his knees. "You already know the answer to that question. It is why much of your fear stems from guilt. It is not just that you failed to protect your mate—it is also that *you* were the one to hurt her." With a sigh, he stares into his bottle. "You ought to know better than to ask questions with answers you dislike of those who cannot lie."

Zylus steps forward, back tense, sweat streaking down the center of his shirt. "What caused it?"

"Five years of nurturing a longing that you could see no end to. Your mate was content with a sliver of you. You couldn't bear the idea of taking it from her. Meanwhile, her life progressed, slipping away from yours unless you took action you knew she would reject." Pollux's jaw clenches as he runs his thumb against the spout of the bottle. "You do not want to lose the half of your soul that has renewed your purpose to live. Were I provided such a blessing, I, too, might find myself crippled with fear." He attempts another sip, then tips the bottle upside down and sighs. "Time's up."

He stands, and both Zylus and I trip backward. *Tall* doesn't begin to describe him. I thought *Zylus* was tall. Pollux is a mountain. Intimidation seeps from his every pore.

Zylus fixes my body behind his, shielding me from the pounding waves of the dream eater's presence. I curl myself against his shaking back and close my eyes, trying to regain composure. I still want to play with the spiders. And take pictures. Pollux isn't *bad*. I know he isn't *bad* because Zylus wouldn't have brought me before someone that leaves him so helpless if he were. I need to calm down.

"Wait," Zylus croaks. "I haven't been able to hunt it down. We came hoping you'd know where it's hiding."

"Where do fears usually hide, Zylus?"

I peak around Zylus's arm, find Pollux remaining on the steps, imposing...tired. Something about him is strictly exhausted, and I guess I didn't notice it before when I was facing him more directly. Now, with Zylus separating us, his weariness is unmistakable.

"In the shadows?" Zylus asks.

Pollux rolls his red and black eyes, then he touches a finger to his chest.

My skin goes icy.

"Even if you defeat this creature when it seeks you out again and materializes from the shadows, history will repeat itself until you overcome what's in your heart. Cats are made of fear, but you cannot afford to let it become an entity that controls you. Rest assured: I am in no way concerned for you or your mate's wellbeing." After saying so, he turns, climbing the steps, and the door behind us eases open with a long, low whine.

Chapter 21

~~~~~~~~~~~

My impulses need to take a long walk off a short pier.

"Just *don't* be scared. Drink more water." I push my hair behind my ear and pour a box of macaroni into a pot of boiling water. "Have you tried *breathing deeper*?"

Zylus, splayed across one of the kitchen nook booths with his feet perched on the windowsill, drags his hand down his face and tilts his head back off the edge of the seat to stare at me. "I don't know how you manage to be so condescending and so comforting at the same time."

"*Yoga*. You should try meditation."

"I am in true awe of you."

I stir the sauce I'm simmering. "You know what? I bet this is Mercury's fault. Retrograde sneaks up on the best of us and causes us to create boogeys all the time. I prescribe *essential oils*."

Zylus remains horizontal, watching me. "I keep looking for a sensation of anger, but it's not there. This is *my* fault. All of it. I should have been content to remain your cat. I got greedy. I—"

"You didn't want to watch me die." My tone bites a little more than I expect it to, but we will not be unpacking the reasoning behind that. Nope. We are making dinner. "Greed's debatable considering the fact most people don't want to die. Think of all the books I can read now that my lifespan has an extended warranty. Very little stresses me out more than an ever-growing TBR and the impending tick of Father Time." Wiping my hands on my apron, I face him. "Speaking of. Father Time. Actual person?"

"Human personification of a concept, not a real or accessible entity."

"Santa?"

He laughs, dryly.

"Oh good. I always hated that guy. Nothing like an uninvited guest whose one job is to judge you while you're still trying to figure out how to be a person. What about... the Easter Bunny?"

"Of the most notable childhood myths, tooth fairies are real. Not in the same context, though. They're far more... devious."

"Do I want to know?"

He pouts. "I am uncertain. You are...so..." Heat fills his cheeks as he looks elsewhere. "Wonderful." Curling up on his side, tucking his legs all the way under the table and across to the other booth in a *biiig stretch*, he murmurs, "You're really not upset?"

"I already processed everything when this started in severe depth, Zy. This information turns this problem from something unknown and ominous into a Scooby Doo villain. Not only that, if your fear was of losing me and we've just learned that this thing can't kill me without turning your fear into anger, there's nothing to worry about. The problem's solved itself. We get to laugh and gloat next time it shows up until it poofs out of existence." Turning back to my sauce, I whirl a finger in the air. "What an effective deus ex machina, story gods. Die and burn for making my story stupid."

Zylus sighs. "I don't know how you reason this threat away so completely when you still respond physically to the name *Alice*."

A shudder goes down my spine. "For your information, Alice is a real problem. She hates me."

"She does not."

"Last time we went to the bookstore, she looked at me funny."

"Did she?" Zylus drones. "Whatever will you do? A perfect stranger may have looked at you funny. This is it. Will you ever recover?"

"Sir." I turn back around, scowling. "I'll have you know there are only two things I care about in this world—absolutely everyone's opinion of me, and books."

"Also, food."

"*Also, food.* Three things. I'm at max care-pacity."

Zylus's face breaks out in a grin before he laughs and shakes his head. "Oh, how I love you."

My stomach flutters, as though it's trying to tell me of a *fourth* thing I care about.

Pulling himself upright, he stands and tucks his fingers in his pockets, approaching slow and deliberate. He stops, too close to me. If I breathe in, I might begin describing his scent, so I'm *not* going to breathe anymore.

Who said I needed to, anyway? Sounds like a scam.

My eyes meet his, and he's unwavering. Present. Something magical and mine.

Bending forward, he kisses my cheek, slips his fingers into my hair, and—

"My sauce..." I say weakly when his lips are an inch away.

He stops, but he doesn't move back. When he speaks, his breath touches my skin—warm. "Is that a *no*?"

Thoughts stalling, I remain frozen in front of him. It's not a *no*. I didn't *say* no. But what was I trying to say? Am I scared? He's been considerate and not initiated anything since the first, and only, time we kissed before, and of course I've not initiated anything either, but it makes sense if he's afraid of losing me emotionally for him to want some reassurance now.

It's a logical step to take in further removing power from the boogeyman.

The breaths I swore I wasn't going to take filter into my sticky lungs, getting stuck in the damp passages. My stomach tips and tumbles and rolls. I'm a little dizzy, and my heart...it's thumping hard against my ribs, sending a thundering sensation down into my toes.

What am I scared of? I can't let *my* fear become the source of the monster's power. I do not authorize a trade off here.

Zylus slides his fingers out of my hair, letting his thumb rest against the line of the pulse in my neck.

He moves his thumb, leans forward, and kisses my throat.

My eyes close.

Kiss. Lick. Nip.

I swear, and my knees go weak, so he catches me in his arms, stabilizes my body against his, and...holds me.

Against mine, his chest fills with air, and very little in my life has ever felt so utterly right. Normally, even day to day, it feels like I'm existing in the wrong body on the wrong planet. Simple tasks are too much where arguably harder ones don't faze me.

Can't wash the dishes, but I'm going to build a new raised garden bed... Why dust when I can repaint the bathroom? It's no wonder why my parents were fed up with me all throughout my childhood. I'd spend hours rearranging the toys in my closet so they lined up like Tetris blocks, but I threw tantrums when asked to vacuum the living room.

In a world where I've learned to call myself *lazy* and *picky* and *disagreeable*, finally I know what it feels like to be wanted. As I am. Regardless of the thousand moments of *me* he saw when I didn't know he was looking.

That must be why I'm scared.

I wouldn't know how to lose him, either.

"Are you sure you're scared right now?" he whispers into my hair.

"Am *I* sure of an *emotion*?"

He exhales a laugh.

"If I'm wrong, just tell me."

His arms tighten around me, reluctant, then he murmurs, "Not this time. May I kiss you?"

He smells like sweet grass.

I swear, pulling back some. Still trapped in his arms, I look up into his eyes. "Only if you promise to disregard my last thought."

"Promises are oaths, and to break an oath is to risk punishment worse than death. In all my years as a faerie, there is but one promise I am willing to make." He touches his lips to my forehead. "Right now. To you."

My face heats as he tips my chin up in his palm.

"I promise to love you into eternity, starlight, until the last of the heavenly host winks into darkness. With every breath, every touch, every moment I feel your heartbeat in my soul, I will love you." He smiles, and I am annoyed at how his beauty draws me in, like flies to a corpse. "May I kiss you?"

"Are we getting married? Is this fae married? This feels like fae marriage."

He grins in a way that shows off his fangs, then he says, "I do."

My sauce bubbles obliviously behind me as my lips part. I stare—ahem, *quite* romantically—at the crazy vampire cat, who appears to be announcing marriage oaths in my kitchen before pasta dinner. Appalling. Who does he think he is? What makes him think he's allowed to do this?

Wasn't he just throwing a kitty tantrum at the table?

He expects me to want to marry a cat man who drinks blood because it helps manage his heart condition?

It's a joke.

I've missed the punchline.

He's insane.

He must be insane.

Why else would he *want* to marry a useless woman who can barely hold a conversation, disdains the world beyond her cottage, and collapses in on herself at a moment's notice? *That's* what he wants to bind himself to with promises he can't break?

Ludicrous.

His thumb swipes across my damp cheek before I realize I'm crying.

"I don't need an answer right now. You can think about i—"

"I do." A lump catches in my throat, and my vision blurs as I hold back the rest of my tears. I'm insane. I'm completely mental. Just like all the kids told me while I was growing up. But, swear words, I am *free*.

Zylus stares at me, his aghast expression pairing oh so well with my trembling lips and wet lashes. "Y-yes?" His voice cracks. He clears his throat. "You…we…*yes*?"

Sharp, I nod once.

A laugh explodes from him. His hands brace my waist, effortlessly lift me, and spin me around. His mouth crashes into mine—smiling against my lips.

The salt of my tears fuses our mouths together as he cradles me closer and closer, still twirling. He feeds a curse against my tongue before stopping short and caging me against the counter by the sink, deep breaths rattling his lungs. His forehead hits my shoulder, and his joy washes over me like a tide. "I shouldn't do that on an empty stomach." His arms circle me, his hands clutching. "I love you."

"I..." My mind clouds, static. Marriage. Am I married now? Did I just get married? Is this legal? I will need to consult with Cael. Maybe I should ask Pila when the next fae court takes place, then, you know, casually pencil that into my schedule.

Crap.

No.

I don't want to shut down *now*. I *can't* shut down now. Is this my wedding night? Technically, we didn't have a *wedding*. We just said fancy words to each other in my kitchen while tomato sauce stained the stove.

What have I done? Since when am I so impulsive? And *why* do my impulses rear for romantic things?

No one should make life-altering decisions before dinner.

I love my cat: the squishy black thing that came when I called—because, unbeknownst to me, he understood English. My cuddly baby. I have not loved another person for years. What if I've forgotten how?

"You haven't," Zylus murmurs, tilting his head slightly enough that his nose brushes my chin. He plants a delicate kiss against my jaw. "You've only forgotten what it feels like."

"Cryptic."

"Really?"

"I think my sauce is burning."

He releases me from the tangle of his arms, and I meander my way to the stove, turn down the heat, and scrunch my nose at the tiny speckles staining the area around the pot. If the macaroni's overdone, I'm rioting.

Getting the pasta off the stove, I head to the colander in the sink, specifically keeping Zylus out of direct sight.

I feel untethered.

Confused.

What possessed me twenty seconds ago? *I do?* Seriously? Me? *I* do? Those are words I never thought I'd say.

While the pasta strains, I lift a hand, wipe tears from my cheek, and swallow hard.

I never thought I'd get married. I told my parents I wouldn't. Guys were gross and no one was nice to me, so whenever anyone asked if I had *a special someone* all throughout high school, I stared at them until they regretted speaking to me. I only verbalized the decision to my parents because I needed them to know grand kids weren't on the table, and never would be.

Grand kids.

Children.

Wedding night…

"I need to go for a long walk in the woods." Turning on my heel, I abandon the pasta in the sink.

Zylus catches me by the wrist, and I whip toward him. "Unhand me at once."

"It's late."

The place where he's touching me tingles with foreign things that have only ever appeared in response to him. I crunch those feelings into a wood chipper. "I require the night sky and the frigid caress of an icy wind."

"Sit by an open window."

Biting my cheek, I hook my fingers under his in an effort to pry him off me. He doesn't budge. "*Zylus.*"

"Willow."

"*What?*" I think I'm crying again. Or still. I'm not actually sure.

"It's okay."

"*What's* okay? Specifically. And, oh yeah that's right,

okay means *nothing*. I am *not* well. I don't think I have *ever* been well. I-I'm *messed up*, Zy. Why can't you see that? Everyone else sees it before I realize what I'm even doing wrong." Giving up on getting him *off*, I plunge my fingers into my hair and grip the roots. "You hunt *mice and moles*. You drink *blood*. And I— I just *married* you?"

"You eat red meat and sushi. Heck, *humans* drink blood, too, Willow. You can buy it in freezer bags at Asian markets."

My mouth snaps open, but no words come.

"Take a breath."

I don't want to. Just because he's told me to, I don't want to. His voice is too charming, and I can't stand how it makes me feel.

"*Starlight.*"

Sneering, I force air into my lungs, drink it down like a heaping helping of blood pudding, then let it out slow.

He lets my wrist slip from his fingers once my head's a little less dizzy. Patiently, he says, "I require nothing from you tonight or any other night. You are mine, and I am yours. The knowledge of that is enough. We can have dinner, read a book, and go to bed. Just like we have every other night this week. You have absolute control over how everything between us progresses."

My jaw locks, painfully tight, spearing an ache through my forehead. "What about you? What do you want?"

"I want to see my wife happy. Constantly. In her own beautiful way." His eyes glisten when he smiles. "I adore you, starlight. The fact you wanted to be with me, even for a second, brings me so much more joy than you can possibly comprehend." When his eyes close, a tear traces down his cheek toward his jaw. "For a moment, nothing felt wrong."

I catch the droplet on my fingertip before I realize I've

approached him.

I've done it again.

I've let my guard down long enough for the hypnotic aura surrounding him to take over my senses.

Clenching my fist in my skirt, I grimace at the pasta in the sink. "You're not allowed to *my wife* me."

"Okay."

"It's way too…domestic. I am diametrically opposed."

"I understand."

"I will also not think of you as my husband. Because that is weird."

When I flick my gaze toward him, he's staring at me with an odd light in his eyes. Something intense in his expression makes me shrink back.

"We will never have children. I hate them. They're mean. And I don't know how to raise any so they *won't* be mean."

"Our children would be angels."

"They would be monster vampire-human-pixie-dryad hybrids. They'd probably wear shadow capes, sit in corners full of spiders, and hiss at the sunlight."

His brows dip slightly, that infuriating smile unmoved. "So they wouldn't take after me at all?"

"I resent that."

"You don't."

I don't.

"I mean it. No kids. I'm telling you right now if we ever do anything that could result in the existence of a child, Faerie better have really good contraceptive."

"It does. I'll take it."

Wetting my lips, I let the fact *he'd* be taking it, not me, sink in. Not that we're going to…or anything. But anyway. My expectations are at human female levels of low. Some faeries come with deer hooves and fox tails and four knuckles per finger and two elbows per arm. As if sexism is even in their vocabulary.

Wait a second.

I don't have a sexist husband.

Score.

Blush warms his cheeks before he covers his mouth with a hand.

"What?" I snap.

He shakes his head. "You said you wouldn't think of me as your husband. But I swear I just felt the sensation of it."

Oh. Did he now? Lovely. In that case, he can now feel the sensation of many expletives. "I have regrets."

"Well, you are not bound to the oath of your word, so you are welcome to pretend nothing has happened."

"But something *did* happen."

"Indeed."

"And it's a big something."

"Yes."

I can't drag my eyes off him. He's half leaning against the counter, blushing down at his bare feet, and I have the oddest feeling he's been standing too long and hasn't eaten in too long, but he's beautiful in ways I have no words to express. It's not the physical beauty or hypnotic pull, either.

It's the way he is genuinely, blissfully happy to be with me.

I mutter a curse as I scrub my knuckles against my burning cheek and take a wary step backward.

I have never had that before.

It makes my chest swell with the terror of one day waking up…and finding it gone.

Chapter 22

Sorely unprepared for this character development.

"What are you doing?" Ollie, holding a platter covered in aluminum foil, blinks down at me where I'm crouched in my front yard.

I puff a white strand of hair out of my eyes and glare at him. "What does it look like I'm doing?" And why in the world is he here so early? I know he mentioned how he'd be by with a snack for *movie night next week* a week and a half ago, but movie *night* doesn't start for another hour. At least. Right? Or...have I lost track of time?

"It looks like you're making a bed."

"Very good assessment. I diagnose you with perfect eyesight." I continue sanding the back-board I've spent all day carving.

"Why are you making a bed?"

Because. Mine is too small. Because. Beds are expensive. Because. I *can*. "Because," I say.

A funny look twists a gleam into his eyes as he peers at the logs Zylus helped me pick out and cut down, assuring me the whole time that Pila wouldn't be mad and I wasn't stealing any faerie homes. Stupid Zylus and his stupid face. "Zy," I mutter as I keep on furiously sanding.

"My love?" His arms wrap around me from behind as he spills from my shadow.

"Your friend's here."

He tenses. "Oh." Straightening away from my back, he clears his throat. "Hello."

"Hi."

Something unspoken passes between them, and it occurs to me they may have a mental link similar to the one Zylus has with me. I don't remember the exact rules he mentioned, but it had something to do with exchanging blood. I've seen at least half of an exchange, and they are impressively close friends.

It wouldn't surprise me.

And I'm not jealous at all.

"We are not talking about you in our minds, starlight," Zy notes.

Ollie smirks.

"Oh, hush." Zylus crosses his arms.

"I didn't say anything." Ollie pushes the tray he's holding forward. "Lemon square?"

He brought lemon squares? Pausing, I look up through the clear bottom of the glass tray above my head. I like lemon squares.

Zylus chuckles and meets my eye, which shouldn't make me blush, but I think it does. Warmly, he says, "Darling, how can we help you shut things down for the night?"

After both Ollie and Zylus help me pack the half-finished pieces of what will soon be my new bed frame into the safety of the house, I get started on tidying myself up.

Pila arrives later, with brownies and Cael, and…I didn't even invite them.

Come to think of it, I didn't actually invite Ollie either.

Did they all just unanimously decide we were having another movie night? Did they have fun two weeks ago? Do I have a friend group?

"Willow?" Pila asks perhaps seven to ten seconds after I've mentally lost the conversation—something about how she wants to help me finish my bed and she loves woodworking and I should have called her to begin with?

Yeah, that feels about right.

Squeezing my eyes shut for a moment, I turn off my popcorn machine then dump the contents into a bowl. "Sorry. It's been an odd few days." Not because anything has changed, really. Just because the air feels different now that I'm "married." Since Cael's here, I should ask him about the legalities. Except then that would alert everyone of the news. And I don't know what to do with *the news* myself.

In a lot of ways, being in a relationship is more daunting than facing a boogeyman.

Or...maybe it isn't.

Maybe that's just how it feels for me, because I'm *me*.

I'm supposed to want to tell my friends about an event of such magnitude. But the only person I feel comfortable talking about it with is Zylus. And so we have. A lot. All night. In my tiny bed with his man arms around me because I need a little more than *meow* while I parse my thoughts.

Yes, the past few days have made it more than clear my little daybed is too little.

Hence, the making of a bed today.

AKA the only logical option.

I've already ordered the mattress.

"Are you well?" Pila asks, genuine concern tainting the words in a way that pulls at my heart.

Mentally? Ha, ha, ha. Physically? Well enough.

I pivot. "You know what? Something doesn't add up."

"What do you mean?"

"Ollie got here first. Before sunset. Even though last week he was late, despite being told to come an hour earlier, which implies that he is often late."

Pila's lips part, then her brow furrows. "That is odd."

Something pricks my chest, painful, *Zylus*, so I abandon

the popcorn bowl and march into the living room. "What's..." Surrounded by Zylus and Cael, Ollie sits on the couch—crying. My mouth fills with sand, and I whisper, "...wrong?"

Ollie tenses, scrubs his face, and pulls away from his friends. Standing, he forces a smile that doesn't quite form his dimples. "Wrong?" His head tilts. "Everything is normal."

Normal is not synonymous with *okay*. Actually, given how often Zylus likes to toss *okay* around in a shallow but comforting dismissal, the absence of that pathetic word leaves me anxious. *Okay* means breathing. Who isn't breathing?

I meet Zylus's eyes.

Stern, Cael stands, wrapping Ollie up in both his arms and wings. I watch the werewolf crumple again as Zylus makes his way to me.

Quieter, I say, "Zy, what's wrong?"

He forces a smile and opens his mouth, but the expression deteriorates before he can find the energy to get any words out. Fists clenched at his sides, he murmurs, "We've been invited to a funeral."

A funeral.

"For..."

Zylus curls his arm around my back and guides me into the kitchen, past Pila's stricken expression. Once we're standing alone by the kitchen table, he says, "Elsie, starlight. Ollie's human passed away this morning."

Pieces of my heart shatter like Corelleware. The image of the old woman sitting by herself in the window of Ollie's little house hits me, and I sink into one kitchen booth.

Zylus crouches in front of me, taking my hands in his.

"Ollie..." I whisper, but nothing more comes. He's not okay. He might be breathing, but because someone precious to him isn't anymore, he's not okay. There's nothing to say. I already know from experience that no words can ease the damage. Bad feelings swarm into me, too cold and clammy, making everything overwhelmingly wrong. "Does Ollie have a place to live now? Is Elsie's family going to come and take him away, thinking he's a chihuahua? Does he… would he want to stay with us? We'll have an extra bed soon. I can begin building a guestroom."

Tears fill Zylus's eyes, but he buries his face against my hands before one falls into my palms. His hot, damp breath shakes against my fingers as he kisses them. He swears. "I love you. I love you so much." He swears again, voice breaking. "Ollie has plenty of places to stay. The forest is home to many fae, and—"

"But it's winter." My tone bites. "It's *cold* outside."

"He won't be outside, love, not unless he wants to be. Cael's palace is always open to those of his domain. Even Pollux would put him up, would that not be utterly horrible. He will be cared for. We care for each other. All of us. Whether we know one another or not, and—" He rests his cheek against my hands, gripping them tight as he curses once more. "—you are so completely one of us."

Biting my cheek, I try to pull my hands free. "I'm not… I wouldn't offer for just anyone. But he's *your* friend. And, you know, he's totally just a little puppy. So—"

Lifting his head, Zylus looks up at me, solemn. "You are so adverse to compliments, starlight. Pay it no mind if it bothers you to think about."

This entire situation bothers me to think about. My body is aching. I need a distraction from this reality, but the idea that Ollie doesn't get to escape the truth since his entire life is about to change completely keeps me from banishing it from my thoughts. "Does Ollie need you right now?"

"Perhaps."

"Go be with him."

"My fealty is to you first, my prince second, and Ollie third."

Jerking my hands free, I slap them to his perfectly handsome cheeks and glower. "This is where soulmate stories get problematic." I bend and press a tear-stained kiss to his lips. "I will be fine. My secondhand sorrow can't compare to what he's going through. Right now, he needs his friend more than I need a mate. Okay?"

Taking a breath, he nods. "Okay."

Our foreheads touch, then both of us linger a moment before he pulls himself away.

★

The funeral exists in a world apart.

It's sunny, because pathetic fallacy is a tool only used in books where the authors are occasionally kind and allow their entire world to mourn for the loss they create.

It was sunny when my grandmother died, too.

It was sunny when they laid her in this sprawling yard, just a few rows of plaques down.

Headstones from generation to generation bear the same name near where Elsie lies. Brittle grass overcomes paper flowers all around. Unrelenting sun bathes every inch in sight.

This is too much like that day. Sobbing families standing around a deep hole. One black coffin shining in a sunlight that should have had the decency to tuck itself away. A sinking, dark feeling crawling out of my chest.

The biggest difference between that day and this one is my perspective.

This time, I'm sitting with Zylus on the cold grass because he can't stand for very long. Peering past human legs at the way sunlight dances across the woodwork, I hold back tears. Ollie. Ollie is the only fae quietly watching on the edge of the hole, a single too-large flower from Pila in his hand. Behind us, Cael looms, running his fingers through Zylus's hair. His large wings shield us from *the rest* of the attending faeries.

And there are so many.

Unseen. Unheard.

The fae came.

I wonder if they always come or if they're just here for Ollie. I wonder if when someone who no one mourns passes, they come. I wonder if when everyone but one broken teenager has stopped mourning whether they wait with her in a solidarity she never knew was present while her body ached and her only friend—the only one who really understood her—left her completely alone.

The ceremony proceeds; the humans collect and siphon away; the fae remain.

I don't know how many hours have passed before Zylus pulls himself up, lets go of my hand, and paces past Elsie's new quiet neighbors to Ollie's side.

In the exact moment Zylus pulls Ollie into his arms I realize two things—

First, I am among the ones I have longed my entire life for. I have a place in a community that doesn't scorn the different. I have a place in a community that welcomes care and compassion and kindness simply because life is a gift worth sharing. The friends I've barely met would not hesitate to help me if I asked. The magic others fear and misinterpret protects me.

For the first time in my life, I am safe.

Second, I am afraid. Despite the overwhelming proof that kindness now surrounds me, my history poisons my blood and feeds liquid terror through my veins.

Losing this would kill me.

I don't know how to feel secure when my entire body revolts at the slightest change.

For the first time in decades, I believe in a care that transcends what I've been taught to expect from people, but my past expectations leave me raw.

Love and fear exist in the same space.

To love something—*really* love something—is to fear the moment it goes away.

Trust can't help me, not even if I now exist in a world where *trust* is stable and lies are impossible. Truth doesn't spare someone from this.

Opening my heart up to what I am desperate for means being afraid of losing it.

Life is loving, so life is fearing.

From the first moment Ollie chose Elsie to be his human, he knew their time wouldn't last forever. He chose to love in the space between anyway.

"Willow?" Cael's stable voice draws me softly from my thoughts. He lowers himself beside me, wingtips grazing brittle blades of grass, and catches a teardrop on his thumb. "Are you well?"

Zy glances my way, registers Cael wiping my tears, but makes no move to abandon Ollie.

Paranormal romance wouldn't hear of it. Another man speaking to the male lead's mate is cause for riots, fire, bloodshed.

I have long since come to understand this isn't the *paranormal* romance I thought it would be. This is something else entirely. Something far softer.

Sniffing, I wipe my own cheeks, glad for the industry-level Amare eye liner I'm wearing. It neither runs nor streaks, and I'll have to take it off with a crowbar later. "I don't know what I am most of the time." There's *good*. There's *bad*. There's nothing. I've lived so long with *bad* that *nothing* became my *good*. Good burned me out anyway. The only *good* I've accepted for years is reading a book and literally vibrating through the sweetest moments until I'm so tired the only logical conclusion is nap time. Right now, I am crying. My body hurts for Ollie. I am beginning to believe that love and fear are one in the same. In the past few months, I have experienced changes that have rewritten my entire world. This moment reopens a raw wound of grief I know will never fully heal.

Despite it all, if given options, I would choose here.

"I can take you home if it's too much," Cael offers—like he's not a very important person, like his duties as a prince mean *caring for everyone* instead of sitting on his throne and making demands.

I shake my head. "I'll stay here."

"If you're sure." Smiling, he rises and finds his way to Ollie and Zylus.

Picture-perfect friends. The storybook kind. The cartoon movie sort.

Through thick and thin, they'll be there for each other. Nothing can tear them apart or bring them down. Together, they fall. Together, they rise.

While the scene enamors me, Pila settles herself on the ground at my side, awakening the grass around her to lush green. Gently, she hands me a large flower filled with Lesta's tiny, whimpering sobs. "Things like this hit the pixies hard," she says. "Are you well?"

I am bad overcome with nothing. A hollow, chasm of disassociation, faintly aware I am not doing *well*. "I must be relying on the dryad in me right now."

Pila rests her head against my shoulder. "When we become bushes later, maybe we can share the same garden patch."

"I'd appreciate that."

"This is what Zy couldn't bear the thought of concerning you," Pila murmurs. "We've attended several funerals like this. Ollie doesn't like being alone, but his pack doesn't suit him, so he adopts humans. He wants someone to care for, someone who cares about him, and his position in his pack didn't offer that."

"There's a hierarchy?" I ask. How very...on-genre of werewolf, or werecanine, packs.

"I'm sure he's mentioned that he's the runt of his litter before. One of his brothers became alpha, and since werecanines carry many animalistic traits he doesn't resonate with, there's a lot of tension he tries to ignore when they're together. Sometimes when you're different, you feel outcast. And sometimes when you're powerful, you unknowingly make the weak feel weaker. Cael took Ollie in when he left his pack a couple hundred years ago. This town, Cael's domain, reflects his spirit and welcomes those who do, too."

"So not all fae are this kind?"

"None of us is infallible. The good among us do not act unprovoked, but for those of us who can bear more than one emotion at a time..." Pila tucks her finger into the flower, letting Lesta wrap her entire body around the golden brown skin. "...we do not have the opportunity to be wholly good or wholly bad. There are many ways to justify meanness. And, on occasion, oblivion does it for us."

Ignorance is a weapon wielded by the blissful. "Zy said Ollie would be cared for, but do you know what he's going to do now?"

"Usually, he finds places to stay in the forest for several years, then when people have all but forgotten that a little spotted chihuahua once graced the town, he finds someone lonely who needs him as much as he needs them."

To think even the fae run from the feeling of inadequacy toward whatever might give them purpose.

The desire to love and be loved goes so deep. It's almost a blight on the soul.

"Pila, can I ask you a personal question?"

"If you'd like."

"Will you have to wait hundreds of years before you find your mate?"

She chuckles. "Dryads do not wish for mates, nor do they have them. We belong to nature and connect in ways outside the romantic. Zy must not have mentioned it because the concept that you may never love him or want him in the same way is one of the things he fears."

Well, that brings up several questions. Most prominently: "If dryads don't care for romantic connection…how come I exist?"

"Love offers regardless of desire at times. Love is not synonymous with romance. I have told you before, nothing in this world is as black and white as parts of you wish they were. The fragments of you that become one thing fully wish for completeness. It takes effort to see the beauty in the gray, but it is filled with opportunity." She strokes Lesta's head with a free finger until the tiny creature's sobs quiet. "After all, it is not about whether or not the glass is half empty or half full, it is about discerning what fills it and whether or not it is enough of what you need at a given time."

She's not wrong.

I swipe my thumb against a soft petal of Lesta's flower. "Do you think Zy was disappointed when I didn't jump into his arms the moment I saw him in his not-cat form?"

"Probably." Pila yawns. "Although, I would assume he knows an illogical desire when he has one."

Swallowing, I cradle the flower bed closer to my chest.

"I mean…do you think he's disappointed that someone like *me* is his mate?"

"Someone like you?"

"Someone who doesn't want him in the same way. At the very least, someone who has no idea how to want him in the same blinding capacity. Someone who may not even be capable of it."

She hums, softly. "Sapling, that is a question to ask him, not me."

Again, she's not wrong. But who has the nerve? Raise your hand if you have the nerve. Oh look. My arm has not moved.

"That is also a question you may want to ask yourself."

My brow furrows. "What do you mean?"

"You are not solely dryad. It might be a touch too soon to assume you are not growing into wanting him in exactly the ways he craves."

I bite my cheek. "That sounds scary."

"It might be." Pila hums. "What matters, however, is that you do not let fear stop you from daring to love."

If fear and love are the same, that might be a tiny bit difficult for me to figure out.

Chapter 23

I've made my bed, now I must lie in it.

The best place for an existential crisis is, and will always be, on the bedroom floor. I stand by that. Even though I am currently lying down in my new king-size bed, contemplating life, staring at the ceiling, and patting the little head of the little vampire cat on my stomach.

It's late. I should have turned the light off over an hour ago. Instead, I'm breaking down the concept of love as though Zylus can't feel the sensations of my thoughts with surprising accuracy.

Love is being afraid. Constantly. Start to finish. Love is choosing to fall even if you're afraid of heights. Love is *never* not falling again, lest you fall *out* of love, which is really just a nice way of saying you got lazy. People don't *fall out of* emotions. That's like suggesting you can *fall out of* an anxiety attack. No. Emotions are caused by *something*, and if you stop feeding that *something*, the emotions die. It's a conscious choice when people stop nurturing anything—whether someone takes responsibility for it or not.

Love is trusting another person in spite of fear. Love is saying, "Yes, you *will* catch me. Yes, you *are* waiting. Yes, I believe that if I allow myself to plummet, you will not allow me to get *hurt*."

Trust.

Ick.

I have problems with trust. One might even call them

trust issues.

"And you're partly to blame," I whisper at Zylus as I pluck his front paws up, thumbs to beans.

His eyes floppily open, and it occurs to me he may have fallen asleep while I was contemplating the love triangle in the book series I've been reading to distract me from the funeral residue over the past few days. It's kind of impressive that he found those thoughts so calming, considering the contemplation consisted of do I a. finish reading, or b. resort to arson.

A lovely little ritual book burning with all my newfound friends would be positively delightful.

There's nothing I hate more than uncertainty. It messes me up.

I can't stand when certain foods touch. I don't know how Idiot McStupidface can stand back-and-forth dipping between two perfectly acceptable men. Pick one. Commit. The end. Thank you.

Zylus's eyes go eepy again, one falling closed before the other, so I shake him. "Excuse me. I know my thoughts derailed. But I did speak to you."

In the next two seconds, I lose my emotional support toe beans in favor of Zylus clasping my hands above my head. He flicks his tongue out against my cheek. "Forgive my insolence, starlight. What were you saying?"

"You are part of the reason I have trust issues."

His eyes widen. "Me?"

"*Me?*" I mock, rolling my eyes. "I don't even know how many times you coerced me into belly rubs that ended in bloodshed."

He curls his lips into his mouth, poorly hiding a smile as he glances off me. Stroking his index finger against my palm, he says, "In my defense, were you ever truly fooled?"

"I said, on numerous occasions, 'If I rub tummy, this time you're not allowed to scratch me. Okay? Okay.'"

"You imagining my compliance is not going to hold up in a court of law."

"You were a bad kitty."

He leans in close, eyes practically *glittering*. "I am the *best* kitty." Cautiously, he touches a kiss to my lips, pulls back, meets my eyes, and brightens when I don't chide him. Without restraint, he moves in again.

"Zy."

He tenses, an inch away. "Yes, my love?"

"Am I strange?"

"In my favorite ways."

That's a *yes*. I frown. "Example."

He kisses my jaw. "You're perfectly calm. Even though I have you pinned to the very nice bed you made for us so we could be comfortable together each night. Even though my promise that I wouldn't bite again until you asked doesn't extend to so, so many other things. Even though you claim to have trust issues involving me. It is remarkably, completely, and utterly strange how you react to the world, and I adore it."

I squeeze his hands, watching his cool façade melt into blushing cheeks and hungry eyes. He licks his lips, scans me from the top of my head down my nightgown, and lets out a slow breath. "Careful. I am desperate for you."

"If I never let you bite me, will you still love me?"

"I will love you forever whether you let me bite you or not."

"What is love?"

He presses his lips to my forehead. "Selflessness."

My mouth opens, but it takes my brain a long while to comprehend that answer. It's so much different than my conclusion of *fear*. Zylus trails kisses across both my cheeks and nestles into the divot between my collarbones before I can so much as begin to gather my thoughts. Wings beat in my chest—strange, unfamiliar, faintly nauseating. My body's too hot for comfort.

I'm starkly terrified, but if the boogeyman shows up and ruins this, it will be all too predictable, and I will spend the rest of my ages cursing the story gods for being bone-dead stupid.

"If you're selfless, then I'm selfish," I say. "How do people love each other when someone always takes more than the other gives?"

"If I'm selfless, and you're selfless, then we take care of each other instead of ourselves. I see to your needs. You see to mine. When something is too much for either of us, the other fills in. Love isn't complicated or difficult. It doesn't keep a record. It *wants* to give. So many people are just too afraid to ask for what they need because needing something from someone else makes you vulnerable and dependent."

My jaw clenches. "Not only that, there's no guarantee your need will be fulfilled. Especially when you *need* something, rejection is scary."

"Everything's scary."

"Wise words from a scaredy cat?"

"I'm flattered you think me wise."

My mouth betrays me as the touch of a smile tips one corner up.

He releases one of my hands so he can trace the expression with a fingertip. His eyelids lower. "I would dream of this...in the quiet moments when you'd fall asleep with a book on the couch... I'd listen to your heartbeat and lie awake for hours, wanting you."

Slowly, my smile drifts away.

"I longed to talk to you, to touch you, to care for you.

But I feared rejection as much as I feared losing you, so I did nothing and wound up on the precipice of both my worst terrors coming true. Everything is scary, but if I could meet you for the first time all over again, I would show you the truth the moment you brought me home. I would have begged for you openly in every moment that followed." His fingers thread into my hair, stretching the long strands out across the pillow beside me. "I don't regret the time I've spent with you, but I've let my own fears keep me from loving you in the way you've deserved for so long."

"I think love and fear are basically the same."

He pauses arranging my hair in order to meet my eyes. "You do struggle to tell the difference."

"I…" I watch his eyes. Lips parted, I ignore the blaze crawling up my neck. "Zy. What am I feeling right now, for you?"

"Must I reveal my own confession?"

I take in a shaking breath. "Zylus. I have never been more scared." Clutching his hand, I lift my free palm to his cheek, cup his face, and search his eyes. "I've not let myself love someone since my grandmother died. I don't know how Ollie says goodbye over and over. I don't know how he manages so much heartache when one tiny thing going wrong renders me helpless. Aren't you disappointed?"

"In…you?"

"That *I'm* your mate. At the funeral, Pila told me dryads don't have mates. I don't know how to want to be yours. I'm scared my love will never be enough if ever I figure out how to express it. I'm scared that the emotions I can handle will always be too shallow for you. I—"

He kisses me, claiming my mouth, deepening the caress, stealing every last ounce of my air. "Hush," he whispers against my tongue. "If you were incapable of being my entire world, you would not be *my mate*. That's what you told Ollie. That was the truth." He swears. "You are enough if you never let me touch you again. You are enough if you never tell me you love me. You are *enough*. You are the kind of woman who built a bed so I could sleep comfortably with you. The kind of woman who offered to construct an entire room so my friend would have a place to stay. I resent the people who taught you to think so poorly of yourself." He presses my hand into his skin and lets his eyes close. "You have a beautiful soul, and it is mine, and that will always, *always* be everything."

"You're sure?"

"I have never been more certain of anything else in my life." Letting my hand slip from his, he curls his finger beneath my chin as a pained smile overcomes his much-too-beautiful face. "Besides. Even when you find it hard to identify for yourself, I can *feel* your care, Willow. You'd rather roll your eyes and say something sarcastic than admit it, but I've no doubt in my mind you would do anything for me. I wouldn't even need to ask. The moment you see someone in need, you pick up on it. Your feelings aren't too small to see." He kisses my chin. "They're too big to comprehend."

I'm not going to cry. I'm *not*. I've cried too much over the past few months, and I'm already in bed for the night—which means I need to reserve my fluids. Swallowing hard, I turn my face away from him. "I love you," I mumble, flicking my eyes toward him, back away. "Don't I?"

"Quite a bit. Rather reluctantly, too."

"Does that offend you?"

"No. I love how you can't help yourself."

Letting my eyes fall closed, I release a bitter laugh. A swear whispers past my lips. "I can't lose you."

"You won't."

"How do you know that?"

"I have lived over a thousand years with far less to fight for. There is no future in which you lose me."

"What about the boogeyman?"

"I am less afraid each day, so I would not be surprised if the boogeyman vanishes entirely. Like Pollux said, it is nearly helpless if I overcome my fear."

I blink. His words process. My eye twitches. "Wait. Wait just a second. You mean…you mean that's it? You've overcome your fear of losing me?"

"It no longer cripples me. In some ways, fate deemed I face it, and now that you know the truth and hold nothing against me, I have come to terms with my guilt. I will *never* let harm come your way like that again. Without physically facing my fear, I may have lost you entirely, so in some ways, I am grateful my mistakes allow me to spend an eternity making it up to you."

I stare at him, gaping. "We *really* deus ex machinaed this? Not even. We machinaed so well we *skipped* the climax entirely?"

"Would you…prefer a vicious battle to the death?"

"No!" Untangling my other hand from his, I cross my arms. "It's just…there was *supposed* to be a vicious battle to the death. You end up mortally wounded. And in a fit of passionate fear for your life, I give you my blood. Revitalized on the power of love, you vanquish the foe. It's night time. Midnight. Moon high. Full. Gleaming. *Somehow* we completely neglect the monster guts splattered across my lawn and the fact my chickens will *definitely* need therapy later in favor of making out. Cue smut."

Zylus is *very* red in the face by the time I've finished my tirade. He clears his throat, opens his mouth, covers it with his hand, and closes his eyes to take a steadying breath. His fingers shake against his jaw. "We can skip straight to the s—"

"You should think twice before finishing that sentence."

He nods. "Right. Yes. My apologies."

I huff, sagging a little. "I guess I should be used to the universe neglecting my expectations by now. This isn't some dramatic story. It's just normal life."

"Sorry."

"No, I'm sorry." I chew my lip. "It's not...you aren't, and Ollie isn't, and none of the faeries are a stereotype. I'm still learning what's...*normal*."

"Disappointed?" he asks.

Lifting my attention to him, I let the quiet of the moment consume me. "No."

My kitty. My vampire. My husband. My Zy.

I love him.

It's scary to love someone. It's scary when things aren't the way I expect them to be.

It's scary when you're different. It's scary when you're not *normal* in a world that mocks even harmless absurdities. There's so very much to be scared of.

It's so easy to let fears lock you up in a box in the woods with your garden and your chickens and your ire. If you ignore what scares you, it can't hurt you, right? Or maybe it just can't hurt you as loudly. Maybe it still cuts deep when you aren't looking.

Like a monster in the shadows, it appears when you least expect it and tries to rip everything you love away.

The only life worth living is the sort where you allow yourself to love, so the only life worth living is the one where you continually overcome your fears. Of rejection. Of heartbreak. Of pain.

The last thing I can overcome is the vampire biting thing.

"Zy?"

His throat bobs, and I know he's felt the direction my thoughts have strayed before I say them aloud.

"It needs to cease being an unknown if we're going to move forward, right?"

"Are you sure?" he whispers.

"It's all part of the vampire romance. If I'm leaning into accepting my place in it, I should at least consider that this is an aspect of it."

"I thought you were very against the idea of subscribing to a *vampire romance*."

I shrug. "I'm live, laugh, loving into fresh spaces. Getting out of my comfort zone. Trying new things."

"Do please continue setting up this highly romantic moment with office poster quotes."

"If I don't like it, I'll just *hang in there*."

Sitting back on his knees, he covers his eyes with both hands. "If you don't like it, I'll stop."

"Don't imply you'll be able to stop. That ruins the *vampire romance* mood." I sit up with him.

He peeks at me through his fingers, the opposite of amused. "We need to talk about the red flags in your books."

"We do not."

"I'm very concerned."

"Bite me."

Tension filters into his limbs, and it ripples along my flesh, raising the hair on my arms. My heart won't settle.

He cups my cheek in his palm. "Where?"

Something in his voice vibrates with need, and my blood heats to a boil. This is actually happening? Really? Who am I if I *want* it to? Just another insipid main character hyped up on liquid stupid?

Or someone who *character arced* her way into being

brave enough to trust someone won't hurt her—even when everyone else has?

I tilt my chin and refuse to meet his eyes as I bare my neck.

"Look at me." Something raw ties up his voice, and I shiver.

"No, I don't think I will."

He exhales a laugh, pinches my chin, and forces me to face his way. His green and blue eyes peer into mine—too gentle. His pupils swallow the shades until only slim rings of color remain. Leaning in, he kisses my temple. "You are everything to me."

I grip the hem of his black shirt and say the only words I can come up with to express the *too much* I'm feeling right now. "...thank you."

He breathes a curse suffixed with my name into my ear, then his mouth settles against my skin, damp, open. His teeth graze my neck, testing the waters, giving me time to change my mind. With each moment that passes, I settle a little more.

When he bites, one of his hands is fisted in my hair, the other trembling against my waist. A small, grateful sound escapes him, and heat builds in my chest.

It's aggressively languid. Soft strokes and tender kisses. Painless.

He leaves off with a lingering press of his lips then shyly, questioningly, shakily meets my eyes.

I watch him in a daze, processing the absence of all pain, processing the way he's looking at me, processing *everything* I've neglected to think about. "Hm."

"Hm?"

"Hm." I kiss him. "Yeah."

A jolt of excitement lines his tone as I topple him back. "Yeah?"

"I don't mind that."

"You don't..." His fangs glint in his smile. "Really?"

"Really. I love you. A lot." Hands pressed to his shoulders, my nightgown flared around his hips, I grin. "Sorry it took a while to figure out."

He shakes his head. "No. No, you can always take all the time you need."

I kiss his nose, and his breaths turn uneven. "I don't want to waste any more."

"No time near you is wasted, starlight. No matter what it's spent doing."

"Oh, good."

"Mm?" The mumble pours into my mouth.

I break away. "A lot of it is going to be spent reading."

He laughs.

"Even though..." I trace one of his pointed ears with a fingertip. "...my expectations are ruined now. I'll have to switch to the fantasy stuff. Like self-help."

He flashes me a toothy smirk. "What a disaster?"

My eyes roll. "Sir."

Trapping me in his arms, he knocks his forehead into mine. "Willow."

Warm. "Yes?"

"I love you."

My heart thumps at an erratic beat. "Immensely?"

"Beyond comprehension. In ways you shall never manage to process nor fathom. Not in decades, nor centuries, nor eternity."

I bite my lip. "So...immensely?"

His laugh consumes me with a sensation of utter peace before he says, "Yes, my darling. *Immensely.*"

Epilogue

No regrets.

Several months later

"And then Little Red Riding Hood decided that bad children should be eaten by nice were*canines*, so she apologized for almost stabbing Christie with her toy scissors in kindergarten that one time. Even though Christie deserved it. The end."

On the other side of the room from my wife, my heart flutters as I watch Willow read her own version of every single fairytale she can get her hands on to the group of enraptured children who, just a few horrifying tales prior, swore up and down that *they'd heard it all*.

It's a sight to behold, that's for sure.

I never would have suspected my Willow to voluntarily sign up for reading hour at the Mountain Vale Public Library, but there she is. Being beautiful and stunning and brave.

"Why has no one kicked her out yet?" Ollie asks, half-sitting on the table I'm seated at. "Is she allowed to indoctrinate the next generation like that?"

"Leave her alone. She's perfect."

"She's paying some nice therapist's future salary."

"Do you want to hear about indentured mice?" Willow calls.

Many hands go up, several children sputtering a

question about what are *indented mice*.

In utter deadpan, Willow says, "Indented mice are mice positioned a little further from the margin than the others. I asked a yes or no question."

The resounding *yes* is near-deafening.

"Oh, I love her," I exhale.

Ollie snorts. "Correct me if I'm wrong, but isn't she wearing your clothes?"

I clear my throat and scan the wisps of my shadow caressing her body. "She's been into design lately. Drawing all sorts of outfits." Then trusting me to clothe her. Be with her. Keep her safe, even in public. Trusting *me*.

Ollie whistles.

"Do shut up."

"No, no. Don't mind me. I'm just egregiously jealous."

Pulling my attention off my perfect (flawless, lovely, amazing, outstanding, darling, precious, etc, etc, etc) wife, I focus on the odd edge to Ollie's smile. "Are you tiring of bed hopping already?"

"You make me sound like a courtesan."

My eyes narrow. "*Weren't* you a courtesan for a little while?"

Ollie stares blankly ahead. "Anyway. Yes, I miss living in a boring little house with a nice little human who expects absolutely nothing from me."

I smirk. "He longs to return to the one-brain-cell life."

"I function debatably well under such conditions."

"Debatably." My gaze shifts back to my queen, my light, the beginning and end of all things in my world, knowing full well *anything* can be debated. There are people on this planet who still believe it's flat, after all. My drifting thoughts slam into place, and I jerk my attention back to Ollie. "What did you say?"

He's not looking at anything; rather, he appears to be

looking *through* everything up until the moment his eyes close. "My...mate. I saw her. Here."

"When?"

"Yesterday. She was moving in." He wets his lips. "Just a few streets down from where Elsie and I used to live. Nearer the woods." Pain creases his brow, and he utters a swear. "She's...*beautiful*, Zy." He curses again, swiping his hand over his mouth. "But I can't explain what I'm feeling well."

"She's human?"

Ollie nods toward Willow as his eyes reopen. "Like Willoughby."

I wish I knew how my precious angel garnered that nickname, but neither of the rascals will tell me, and attempting to decode the sensations she gives off when she's thinking about it are nearly impossible. It's tied up in too many references I simply do not understand. "If she's like my mate, you'll have to turn her," I murmur. "I recommend introducing the idea sooner rather than later, so you don't risk—"

Ollie snarls, lip curling and dark eyes flashing. "*Don't*." Squeezing his eyes shut, he shakes his head. "Sorry." A bitter laugh leaves him, and he sinks deeper back against the desk, stuffing his hands in his pockets and slouching. "Turn her. Right. My lovely little mate is going to let a chihuahua bite her beneath the light of a full moon so we can go yipping through the trees together."

"She's *yours*. Whatever form you feel most comfortable taking, she will accept."

"She deserves better. I've barely seen her, but I already know that. She deserves *better*."

Scowling, I stand, glare at him, and say, "Then *be* better. You and I both know you're capable of so much more than you show. Be. Better." With that, I navigate through the sea of children toward my mate, who is cheerfully educating them on the risks of doing things for food like Cinderella's mice. She's the only one who can see me, and her little nose scrunches at my approach.

Sensations flood toward me, growing stronger the closer I get, a melange of emotions and spotty words. How dare I interrupt her teaching time. I'm supposed to be playing with my friend like a good kitty. She can't take me anywhere. Dang. She loves me. So, so very much.

I melt, from the inside out as the ocean of her adoration overwhelms every droplet of ever-present snark. Her mind is a beautiful little playground of rolling eyes and reluctant smiles. Unlike once upon a time, now it is also filled with unbridled joy, a sense of soul-deep belonging, and remarkable love.

Just being near her serves so much comfort.

"Starlight. I'm hungry."

She ignores me.

"Starlight."

She turns a page. "And here we see that poor little mice are being forced to make clothes. In the original story, Cinderella just cried a lot, and everything was well."

"Starlight."

She points starkly at her group of gathered minions. "Don't let modern propaganda tell you it's not good to cry. Just make sure you cry on trees. The dryads will appreciate your kindness, and the saplings will grow into magic willows that can do anything."

"Starlight."

Willow sighs, slapping the book shut. "That is all for today. Next time I'll teach you about taxes."

"Please don't try," I comment.

"I can and will, Zy."

Can't and won't. I handle her taxes. She barely

understands what insurance is or why she needs it.

Sighing, she smiles. "If you learned nothing else from this afternoon, remember this, kids, challenge everything you believe is normal. Ask every question." She holds her hand out for me, and I go to her, drawn in uncontrollably—like Cael to a headlight. "And when you find something new, treat it with kindness."

The second our palms meet, I steal her from their perception, tucking her beneath my arm as the uproar over her disappearance begins. "Will you ever stop abusing my abilities?" I whisper into her ear as we duck out into the early autumn air. Blessedly, summer has come and gone. I survived. In fact, thanks to my amazing wife, I may have *thrived*.

"*Our* abilities. Thank you." Her eyes glimmer, all rimmed in dark shades that faintly glitter in the sun. "Did you see me? Did you see me doing a *children*?"

"And you only hissed once."

"And I only hissed once!" She stands a little straighter, trotting down the sidewalk in her four-inch platform shoes. "New record. I'm proud of me. You should be proud of me. Express your pride at once, husband."

"Immensely proud. I'll not clarify for what."

"I'll accept it." Tossing her hair back, she says, "I'm going to say hi to Alice and get new books before dinner. Will you manage?"

By her side? I'll do better than *manage*. "I suppose."

Grinning, she cradles her arms in front of her chest. "Kitty."

I don't ask questions. I just melt into her arms, stand against her shoulder, and lick her neck. With a giggle, she touches her head to mine. "Love you," she whispers.

And everything in our perfectly normal little world is complete.

Uh oh

Well, except for one…last…little…loose…end.

Several months earlier

Sunset bled into Pollux's sensitive eyes as he trudged through the winter woods. Heaven knew why he was out there, tracing down the agony of his own kind. It wasn't as if he *cared*. No. It just tasted so…

Bitter.

Hopeless.

Nostalgic.

The scent of fir trees filled his lungs as he breathed in, letting out another weighted breath.

Lovely place, the woods. Better at night, definitely. But of course he favored the darkness.

Darkness held no expectations for something like him. It beckoned sweetly into its embrace and let shadows be shadows.

Stopping beside an overgrown bush, he crouched, pulled away the branches, and looked at the pathetic creature huddled in the growth. How laughable that this thing had managed to scare a vampire to tears. How pitiful that such a tiny thing could be called a boogey*man* at all when it was barely an infant.

Large, black eyes opened in the small, dark face. Ragged breaths rocked its misshapen chest. Perhaps no one else would see anything but a monster made of weeping ink and gaping chasms, long nails and sharp teeth.

Pollux couldn't see anything but a despairing, hurting child.

"Hun...gry."

His chest pinched. He needed his liquor. Something strong.

A weak hand reached for him. "Hun...gry."

"I know," he murmured. "Do you think I'll feed you?"

The tiny claw-tipped hand stopped moving for him.

"You hurt someone very badly. Scared someone I..." He rocked his jaw. "...tolerate."

He'd not say *like*. He *liked* Pila and Cael. Ollie and Zylus were people he tolerated and respected. He couldn't begin to imagine the energy it took to survive as freely as they managed when their terrors and insecurities left them so tremendously crippled.

The little body gave up, curling in on itself in the damp brown leaves, preparing for the moment when it would no longer have the strength to cling to the physical plane. Already, it was working a feat by sticking around. Naturally, a creature born of vampiric fears would bear innate strength of will.

Pollux muttered a swear. He *really* needed a drink. Holding out his hand, he gathered enough liquid terror from his veins to create a sizable, shrieking orb of the stuff in his palm. "If you accept this, you accept how easily I can take it away. You will pledge yourself to my rules."

Its mouth watered, shaking hands reaching.

He drew the relief back. "Do we have a deal?"

The child nodded. "Y-es."

He tossed the morsel its way. "Then eat up, Andromeda."

So she did. Quite gruesomely. Licking her lips and fingers and claws until not a speck remained. After she was finished, she looked more like him. Almost human. Never quite. Blue eyes instead of red. Dark skin instead of pale. A curly bundle of beautiful brown locks spilling around her little cheeks.

Great. He'd have to educate himself on proper care for curls.

His eyes rolled, but he moved under the brush and picked her up, cradling her in his arms and tucking her face against his chest where the dying sunlight wouldn't burn her light-toned eyes. As the shadows increased over the land, he stroked her hair and muttered, "It's almost night, dear."

"Time to hunt," she whispered.

And his teeth flashed in the final, blinding rays.

Acknowledgments

You know who you are.

You know what you did.
And you probably have an N in your name.

Keep reading for bonus content.

But Wait… There's More.

Read Ollie's story in *Falling in Love with my Chihuahua Shifter*!
    Doliver Talon has never been *the good guy*. He's sexy. Carefree. Always up to mischief. Always ready for a romp around in the woods, or, you know, wherever. Honestly, as the overlooked runt in a litter of seven, he'll take whatever attention he can find.
    Life is all about living in the moment, so he's going to make sure there are a lot of good ones.
    Problem is, when his mate shows up in the small, mythical town of Mountain Vale, no distraction compares to the soft, chestnut waves of her hair, the beautiful bright hazel of her eyes, or the intoxicating scent of her presence. She haunts him like a nightmare he never wants to wake up from.
    He's nobody's hero. Nobody's *forever*. Nobody's first choice.
    But if she's willing to let him, he's willing to pretend.
    At least until the truth finds him out.

Reader Expectations
Heat Level: Fade-to-black, innuendos, no cursing, sensual description, mentions of sex
Notable Tropes: Secret identity, reformed rake, forced proximity, underdog, loyal to the core, alpha in disguise
Triggers: People pleasing, low self-esteem, abusive family situations
Style: First person present, single POV
Stress Level: Low
Ending: HEA

Prologue

Applesauce is an excellent egg replacer. Puppies are a phenomenal man replacer.

Today's Nature Walk for my Mental Health is sponsored by Heartbreak.

I inhale the fresh air and ignore the crushing need to cry that presses on my lungs. Noah wasn't the love of my life—he was just some guy. I will *not* be hitting him with my car, though. Because that's wrong.

And, also, on an entirely unrelated note, I no longer know exactly where he lives.

I could find out.

I won't.

Sniffling, I turn up my *Can't Be Sad* playlist and adjust my pink headphones as "Caramelldansen" drowns out the nature sounds. If a bear is coming for me, I will not hear it. I will also not hear the crack, crack, shatter of my innocent twenty-four-year-old heart.

Sometimes, people make mistakes.

Sometimes, people move six hours away from everything they know and love—finally having the nerve to deny the advice of their well-meaning, but largely micromanaging, mother—and they wind up with three glorious months of…red flags.

Red flags that move *twenty-four hours* away to be with someone else they met online after sending a breakup text and a selfie of them trying to look pitiful as they board a plane.

Noah was cheating on me before I ever came.

He's probably cheating on whoever he left to be with.

I've dodged a bullet.

Yeah.

Scrubbing my face, I discover that my phone sound is completely up and I'll likely be unable to hear by the time I'm thirty. Assuming I live that long. Assuming the *I told you so* from my mother won't kill me.

She never calls me. I could avoid talking to her until I have my life back *together*. But if I don't call her enough, she's upset when I do. It's a lose, lose situation where I either avoid her and wind up brutalized for more than one reason, or I let her kick me while I'm down.

Glancing behind me, I lift one muff off my ear and scour the woods.

Long story short, really hoping on that bear right about now.

"Nyan Cat" begins shrieking into my skull, and I lurch, snapping my headphones back into place, grappling for my phone, and mashing the volume down button.

Once the screeching siphons away, I exhale.

If I die in the woods, I won't have to deal with any of my problems. My parents will get upset as the weeks drag on and on without hearing from me, then when some other wanderer locates my decaying, bear-mauled body and the police identify me...they'll regret all their anger. They'll say *we told her so* at my memorial. All their friends will agree. My tombstone will say *Here Lies Brittny Page. Why, oh why, didn't she just listen to her mother?* My sister will lift a bottle of sake, dump it out on my grave, and recite some haiku about a butterfly finally escaping the cocoon.

My mother will yell at her about making me drink.

She'll yell back about how I can't drink if I'm dead.

With any luck, she'll get my laptop when they divvy up my meager belongings.

Not that there's anything...*bad* on there. Just. Just a lot of love stories at various stages of completion, at various levels of grammatical correctness, and with various amounts of trauma dumping.

My sister, Alana, will see the story where the main character's sister abandons her to go off into the world and live her life as *Wow, Brittny loved me*. My parents will see the story where the main character struggles with how her parents have made her feel suffocated and unworthy as disrespect—a final insult, proof I really was a horrible and ungrateful daughter. After all, wouldn't I be alive right now *if only* I'd listened to them? *If only* they were a little more suffocating? *If only* they made it impossible for me to leave?

Blinking, I rediscover the woods, the quiet, the scent of spring, bursting to life. Sun scatters across the brush, brightening the green hue.

I slip my headphones down around my neck, remember I *am* alive right now, and let wraith-like calm seep into my bones.

Pro: I love Mountain Vale. Having access to the sprawling forest that surrounds the town in my backyard brings so much more peace than I know how to describe. It's private. Safe. Even if my brain runs away with gruesome tales of my demise, I prefer natural selection by means of bear attack over the *if you don't get in and out of this store in two minutes, you will get kidnapped and sold*. The stories that invaded my head in the city centered around evil people making evil choices to hurt others.

The concrete jungle with its high-rise buildings, congested streets, and stacks of apartments flooded with strangers didn't suit me.

Pro: I am a homeowner. Sure, I'm still making payments, but I was at least smart enough to house-hunt under an assumption of *this is where I will raise a little family with the person I love*. It's my dream home. In my dream *quiet town*. All I need now is some *dream guy* to appear and sweep me off my feet like in the cheesy stories I throw together whenever I'm distraught that life isn't as simple as I swear it once was.

Con: My job is very demanding of my mental, emotional, and physical energy... The past three months have made that clear. Being an assistant is hard.

Pro! I *have* a job. I can make my house payments. Buy food. Get a hummingbird feeder.

I should do that right now, actually. By the time hummingbirds start showing up, I'll be over Noah. I'll be a new woman. They'll look in the windows at me and say *wow, look at that, that right there is a well-adjusted human*. And I *will* be a well-adjusted, mature, stable adult human. I will *not* be crying into a carton of ice cream and watching whatever heart-wrenching anime movie Alana has sent me to help provide me a little *perspective*.

Honestly, what is up with my sister? In what universe does my being sad warrant her inflicting further emotional damage? You're right, A. At least I've not been trying to date a weird forest spirit thing who dies if touched by another living thing. How silly of me to think my problems could ever compare?

Note to self: if the *music video* makes you cry, *don't watch the movie*.

Also, never trust your sister. She is one of those people who say *this destroyed me, enjoy*. And I know this. But I keep forgetting.

I miss her.

I wish I could drop everything and stay with her until I feel better. Could take weeks. Or months. If only she had a house, she'd put a sign on her basement door that said *Brittny's room, please knock*, and I'd live there with her forever, watching anime, hugging borderline-inappropriate body pillows, and crying because real men aren't half as decent.

Con: Alana does *not* have a house. She has made a career out of pet sitting from one place to the next, and while she has forged relationships with dozens of people who don't mind her living in their houses and eating their food, it is frowned upon for her to invite someone else along, too.

Not only that, in Alana's opinion, getting over one mistake means making a bigger one.

What will Alana do next! And as long as it doesn't involve arson, isn't that lovely?

I envy how low she's made our parents' standards in regard to her drop. She saw our mother's stifling requirement of perfection and immediately started stacking disappointments. For Alana, passing with C's was amazing. For Alana, every day she's not in prison is a grand win.

For Brittny, honor roll wasn't enough so long as there was a *high* honor roll. For Brittny, *perfect* is never *perfect* enough, and the one time Brittny tries to do something on her own, something she *thought* would make her feel whole and loved and *right* for the first time in her life, it's arson. It's prison. It's drugs and alcohol and living out of a cardboard box on main street.

The tears I've been holding back trace down my cheeks as the sheer *weight* of this mistake settles on my shoulders.

I am alone in a different state, hours away from anyone who can give me a hug. Overworked. Underpaid. Pretending I grew up in an environment that let me have responsibility instead of making me feel like I couldn't do even the simplest things correctly on my own.

This is a disaster.

And I'm going to fix it with thirteen hummingbird feeders.

Wiping my cheeks, I sniff, force down a hard swallow, and gather something like fraying resolve.

This is the last relationship I'll ever have. They aren't worth the trouble. From now on, I will train hummingbirds to sit on my palm and drink out of little plastic flower cups. From now on, I feed the crows and teach them to bring me shiny rocks. From now on—

A tiny *yip* freezes me midway to putting my headphones back on.

I stop, assess my knowledge of bears, and turn once I'm certain they don't sound like squeaky toys.

My heart stops.

There, sitting perfectly in the center of the clearing, is a tiny, tan and white chihuahua.

Its big brown eyes focus on me, searching.

Releasing my headphones, I crouch slowly and whisper, "Oh my goodness. Hi."

It yips again, stands, takes one cautious step forward toward my outstretched hand.

"You're so cute. Hi, baby."

It stops. Its eyes flick off my hand.

"I won't hurt you. Do you have a family? Are you lost?" It's not wearing a collar, but it's also not dirty. It hardly looks like it's been out here for very long. I've heard rumors that an alt girl lives in the woods. Maybe this is her puppy?

Maybe this is a perfect excuse to meet the alt girl in the woods and make a friend.

Oh my goodness.

I love that plan.

Reaching into my pocket, I pretend to pull out a treat. "You want this?"

It inches closer.

I move my hand, but its eyes stay locked on mine as though it's entirely uninterested in whatever I may or may not be holding. Might be too smart for me, this one.

It stops a foot away from me and sits.

When I reach for it, it closes its eyes but stays put, letting me pluck him up into the cradle of my arms. "You're a timid thing, aren't you?" I pet his little head, and he melts against my chest.

The idea that he might belong to someone else guts me, but I can't steal someone's dog. That's wrong. Too wrong to even think about.

My every step weighs me down as I navigate through the trees toward the other side of the forest, where the cluck of chickens cushions a quaint cottage. "This is where the person people call a witch lives...?" I murmur. Holding puppy up, I ask, "What do you think, baby? Terrifying or no?"

The tiny boy cracks one eyelid, then scrambles.

"Oh!" I catch him before he leaps out of my hands and hold his wriggling body steady. "Okay...maybe you find cottages threatening."

He yips, imploring, as I start up the stone pathway to the front door.

"I'm positive she's not actually a witch. People are just mean to people who are different." Tucking him under one arm, I knock. "Hello?"

"Zy. A human."

Beyond the door, a cat coos. A few moments later, the door swings open to reveal a towering man in all black, rubbing his ankle with one bare foot as he scrubs his eye. "Mm?"

"I...uh..." I clear my throat, cast a look inside at the incredibly plush living room. A woman with white streaks of hair framing her young face sits on a couch with a book in her lap titled *How to Turn Your Husband into Your Book Boyfriend*. Without smiling or lifting her attention off the pages, she laughs.

The man cocks his head against the doorjamb, blocking my view as he fully opens his eyes. One green. One blue.

They widen while I'm stuck in an inferiority complex. These people are *stunning*. What? Did I brush my hair today? I should have worn makeup. Does it look like I was just crying and lamenting my untimely demise in the woods?

I wet my lips. "I'm so sorry to bother you. I just found this puppy on a walk." I present him, even though now he is thrashing with vengeance in an effort to escape. "I thought he might belong to you."

The man's eyes home in on the chihuahua, and the little boy cowers, tucking his white-tipped tail.

The woman's head pokes out from behind the man's broad chest. "Pupp... Oh."

The man nudges her, lifts his brows.

Her mouth drops open, then her gaze flies toward my face. "*Oh.*"

In unison, they flash brilliant smiles so white my head spins.

I take a hesitant step back and cradle the tiny dog against me. His limp body sags deeper, and his little head taps into my chest at a gentle, consistent rhythm. He whimpers.

"He's not ours," the woman says.

"You should absolutely give him a nice home," the man notes—something in his voice so soothing I want to do exactly what he says.

"But never lock him in the bathroom with you accidentally while you're changing or taking a shower." The woman points a finger at me, suddenly intense. "Trust me."

I don't know why, but I do. I stammer, "So...he's not yours?"

"He doesn't have a home, and if you take him to the pound, they will kill him." She folds her arms. "Then you'd be a murderer."

"Darling..."

"He looks like the kind of dog who'd hold a grudge and haunt you for the rest of your life, too."

"Okay, sweetheart. That—"

"Basically, take him home. Welcome him into your heart. And love him forever." She gasps, pushing white strands of her hair over her ear. "*Also*, Thursdays."

This is such an out-of-body experience. Normally, *I'm*

the one confusing the people around me with my inappropriate dialogue and disconnected lines. In that way, it's almost refreshing to be the one utterly lost. "Thursdays?"

"Thursdays are movie night. All Thursdays. And the invitation never expires." She rests her head against the man's arm, looking like a picture perfect match for his dark outfit in her white ensemble. "Every Thursday at eight, you're welcome to come by with your puppy. There will always be popcorn and water. This household is not responsible for any other snacks, but many do appear."

"Like…magically?" I ask.

The woman's smile turns nearly feral. "Now, I said *nothing* about *magic*."

The man clasps his long fingers over her mouth. "And she probably won't say anything about magic. Because that would be overstepping into someone else's story. And the likelihood we would do that is a percentage, right, my love?"

The woman makes direct eye contact with the man, then bites his hand.

Against all logic and reason, the man's pale cheeks tint red.

I take a step back, clear my throat again. "Right. Well. It was lovely meeting you two. I'm going to buy some hummingbird feeders now. I mean, dog food. Well. Both. Sorry again about disturbing you." Turning on my heel, I flee.

"You scared her off, starlight," the man chastises.

"Oh, she'll be *fine*." The woman laughs. "And…you know…she'll also be back. Eventually."

The door closes as I retreat, clutching my puppy to my chest.

My puppy?

My heart skips a beat, and I look down at his pitiful little face, pinned ears, and whimpering eyes.

"It's okay," I whisper as I adjust my pace away from *fleeing* and more toward *leisurely woodland stroll*. "Sometimes people who are confident in their own skin have big personalities. And sometimes those personalities can freak people like us with smaller ones out."

He lifts his face, regarding me dryly. I don't know why—childhood trauma probably—but I can't shake the feeling that he's judging me. He yips.

I fall in love.

Smiling, I kiss his little head. "I think I'll name you... Oxford."

His head tilts.

"Like the comma. Not anything else that *Oxford* reminds you of."

He blinks.

"With an Oxford comma, items in a series that might be confusing are a little clearer. Observe: we are going to go to the store *comma*, get hummingbird feeders and pet supplies *comma*, go home *Oxford comma*, and cry into a tub of ice cream together."

He stares at me. Like I am insane and he is afraid for his life.

"Okay. I know you couldn't *observe*, since I was speaking, but if everything I'm saying were written down, you'd get it." I cuddle him closer and remind myself he's a tiny chihuahua and has no reason to hate me. If he does, though, I'll bribe him with peanut butter until he's forgotten why he hates me. Softly, I say, "Basically, we're going to be just fine. When one chapter ends, another begins. Noah breaking up with me wasn't the end of anything. It was the penultimate item in a series of unfortunate events. You're the comma indicating as much."

The real story starts now.

Chapter 1

It's a lovely day for bad decisions.

One year later

"A—" My sister cuts me off, leading into reason four hundred of why I should get a dating app, start swiping right, and *get back out there.*

"*Food*," she states, then she says something in Japanese. Or Korean. I'm uncertain if she's been watching an anime or a K-drama in the past twenty-four hours. "Think about all the free food you could get on dates."

I adjust the little sombrero I'm putting on Oxford and roll my eyes. "Think of all the tabs horrible guys would leave me with. Think of all the awful men who would assume I owe them something if they buy me a ten dollar meal at Steak 'N Shake."

A momentary reprieve followed by, "Why are you going on a date at Steak 'N Shake?"

"I like their cheese fries."

Alana sniffs. "Okay. Fair point. But opt for something a little fancier on a *date*."

"Like Taco Bell?"

"Try again."

"If I *opt for something fancier*, I won't be able to afford it when I'm left with the bill." I hand Oxford a tiny stuffed taco. He looks at it, then at me, then back at it before gingerly biting it. I beam, tuck my cell phone receiver away from my mouth, and whisper, "Sit, baby."

He plants his cute patoot in his cute poncho down with

a snuffly dog huff.

Alana drawls, "Can't you tell when a man's going to be a jerk from the first moment you see him?"

"Unfortunately, no."

She rambles something that I'm *pretty* sure *is* Japanese, then mutters, "The real world sucks. If life were an anime, the good guys would come backdropped by sakura blossoms."

"Mhm. Time would slow down, angels would sing—"

"Angels wouldn't sing. Both time and the music would slow down as they run their fingers through their hair and catch sight of you. Stay with me, B. We don't want *American cartoon* reality. We want *Asian romance drama* reality."

"We're not Asian." And I'm pretty sure I don't want *any* kind of *drama* to be my reality.

"We're, like, two percent Asian. Remember? I did that DNA test a few years back. And we're sisters. So we're the same."

"Is that how it works?"

"Absolutely."

"Is that why two percent of the words you say come out as common anime phrases?"

"I resent that." I picture her tiny nose scrunching. "All I'm saying is you deserve *at least* two percent of an anime romance in your life. It's your birthright."

"All I'm saying is men are evil, and Oxford is all ready for his photo shoot, sooo…"

"You're trying to hang up on me so you can take three hundred more photos of your dog."

I begin drawing my phone away from my ear. "I can't hear you over how adorable he is."

"Brittny."

"What? Alana? Hello? Oh dear. Oxford, your cuteness is too loud! It's disrupting the cell service! Which is obviously very scientific and cannot be debated." I hang up.

Sighing, I give myself a moment to pretend I'm not a disappointment to both my parents and my sister, then I lift my phone, intending to go to my camera.

Alpha Sister: Scam.

Alpha Sister: I'm worried about you, imouto.

I wince. "I'm worried about you, too, sis." No twenty-eight-year-old should be sending texts half in English and half in romaji, then following it up with seven gifs of crying anime girls. It's juvenile. Cringey.

Brave.

My favorite thing.

I love her so much.

To get on her nerves, I send back the gif of Homer Simpson disappearing into a bush, then I open my camera app. "Okay, love of my life and the only male creature who has yet to hurt me, say *takito*."

Oxford yips, and I get a picture of him dropping his little taco.

☼

"I've fallen for your sunset lips and those earth-shade eyes. The way you move like paradise. After an eternal night, you crest the skies," dolivers_not_trending hits a note that I can't, so I just sink a tiny bit deeper into bed and let him sing to me from my phone. "I've fallen for your heart of gold and that laughing smile. The way you overcome any trial. I know you'll haunt me for a while." Doliver strums his acoustic guitar with tan-and-white spotted fingers, a soft smile playing on his lips. "I'd trade the rest of my life for your sunshine. Whoa, oh. Whoa, oh. For your sunshine."

My heart swells, and I melt, biting my lip. I've been trapped here for three hours. I have work in the morning. I don't want to go. So I've been stuck on Leopard, replaying and replaying dolivers_not_trending's latest song "Sunshine." He is the most beautiful man I have ever seen

—all lean muscle and grace, dark hair and eyes, paint strokes of pure white cutting through his tan skin. He is probably the only man on earth I could still fall in love with.

If, of course, he weren't an internet sensation who is—on all accounts—*actually* trending. Between when I found him something like seven months ago and now, he's accumulated just short of a million followers. His voice—ethereal. His presence—stunning. His manner—elegant. His flirty smile—to die for.

If *perfect* were a person, I'm looking at him.

So when I say that my shriveled up heart has space for him alone, it's a big *duh*. In the last few hours, this video has gained *thousands* of comments from girls who are completely in love with him, too. We are the fangirls. The crazies. The ones who only *end up with the guy* in our extensive fanfiction, which releases weekly on Tuesdays and would make my sister very, very proud if only she knew it existed.

After all, it's packed full of the kind of drama she loves.

The kind of drama my mother would claim is *wasting my talent*.

Personally, I think *wasting my talent* means never finishing the hundred "original" stories I've started. In that regard, my computer is a graveyard of *talent*. The place where my talent goes to die. It's not like I'm writing so I can query agents and wind up in Barnes and Noble. No. I'm just…writing to stave off the collapse of my mental health.

Pretending Doliver's singing his songs to me fulfills that somewhat important goal.

Yep.

Doliver laughs as the chords hum to a halt. "Well. I hope you like it, beautiful. Remember, this one's for you. And only you. I love you."

When the video cuts to the end screen, I let a tiny,

fragile sigh out, rewind, and let him go again.

Honestly, he's probably a jerk. I mean, really. What nice guy looks *lovingly* into the camera at over a million people who may not be following but who are watching, and says *that* stuff? Yeah. Exactly. I bet he's with a different girl every night.

Disgusting.

I roll over, find Oxford tucked in on the other side of my bed, and pet his little head. "You're the only guy for me."

Oxford opens his eyes, looks at me, looks at my phone, and shimmies farther under the covers.

"I know. I know. You hate him. I should trust that. You are the smartest chihuahua in the world. But, see, I am weak to dimples." I show Oxford my phone a second before only his little black nose is visible. "And he has dimples."

Oxford yips quite pitifully.

"What's so important about dimples?" I rest on my back, hold my phone above my head, and watch Doliver sing. With dimples. Precious. I murmur, "I don't actually know. Maybe they're just very…kissable."

My phone drops on my face, colliding with my skull. "*Ow.*" I rub my poor forehead as Oxford pokes his face back out from under the sheets to make sure I'm okay. Surely. He's sweet like that. Puffing, I mutter, "Dimples make boys look endearing. And endearing things are kissable. It's why I'm always kissing you, you know? You're the most darling little puppy a girl could ask for. You don't even need dimples. Just a cute little waggy tail, and, on occasion, a stuffed taco."

Speaking of…

I rip myself away from dolivers_not_trending in order to pull up my Instagram profile, which is one hundred percent a collection of Oxford in various outfits. He's a model. And people love him. And the validation of the three thousand followers who leave hearts and comments helps me feel less alone in this big scary world.

Sure, it's been over a year since I moved to Virginia. Sure, my only real friend is still my sister. Sure, my attempt at making friends with the bookstore clerk at Page Turner *somehow* devolved into my sharing my entire life story and her asking if I was paying with cash or card.

It's hard to be an adult.

Even if I meet someone I click with, then what? Do you just ask for someone's phone number in the chip aisle at Martyn's Grocery Mart? What if they don't text in the same tone and you can't tell if they're happy or bothered by your messages? I'll die first before calling anyone who I don't share DNA with.

Therefore, I'm a terrible puppy mom. Exploiting my cute dog in an effort to simulate human connection through positive affirmations online is not healthy. But it's what we have…

Against my will, I fall asleep while overusing emojis and writing "thank you" with seven u's.

Then, as it is wont to do, tomorrow comes, bringing with it the despair of work.

☼

With a smile plastered on my face, I stare blankly at the cursor blinking on my screen. This is above my pay grade. Far, far above my pay grade.

Office noises fill the small building, machinery humming, printers printing, coworkers I've never shared more than pleasantries with laughing. People are getting their final coffees and heading home for the day.

I am going cross-eyed looking at a spreadsheet I'm making to assess and compare marketing budgets from this year and the five past years.

It's a lot of numbers. A lot of equations. A lot of *is pink too unprofessional or am I allowed to make the accents appealing to me?*

It's my own fault for nodding and saying *yes, yes, of course I can do that* like I knew the first thing about making this sort of thing seven hours ago. Spoiler alert: I did not. Shoving it in with all my other duties of maintaining my boss's schedule, handling her appointments, playing gopher, ordering meals, and, and, and, it's a miracle I know anything about it *now*. Sure, it was my idea. Or part of my idea. My idea is actually a lot different and a lot better, but when I tried to express that, my boss asked for this, so I smiled and confirmed that my idea was probably stupid anyway.

Why do I do this to myself?

Rubbing one eye, I type in another row of numbers, double check them, and start on the next.

Why am I still here?

I'm on salary.

This is my time.

I need to feed Oxford.

I need to feed *myself*.

I've been working here long enough to know that finishing this job doesn't mean returning to the tasks I signed up for—you know, the ones listed on my employee agreement. It means another meeting where another idea for success and growth will appear that adds fifteen more things to my plate.

Because I hold my plate up when everyone else goes quiet.

Because my boss smiling and praising my accomplishments makes it all worthwhile.

I'm cheap.

I'll do just about anything for the price of one (1) compliment. One little line that proves you don't hate me, and I'm wagging my tail, dead set on making sure you *never* hate me. Because, if you do end up hating me someday, I will never recover from the emotional aftershocks.

"Brit." Exiting her elegant, glass office, my boss Racheal Watson smiles at me and pulls her purse onto her shoulder. "Don't stay too late tonight, okay? I worry about you sometimes."

My heart jumps at the notion of another human being caring about me, and I smile a little brighter. "I'm fine! I just want to finish this. It's fun."

Racheal lifts a perfectly-tweased blond brow. "Compiling data into a spreadsheet is *fun*?"

"Well, it's nice when all the numbers do all the things I want them to, isn't it?"

She hums, fixing her bangs. "If you say so, honey. I really appreciate all your hard work. I just want to make sure you're also taking care of yourself, all right?"

"Of course."

Lifting her wrist, she glances at her watch, purses her lips, and clicks her way over to my desk, which sits just outside her office door like a sentry. To get to the queen, peasants must go through me. "Actually, honey, I've been leaving first every day this week. I'm making an executive decision. You can finish this—" She taps a perfectly manicured nail against the top of my monitor. "—tomorrow. Head on home."

"Oh, really, it's no troub—"

"I know you're capable of staying here all night doing this and seven hundred other things, but that doesn't mean you should. Call a friend. Go out to dinner. Watch a movie. Do *anything* but this. Okay?"

I bite my tongue before blurting that I *really* don't have anything else of more importance to take care of, no friends to call, no one to go to dinner with. I swallow all the words claiming that this is honestly the only thing I have that brings something akin to a sense of fulfillment. I remind myself I have a puppy to feed. I remind myself I have a *me* to feed. Then I nod. "If you insist."

She does, so I shut things down and wander outside into

the cool spring evening. Sunlight pours across the sidewalk as I make it to my car, put on the newly-made one hour version of "Sunshine," and back out of the lot.

It's about thirty minutes to get home from my office building in a nearby city's downtown, but I wouldn't trade where I live now for the convenience of everything being five minutes away. These roads are empty. I don't deal with traffic to or from. I'm no longer panicking that I'll get in a car accident every time I drive myself anywhere.

Life is great.

In unrelated news, I want to sleep for seven years.

It is that sense of bone-deep weariness that makes me yawn as I pull past the *Welcome to Mountain Vale* sign, through downtown, and past…

I snap my mouth closed as I stop at the only light on the stretch of shops and stare.

My heart rate picks up, thundering, pounding.

It can't be…

Standing in front of the bookstore with a black cat in her basket is *the alt girl from the woods*. Which isn't entirely unusual. I see her around now and again, always with her cat. But across from her? Across from her with his hands tucked in his pockets, stands *Doliver* bathed in the blinding sun.

He is unmistakable.

A tattoo on my brain.

I stare, rub my eyes, question my mental stability.

I'm tired.

Exhausted, rather.

I'm hallucinating?

There's no way.

There are entire *hunt down Doliver* creep pages on Reddit where people have theories that he's not actually real because no one has *ever* seen him in person. He's big enough now that he should be getting recognized. Grocery stores shouldn't be safe. He *should* be doing shows, recording for labels, juggling sponsorships—

The light turns green.

My heart skips as I ease my car around the block, just to find Doliver still standing there, across from the alt girl in her perfect, lacy white dress complete with elegant corset and fingerless gloves.

My dress-shirt-and-slack-clad self envies her femininity. Among other things. Like her confidence. If I were standing across from perfection, I'd be having a meltdown. Sobbing. Screaming. Confessing undying love.

Is she a fan? A girlfriend? It's been a year. Maybe she broke up with the other guy?

Why would they be dating? Why *wouldn't* they be dating? She's beautiful. He's stunning. She gives off anything but the basic vibes I do. Incredible people find themselves among incredible people. It's a fact.

I can't believe it.

Doliver lives *here*. I've never met him. And he's dating the social outcast.

She's the one he says *I love you* to at the end of every video.

My stomach knots at the very idea of that as I turn the corner again and force myself to head home.

"Don't be a fangirl, Brittny." I swallow, hard. "*Don't.*"

For some uncanny reason, a tear slides down my cheek as I pull up the driveway. After I park, I take a deep breath, cover my face, and bite my lip. "What is wrong with me?"

I'm going insane.

I'm jealous of someone I've barely met because of someone I've never met.

And, *worse…*

It's Thursday.

Also by Camilla Evergreen

Could Have Been Sweet Rom-com Series
Could Have Been Us
Could Have Been Closer
Could Have Been Romantic
Could Have Been Real

How to Rom-com Series
How to Turn Your Husband into Your Book Boyfriend
How to Fake Date Your Grumpy Boss
How to Not Be Alone on Christmas
How to Marry Your Single Dad Neighbor
How to Destroy Your Lifelong Bully
How to Confess to Your Childhood Best Friend
How to Find Love When You're Weird
How to Make Your Enemy Fall for You

That's (Para)Normal Series
Falling in Love with My Vampire Cat
Falling in Love with My Chihuahua Shifter
Falling in Love with the Moth Faerie Prince
Falling in Love with the Man of My Nightmares

Printed in Great Britain
by Amazon